AMERICAN LIVES

AMERICAN LIVES

With Love

~~Ron Denby~~

For Gabriel At 21

Because...

Byrne

29 Mar 1990

Knights Press

Stamford, Connecticut

Copyright © 1985 by Ron Denby

Designed by Able Reproductions, copyright © 1985
Published by Knights Press, P.O. Box 454, Pound Ridge, NY 10576

Library of Congress Cataloging in Publication Data

Denby, Ron
    American lives.

    I. Title.
PS3554.E515A8   1985   813'.54   85-4280
ISBN 0-915175-13-4 (pbk.)

Printed in the United States of America

PROLOGUE

New York Times   Nov. 14

PRESIDENT PROMISES FULL COOPERATION WITH TRANSITION; PRESIDENT-ELECT PRAISES SPIRIT OF UNITY

Daily News   Dec. 30

PRESIDENT-ELECT PROMISES WAR ON INFLATION

The president-elect today promised an all-out war on the inflation that has eroded the American economy. In a related development, he further said that traditional American values were our best defense against the problems facing us.

Chicago Tribune   Jan. 9

PRESIDENT-ELECT PROMISES ECONOMIC BLITZKRIEG, ADVISERS SAY

Des Moines Register   Jan. 15

JENNINGS SUPPORTS NEW ADMINISTRATION

The Rev. Billy Jennings today at a rally of *God's People* praised the president-elect, claiming that he was the last hope for the forces of morality in America today. Jennings promised the support of his widespread organization.

New York Times   *Jan. 20*

PRESIDENT INAUGURATED; CALLS FOR RETURN TO THE AMERICAN WAY

The new president at his inauguration called for a return to traditional values. He said that economic problems were the chief problems facing us. He insisted that the new forces of a conservative America could ultimately triumph over the economic and spiritual malaise.

Marion Register   *March 17*

KLAN DRAGON SPEAKS TO RALLY

The Grand Dragon of the Ohio Klan spoke last night at a rally of Klan Youth. He said that the new order in America had arrived and that the mighty voice of the conservative nation was heard at last. He urged all members of the Klan to prepare for the battle against the foes of the American Way.

Daily News   *May 21*

PRESIDENT ANNOUNCES TAX CUT

The president today announced an across-the-board tax cut, effective in the next fiscal year.

New York Times   *June 17*

PRESIDENT SENDS TAX CUT TO CONGRESS

The president today sent his long-awaited and much-heralded tax bill to Congress. There is the promise of acrimonious debate, and whether he will be able, even with the good will usually accorded a new president, to push the bill through both houses remains to be seen.

Macon Post Dispatch   Aug. 4

SCOUT LEADER ADMITS KLAN MEMBERSHIP

Jerry Simmons admitted today that he was a member of the Klan and that he had been teaching battle tactics at scout outings. He said young men had to be prepared to fight against the Communists and homosexuals who were a menace to our free society. "Communists and homosexuals are the enemy," he was quoted as saying.

New York Post   Oct. 15

JENNINGS TO HOLD RALLY IN NEW YORK

The Rev. Billy Jennings announced today that he and his organization, *God's People*, which claims a membership of over 5 million scattered among nearly 77,000 churches across the country, has targeted New York City as the site of their next crusade for America rally. Jennings hopes to appear in New York on Thanksgiving. "The forces of immorality which received a resounding defeat in the recent election," he said, "are still strong. And they are subtle. Even now, the advocates of ERA, abortion and sexual license are banding together to form new centers of influence. Vigilance and the help of God are our only weapon against them."

San Francisco Examiner   Dec. 6

CRACK DOWN ON GAY BARS

The Los Angeles Police today began what some gay activist leaders see as the beginning of a new policy aimed at

gay people. In late-night raids, seven gay bars were simulta-
neously closed and patrons arrested on a variety of charges,
including loitering, soliciting and lewd and immoral conduct.
Randy Asher, newly elected chairperson of the National
Coalition of Gay People, in San Francisco for a speech to
launch a national campaign against Jennings' *God's People*,
denounced the raids as another symptom of an increasingly
repressive society.

New York Times   Jan. 17.

TAX CUT STILL IN LIMBO

The president's tax cut measure is still in congressional
limbo. Presidential advisers admit they had anticipated an
easier passage. The president and congressional leaders are
reported to be seeking a compromise bill.

Daily News   April 2

VILLAGE BLOODBATH

In a swift and seemingly senseless attack last night at a
gay bar in the Village, an apparently berserk man shot and
killed three men, and wounded six others. He sprayed the
front windows of The Underground, a gay bar, with repeated
rounds from a machine gun and then sped off into the night.
There is no information about the identity of the killer or a
motive for the attack.

Chicago Tribune   Aug. 19

Wall Street analysts agreed today that the crippling
inflation rate is still on the rise, having gained new impetus
after the expected dip following the presidential election.
Banks across the country have again increased the prime rate.

Des Moines Register   *Dec. 3*

JENNINGS ANNOUNCES DISPLEASURE AT ADMINISTRATION COURSE

The Reverend Billy Jennings, while still affirming his support for the president, declared today that he hoped for a meeting with the administration and the president to urge them to take stronger measures in the fight against the Right-to-Life and gay groups which he insisted were more powerful than ever. He reminded the president that the party had supported an anti-ERA plank and an anti-abortion plank and voted down the attempt by the gays to be seated at the convention. But he felt that more was required in these areas and that the president and his advisers had not kept their promise in "these important areas of American life."

The Lowe Report: WPXI, Channel 7   Jan. 17

Lowe: Tell me, Senator, do you feel the present administration has lived up to the promise it made?

Senator: No, I emphatically do not. It is clear to anyone who can read that the inflation rate has not been curbed. The vaunted tax cut has become only a partial reality. Not only that, but the honeymoon with big business seems to me to be if not over at least turning sour. No, I do not feel that the promised changes have materialized at this point.

Lowe: Do you see a chance for a turnaround in the remaining year of the term?

Senator: Frankly, no, Not, mind you, that it can't happen, but the policies of the president have not been quite as easy to implement as he had hoped. If anything, the mood of the nation is more divided than ever, and I believe he will have a harder, not an easier time of it in the next year.

Lowe: Do you believe then that the conservative trend that swept him to office is already on the wane?

Senator: No, not at all. It is as strong as ever I think in most areas. But what seems to me to have happened is that the extreme right and the middle-of-the-roaders who elected him have largely begun to part company.

Lowe: Do you think people like Billy Jennings and the many pockets of the Klan are a danger to the national situation?

Senator: I think my views on the Klan are clear. Of them I dissapprove. Of Jennings I can say that I believe him to be a sincere man. And it is difficult to describe a movement of God-fearing people, dedicated to values that are traditional to the nation, as dangerous. I think healthy disagreement is part of our American tradition.

Lowe: Would you care to comment on your plans, Senator Hopkenson, for the next year?

Senator: (Smiling). I will continue to serve in the Senate, and together with my senior colleague Senator Rideau, I hope I will continue to be useful.

Lowe: You have no plans for, shall I say, more active participation?

Senator: The Senate is quite active enough. (Laughing).

Lowe: Thank you, Senator. Ladies and gentlemen, tonight we have been talking with Senator Magnus Hopkenson, who, some speculate, is a potential candidate in the . . .

New York Times   Nov. 2

On the eve of the election, which he is expected to win by a large margin, the president declared that he had won the battle and "turned America around again. Prosperity is here to stay," he said.

Chicago Herald   *June 4*

Jennings walked out of the Presidential Prayer Breakfast, declaring that the administration has "betrayed those Americans who believe in God and the American Way."

New Orleans Sun-Times   *Aug. 7*

Less than two years into his second term, prominent analysts say, the seeming economic miracle which the president claimed seems to be crumbling. Interest rates are steadily rising and housing starts are at a nearly all-time low.

New York Times   *Nov. 12*

Randy Asher, a "gay" leader in the Village declares that "gay people are in a more powerful political position than they ever have been." Asher said that the recent climate of oppression against gay people, far from fragmenting them, has "bound them together into a more unified and determined group." It is widely believed among political analysts that Asher will run on an Independent ticket for the congressional seat due to be vacant in the next national election year.

San Francisco Chronicle   *May 3*

HOPKENSON BLASTS PRESIDENT'S SOUTH AMERICAN POLICY AS BANKRUPT

Des Moines Herald   *Jan. 22*

PRESIDENT CALLS ECONOMIC WOES "CYCLICAL". SAYS NEW INFLATION RATE WILL DECLINE.

Boston Globe   *Aug. 17*

VICE-PRESIDENT SPEAKS IN BOSTON TODAY

Many believe this is the kickoff of the vice-president's quiet campaign to succeed the president.

Albany News   *Feb. 3*

PRESIDENT DECLARES HE SEES A LIGHT AT THE END OF THE MIDDLE-EAST TUNNEL

New York Times   *Editorial*   *July 4*

Surely, in his last year in office, the incumbent cannot still claim that the opposition is responsible for the continued erosion of his once-successful economic policy. That the vice-president has made rumblings that he will run, and on the very same now discredited policies which have failed thus far, is no cause for joy. New ideas and fresh thinking are needed for America.

San Francisco Herald   *Nov. 20*

HOPKENSON ANNOUNCES HE WILL SEEK NOMINATION

Magnus Hopkenson today announced that he would seek his party's nomination for president. Hopkenson has a wide spectrum of supporters from many areas of society who have suffered under the policies of the current administration. Groups as diverse as the United Mine Workers, Billy Jennings' God's People, and the National Coalition of Gay People have indicated they will support Hopkenson. Some analysts fear that such diverse support may not work to his advantage with the majority of the American electorate.

1.

Some stood, waiting. Others wandered, eyes fixed in seeming disinterest. Those more bold shot dissecting glances appraising, accepting, rejecting. A few posed in strategic places, waiting, if they were beautiful, for the inevitable worshipper. Because it was late, the excitement that had earlier charged the air was now more urgent. There wasn't much time. The choreography of the wanderers was accompanied by fewer doors closing, fewer moans of pleasure or pain; the many who had searched earlier were reduced now to the few who had not yet found what they wanted.

It annoyed him to be among the few. He was not undesirable. Long exercise honed him; youth was on his side. But tonight he was invisible, at least to those he hoped would see him. The fervor of the evening was replaced with the *obligato* of his need. Nothing had quite seemed right, though much had been tantalizing. Earlier, a tangle of bodies had provided a few fervent caresses, a kiss, a hand stroking. but none of this aroused him, and his unexcited state soon sent his anonymous contact away in search of more accessible pleasures.

He took one more turn down the dim hall, passed the rows of doors, a few open with occupants hidden in the darkness, inviting or asleep. Stray thoughts invaded: of the time, of tomorrow, of other times, intimate bodies, happy moments. He dismissed them and looked further for someone to hold, to love for a moment. He wanted the exhilaration that can come when the only knowledge between two people is sex: no pretense, names, careers, personalities. Just desire and the union of two bodies with only a single thing to do.

Tomorrow became more insistent. A position paper to write. Two new staffers to settle in. A meeting with the City Hall liaison in the afternoon. Two uppers and a cold shower in the morning would have to do it. He headed for the dark playground on the fifth floor: he could find something there, quick and a release. Love, he thought wryly, would have to come later. As he passed the steam room he caught a quick glance of inspection. He paused, studied carefully an intricate arrangement of pipes that ran up the wall and let his watcher look again.

The test was passed. The ritual began and he followed love down the hall toward one of the cubicles. He decided it was too late for any preliminary stopping and looking and returning and so he followed close behind and into the open door. Without hesitation he closed the door, dropped his towel to the floor and when the strong arms embraced him, he knew that for a while he was home. He had just what he wanted.

On the narrow bed kisses, bites, intimations of mastery. He was ready. When a bottle of poppers was produced, chemical and aromatic, he took a long whiff and felt the lightness, the sexual tension pounding in his head and thighs, and he melted into the stranger, his friend. He was turned gently on his stomach; another hit of the popper and the hard muscled body engulfed him. Hands, rough hands, hot hands, now gripped him by the shoulders, thumbs dug into his shoulder blades. Now, fingers caressed the back of his neck, thumbs curling around his throat.

"Oh, yes, master," he said, wanting to surrender to the pressure of the hands, trying to give his allegiance to his lover.

The soaring singing high of the popper raised him up and he was willing to be the victim of desire.

Lips grazed his, touched his cheek, brushed his ear.

Terrifyingly, whispered, he heard his name.

The face he could not see, the lips he could only feel, had whispered his name.

Panic struck; he struggled, his stomach knotted. He had to get out. No one should know. It was too dangerous.

"Please, please, let go of me, please," he said, but it was hard to speak and he heard the terror in his voice, felt the horror in his heart and realized that the steady rough hands were tightening around his throat. Hot breath seemed to burn his face. Breathing, heavy and not his own, sounded in unison with his own struggling indrawn gasp.

He tried to speak; struggled for breath. His eyes opened involuntarily wide, and he felt the darkness coming, felt his heart straining to burst, his temples resisting the expansion of his brain, his skull not strong enough to resist.

Then the stain of crimson spread across the world, darkened at the center, and there was no more light and no more sound.

In another place a telephone rang.

"Yes, this is contact."

"I've taken care of it, sir."

"Good. Where?"

"In the baths. I had to follow him for a couple of days, but he went to the baths last night. So did I."

"Will he be identified?"

"Yes sir, I made sure there would be adequate identification."

"Good. That will make a point. Leave town, tonight if you can. I'll be in touch in the usual way. I think there'll be something else for you."

April 1   *6:45 A.M.*

The early morning light shimmered around the edge of the blinds. Little patches of sun made a pattern on supple skin. Philip touched the sunny places with his lips, ran his hand down a long sleek line. He got a sleepy good morning and: "It's early."

"Want to?" he asked.

"Sure."

His body awakened into desire, as warm flesh moved against his muscled body. Hands tickled, massaged, cajoled him.

The room became brighter. Morning sounds drifted in. Coffee was made someplace and street sounds began. He was pushed back on the pillows, teeth playfully bit his nose, nibbled his lips, a tongue drew a light sharp line down his chin and his chest. Little bites on his stomach aroused him more and he closed his eyes. Sweetness and gentle motion conjured fantasies: south sea isles, and rolling oceans, pounding surf and rising waves.

When the phone rang he was balanced on a surfboard, cresting on a mile-high wave, about to descend into a long smooth trough of the sea to make the long and wild rush toward the shore.

He reached out and took the phone. "Don't stop," he said.

He cradled the phone next to his ear, eyes still shut.

"Kristopher here."

"Yes," he said after a moment of listening. His voice was alert now, business filled it. "Can you get here by seven-thirty?" He glanced at the clock-radio. It was 6:45. "Good."

He slipped the phone back, and the waves carried him, content, to the shore.

"That was nice," he said.

"I take it that we have to dress?"

"Orange juice or apple," he said, slipping into a dark brown velvet robe.

Nice, he thought, as he closed the door. I'll call again. He walked over to the desk and took a small file box from one of the drawers. He selected a three-by-five card from the rear of the box and jotted a note: "Tuesday night, March 31. Black hair. Research staff. Time Inc. 777-2089." He slipped the card into the file box under R.

He glanced at the Seth Thomas clock on the mantle. It was 7:10. He went into the bathroom, hung his robe on the door hook and shaved, stepped into the shower and washed away the reminders of the night. He toweled, blew his dark curly hair dry, patted on some Hermes and went into the kitchen, raising blinds and opening draperies as he went. The morning sun glanced off his naked body. He never liked to dress immediately after his shower.

Two eggs in the blender, protein powder, orange juice, yeast. He pushed the button and the blender whirred. He poured coffee and by the time the bell rang at seven-thirty he had downed the cup. He picked up a pair of briefs from his bedroom, slipped into them and answered the door.

"Coffee, Frank?" he asked the man he let in.

"No thanks, I'm swimming."

"Come on in while I dress."

He led his visitor into the bedroom, indicated a leather wing chair. He opened a closet, selected a pair of dark slacks, a white linen shirt from a drawer full of them, and a maroon tie. These he put on the bed and sat down on the edge of it.

"So Frank, what have you got that couldn't wait till I was at the office?"

Frank LaMonica smiled. He was used to Philip's ways. The two men had known each other for three years. LaMonica was desk man, nights, at the Village Precinct, rank of sergeant. When Philip had been assigned by the network to dig up some facts on the mob, the unions, and the meat packers in the Village, it was Frank LaMonica who had been assigned by the precinct to be his liaison. The two men liked each other, and since then they had done favors, one for the other, when they could. Frank bent a few rules for Philip, passed on information that it might be harder for other investigative reporters to ferret out and Philip in turn filled Frank's files with some of the darker secrets that didn't always come easily to the police. Most recently, Philip had investigated violent and unsolved crimes in the Village. Frank had filled him in on the number of murders the police could do nothing about, or, as Philip suggested in his story, were unwilling to do anything about. Both men knew there was some danger in their cooperating.

"I think I've got another one for you, Phil."

"Another what?"

"Another dead boy."

"I've closed the story, Frank. I couldn't get it in, even if I wanted to."

"I think maybe this is separate . . . and hot. It's Michael Ross. Know him?"

"I don't think so."

"We didn't either until we got the body out. He works for the Hopkenson campaign here."

"Where did it happen?"

"The baths, on sixteenth street."

"Bad. A politician and gay."

"And dead. Strangled."

"Who else knows?"

"Me, my two men, you, and the management at the baths. But they are very anxious to keep it quiet."

"How long do I have?" Philip asked.

"I'll have to contact the DA, certainly by noon."

"Is that all I've got? Frank . . ."

"I don't know, Phil."

"Frank, you know you can trust me . . ."

"Yes, Philip, and I know if the precinct found out that I pass along to you what I pass along, I'd be in trouble. Don't say it, I owe you one. I'll stall as long as I can."

April 1   *8:30 A.M.*

Philip pondered what LaMonica had told him as he waited for the express elevator in the lobby of the network building. Before he left home, he had keyed his small computer system into the network terminal and come up with what meager information there was on Michael Ross. Not too much: age twenty-nine, Yale Law, worked for a small New York City public relations firm, then into Hopkenson's organization, perhaps through connections. Now media and PR with compaign headquarters. A fairly open public position. Un-married, lived alone in an apartment in Chelsea.

And now he was dead, in a gay bathhouse, and it didn't take a political analyst to know that when the story got to the papers it would cause trouble for Hopkenson, who was, as the news often said, impeccable, above reproach. A dead staff member, and a dead gay staff member, was going to put a blot on that image. Right now, he, Philip Kristopher, had the story and he knew it might be a big one. So after doing the rundown on Ross he had put in a call to Chuck Witter. Charles "Chuck" Witter, Network executive head, and Philip's immediate boss, would be very interested in this one. Philip knew that Witter had personally made large contributions to the Hopkenson campaign fund, and that he was subtly gearing up the network for full support in those quiet ways that men in power can effect without appearing to do so.

Philip stepped out of the elevator at the executive level, waved to the pretty young receptionist, and waited for the private elevator to Charles Witter's office suite.

"Mr. Witter is there, Mr. Kristopher. He's waiting for you."

"Thanks, Marion," Philip stepped into the elevator and pushed the button marked 55.

"Philip," Chuck said. "Good to see you. Coffee?"

Charles Witter stood by the breakfast table near the large windows that looked over the city. He was dressed casually, but expensively: soft gray flannels, taupe cashmere sweater, suede coat. His hair was clipped short, as was his blond mustache. He had a habit of looking sideways that often caught a person off guard, as if he had been found out in a secret. Witter intended that, but his sideways glance turned into a quick smile if he knew he had gotten the advantage. Witter looked much younger than his forty-five years. Philip knew that Witter kept himself in shape. The two of them had often worked out at the private gym on top of Witter's tower suite. Often they concluded some of the most complicated assignments as the worked out on the machines or free weights.

Philip also knew that Witter's mind was as tough as his body: precise, sharp-edged and quick to make decisions. He liked and respected Witter: liked him because he was direct, fair and honest; respected him because he demanded a lot, expected the best that Philip could give, but would back up Philip all the way, even in tight corners. He expected the best, and got it.

"So Philip, another big one?" Witter said, motioning to a chair.

"I think so Chuck. Too big, maybe."

"Let's hear it."

He relayed what he had learned from LaMonica and the product of his own research that morning.

Witter took it in silence, nodding now and then, walked to the windows, back across the office. He returned to his desk.

"Very bad," he said. "Very bad indeed."

"Yes," Philip agreed. "How do we handle it?"

"No one else knows?" Witter asked.

"Not now. But LaMonica can't keep the lid on forever. He has to move soon."

"No," Witter said decisively. "He can't."

"Can't?" Philip said. "I don't follow."

"Tell me, Philip, what do you think it would mean to Magnus Hopkenson if it got out that one of his aides was murdered in a gay bath?" Without waiting, he went on. "It would be damaging, probably enough to cost him the election. The opposition could make a lot of points with that. You know that Hopkenson has to be elected, don't you?"

"I know you support him," Philip said diplomatically.

"So do a lot of people," Witter said, "important people who are worried about the direction things have taken in the last four years. There's a lot at stake here, Philip."

Philip was surprised at the grimness of Witter's tone. He had expected that Witter would want all the information, and he knew Chuck Witter was not the kind of man to rake up scandal for its own sake. But Philip sensed in Witter's determined manner that he intended to act on this himself.

"What do we do?" Philip asked.

"What do *we* do?" Witter shaded the *we*. He looked at Philip for a long moment. "Do you want to be in on this?" he asked.

"I think you know the answer to that one already," Philip said.

"You may have to do some things you don't like."

"I have before."

"Then what you do," Witter said reaching for the intercom switch, "is to cancel all your appointments and go home and be ready when I call."

April 1   *8:15* A.M.

Nelson Beverwyck ducked under the whirling helicopter blades and climbed in next to the pilot. They rose smoothly and soon the long avenues of trees were becoming small below him, and even the vast sprawl of the house rapidly became a manageable pattern, formal and substantial, like his life.

The helicopter caught the wind and scooted before it, across the Sound and onto the path marked out by the Long Island Expressway running below, silver with inching cars.

Nelson Beverwyck always felt complacently pleased that he would be in his office for an hour, long before most of those riders below, many of whom, in fact a very large number of whom, worked for him, in one way or another.

The trip to the city was quick. As they approached the river the sunlight gleamed off the high rising buildings, among them his own lofty tower, sending welcoming semaphores of power.

An insistent beep interrupted his pleasure at the beauty of the scene. The phone light was blinking in time with the beep.

"Yes, Jeffrey, what is it?"

The experienced voice of his private secretary said: "Mr. Witter is calling, sir. He says it's very urgent and he must see you right away."

"I'll be there in ten minutes, Jeffrey. Tell him to come up. We'll have breakfast in the solarium."

"Yes, sir, the usual?"

"For me, yes. Get some sort of protein drink for him. And a little Scotch salmon."

What the hell does he want? Nelson Beverwyck wondered. Probably more advice on running that network of his. I ought to buy the damn thing.

April 1   *9:00* A.M.

Chuck Witter got out at the entrance to the Lexington Avenue building.

"Wait," he said and hurried into the lobby.

He stepped into the open elevator and punched *60*. The car stopped one or two times, letting people off, others on. It seemed to be forever. Finally he stepped out into the reception floor of Beverwyck International, as austere and elegant as Nelson Beverwyck himself. A young man, himself austere and elegant, rose from the desk.

"Good morning, Mr. Witter. Mr. Beverwyck has just landed. Please come with me."

He led Witter to another elevator, this one opened with a key. Inside there were three buttons, marked NB 1, 2 and 3. He pressed NB 3.

A quick surge, then a moment of silence, and the doors opened into a room brilliant with sunlight, glass on three sides, sparsely furnished. A small round table stood in the sun at one end, set for breakfast.

"Mr. Beverwyck will be here in a moment, sir," the young man said. "There's orange juice on the table, or a bar in the corner should you want it."

Witter grimaced at the thought of a drink at this hour and smiled his thanks to the young man who stepped back into the elevator. As the doors shut, from out of a glare of sun at the other end of the room, Nelson Beverwyck appeared, apparently coming through a mirrored door. "So, Chuck, what's on your mind to bring you out so early? Juice? Drink?"

"Just juice thanks. Nelson, we may have a problem."

Beverwyck motioned Witter to the table.

"By 'we' do you mean 'you' or do you in fact mean 'we'?"

"I mean 'we.'"

"Explain. Have some salmon. It's Scotch."

"Michael Ross, do you know him?"

"I know who he is. Never met him. Does something for Hopkenson, doesn't he?"

"Did. He's dead."

"Dead? How?"

"Murder it seems, and in the Village. It looks like sex."

"That is bad. Woman?"

"No. Apparently not. Quite the opposite."

Nelson Beverwyck drained the last of his coffee, and after a moment, he said: "Who else knows?"

"The police, you and I, and Philip Kristopher."

"And he is?"

"An investigative reporter on my staff. He was doing a series on sex crimes. That's why he got called."

"It's obvious," Beverwyck said, "that we have to do something to keep this quiet. Murder and sex are not especially useful ingredients in a presidential campaign."

"Hopkenson's not touched. He's impeccable."

"I know that, but you know as well as I that if this is a homosexual murder, and if that young man was homosexual, then it's going to stain the candidate, if only by association. Just what was his job with the organization?"

"He was assistant campaign organizer here in New York. Media and liaison work mostly."

"Did you ever meet him?"

"Not too likely, though I may have."

"Have you had him checked out?"

"I'm on that now. I've told my office to call here with a report."

"Good. Can we keep it quiet? That's the question. And without involving the candidate?"

"Keeping it quiet is going to be hard. The police will have to notify the family, the DA and compaign headquarters. It's going to break soon."

"Unless we can stop it, or at least slow it down," Beverwyck said.

"Can we do that?" Witter asked.

As an answer, Beverwyck pushed the intercom button on the telephone sitting on the corner of the table.

"Jeffrey, I want you to get hold of Amos Parr in Washington, and Judge Haley in Boston."

"Right away, Mr. Beverwyck."

"Do you think the others can help?" Witter asked.

"I think we need as much influence as we can muster right now, Chuck. Can you at least dampen this at your end?"

"I can handle news coverage for maybe twenty-four hours. That's all. We need to get to the source."

"Meaning?"

"The commissioner, or the DA, or both."

They looked at one another for a moment.

"I think that's possible," Beverwyck said. "I'm sure I could get the commissioner, and Haley the DA. Parr can push the right people in Washington. I'll call New York campaign headquarters. I doubt they'll want this noised about much, and you can handle the news end. That's the hardest."

"I think," he continued, "that all we actually have to do is to doctor the circumstances of the murder. In other words, kill the gay angle. That he's dead we can't help, how and where it happened, I think, among us all, we can."

"Hopkenson will have to know," Witter said.

"No, I don't see why. We have too much invested in him to tell him and let him endanger our investment."

"Yes, we all have a rather large investment in Magnus Hopkenson, one way or another," Witter mused.

"Mr. Beverwyck," a voice said from the intercom.

"Yes, Jeffrey."

"I have Judge Haley on the line. Dr. Parr said he would call back."

"Put the judge on; call Parr back and get him to hold on. Tell him it's urgent."

"Yes, Mr. Beverwyck."

The phone clicked.

"Hello, Haley, is that you?"

"Who else do you suppose it is at this hour, Nelson? What do you want? It's too early to gossip."

"I'll get to the point. One of Hopkenson's young campaign aides was murdered last night and in circumstances not entirely of the best."

"What murder ever is, Nelson? How did it happen?"

"He was killed in a homosexual bathhouse, we think."

"We?"

"Chuck Witter and I."

"How do you know this?" the judge asked.

"Through sources. That's not important now."

"What is important, Nelson, is if anyone else has sources. If the Oval Office gets hold of this, they'll have a field day. It's a perfect diversionary tactic. Just what they've been looking for."

"I know that, and so does Chuck. We've already started work on it, and I've called Amos. Can you get the DA here in New York?"

"Of course I can. He was a student of mine in law school. Not too good, but pliable I recall. Yes, I can have a talk with him."

"Can you promise him anything?"

"Nelson, I am chairman of Judiciary. Let me use my own methods."

"Good. Now I want . . ."

The intercom buzzed.

"Hold a minute, Judge. This must be Amos. I'll put this on a conference call."

He pressed a button. "Hello, Amos, it's Nelson."

"I know it's Nelson. What's so all-fired important that you had to pull me off the golf course? I'm with the Secretary."

"I'm with Chuck Witter and the judge is on *our* conference line." He emphasized "our."

There was a moment of silence.

"What's the problem?"

"I need you to pull a few strings, Amos."

"What kind of strings?"

"Can you get to the national chairman?"

"Well, of course, but if you don't tell me what you're talking about I can't do anything."

"What I'm talking about Amos is that one of Hopkenson's bright young campaign aides here in New York—no one particularly important—has just become important by getting himself killed, apparently in a gay bath. Is that enough?"

"Oh, my God." There was an indrawn breath. "I was afraid it would come to this."

"What do you mean, come to this?" Beverwyck demanded.

Not hearing, Amos Parr asked, "Who was it?"

"Michael Ross."

"Ah yes, young aide, I met him once."

"Let's get on with this," Haley interrupted.

"You're right," Parr said. "Have you done anything? We have to do something, I'm sure you all agree."

"Yes," Beverwyck said, "I have. I've talked with Chuck, who's here now, and I'm going to contact the commissioner, to see if we can keep it quiet. The judge will handle the DA, and you can get to the national chairman."

"Good," Parr said. "What then?"

"Well," Beverwyck said, "I think that ought to do it. If we keep the specific details out of the paper, then we may have it handled."

"I'm afraid," Parr said softly, "that things aren't wrapped up quite so neatly as you might think."

"I don't follow," said Witter.

"It's true," Parr said, "that we can handle this. It won't be hard to downplay this into the back pages. But I'm afraid that is not the problem."

"What is?" Haley demanded.

"I think, in fact I am rather sure, that Michael Ross's death was not a random act of violence which we can simply hide. It was a warning."

"To whom?" Witter said.

"A warning to Hopkenson, and perhaps, gentlemen, to us. I fear that beneath the impeccable surface of Magnus Hopkenson's incorruptibility there is hidden one, tiny vulnerable point, about which I know, which I have never revealed, but which I believe someone else has discovered. You see, my friends, thirty years ago, when we were in college, together, Magnus Hopkenson and I were lovers."

2.

Philip left Witter's office and took the elevator down to his. His secretary was not in yet, though she should have been. He left a note canceling his appointments and saying he could be reached at home.

On the street, he decided to walk back to his apartment and ponder what had happened so rapidly that morning. He headed toward Fifty-Third Street, turned east when he got there, watching the eyes of New Yorkers on their way to work. Some eyes were looking at the sidewalk or dully fixed straight ahead. Others drank in the sunny morning and seemed cheerful, anticipating the day. New York eyes, varied, wary, keeping a corner watch for the mugger or the madman, yet curious and on the lookout for adventure, too. Philip liked New York eyes, even those behind dark glasses for the mystery of it. Sometimes eyes would catch his: some would quickly look away, look down, or pretend it hadn't happened. Often men would look at him, some with interest, speculation, or invitation. Women looked too, though never so boldly as some of the men, and Philip looked back, and often smiled at both men and women. Philip knew he was handsome and he enjoyed the game. As he walked, he felt, as he often did, a benevolent fondness for his New Yorkers, a curiosity above them all. But this morning the walk had other overtones, because he was puzzled, though not disturbed, by Witter's reaction. Witter had reacted in some ways as Philip expected he would, quickly, decisively. But he was surprised that Witter had not ordered him to find out more. And he was intrigued by his strange comment: "He *can't*," Witter had said, accentuating the verb as if there were someone who could keep under wraps the murder of a prominent figure in very questionable circumstances. This was a big story, one that the other papers and networks would field with a lot of display, but one that they had first if they wanted it. Philip didn't like the feel of it, but he knew Witter well enough to know that the man was scrupulous and that he ought to trust him. Witter was also his boss, and so, uneasily, with a sense that for a moment he had lost control of the situation, Philip decided the only thing he could do was what Witter demanded: stay by his phone. He nodded to Harry, the doorman, and took the elevator up to his floor.

Once in his apartment he decided that while waiting he could do some work of his own to be prepared for whatever might happen. He knew that if he had as much material as possible he could do his work most efficiently, and he also knew that if Witter was keeping him on hold he would eventually find out why and be part of the solution to the problem of Michael Ross.

He had worked with Chuck Witter for several years now, coming to the network after a stint on the Coast as a sports reporter. Witter had taken notice of him a year or so after he had come to work at the network when he managed to bring to light the real story behind the Techtron International collapse, and just why its president, Lavin McPhee, had certain investments in Argentina.

Witter had taken Philip under his wing at that time, and in the last few years he had worked closely with Witter, gaining his trust and confidence. Philip knew he owed a lot to Witter and so he waited for his call. But in the meantime he keyed his computer into the network research on Magnus Hopkenson, trying to find out just why such a man could sway someone like Chuck Witter to react the way he did.

Once he had everything, Philip knew he had nothing. All the facts were there: the material that went to make up the official compaign biography. Magnus Hopkenson, senator, upright crusader, liberal but not too liberal. A man of the people with strong ties to big business. A man who stood for God, Home, and Country, but who disavowed affiliation with radical right groups like Billy Jennings's God's People. A brilliant career in the Senate. A brilliant marriage to a woman of wealthy family. Two children. An "important" book on foreign policy, another on "The American Crisis." In short, just what the country needed, a fatherly activist, who would correct the ills that everyone saw, who would steer the country back to the middle course again. The current administration, after a brilliant start, had faltered: things had gotten worse, not better. The bright promises of economic recovery in the end had not come to pass and big business was disenchanted. Witter was big business, the biggest. The rightward turning of the nation had come close to hysteria. Those thoughtful men who saw a danger to national liberty in this as well as the serious danger of increasing presidential power were determined to act for Hopkenson. But not only was Witter big business, Witter was a thoughtful man. Philip could see why Witter might want to "handle" the news. But he wondered if he could.

He glanced at his watch. Several hours had gone by. The early edition of the *Post* would be out. He decided to go out for a bite and pick up the paper.

He was surprised, as he sat in the corner coffee shop, combing through the paper, to find there was no front page headline. The usual quota of death and mugging was there. A sex scandal in New Jersey took up the second page. Corrupt welfare workers were pilloried in the middle section. There was a laudatory editorial about the president's support of the regime in El Salvador "despite some minor infractions of human rights," and many letters from irate readers about the mayor's snub of Billy Jennings. But not until the last page before the sports section did he come on the story: brief, uninformative and to the point, the headline "Hopkenson Staff Member Felled by Stroke."

Philip finished his sandwich and hurried back to his apartment. The evening news—he watched all three channels on his special bank of three TV monitors—carried no mention of the story, save for a brief filler at the end of the NBC local broadcast: "Michael Ross, a junior staff member with the Hopkenson campaign was found dead in his apartment this morning. Medical reports indicate that Ross died from natural causes."

Philip switched off the set and picked up the phone, dialing LaMonica at home. The phone rang several times. LaMonica's sleepy voice answered.

"Frank, it's Phil. Listen, I know you're sacked out, but what happened with the Ross thing?"

"Ross? Oh yeah. Damndest thing, Phil. About three hours after I talked to you—no, maybe four—word came down from the top—I mean the *Top*—to close the file. Seal it."

"Thanks, Frank," Philip said.

"You got *some* friends, Phil."

"That's not the half of it," Philip said, and hung up.

At last the call came. It was 9 P.M.

"Yes, Kristopher here."

"Mr. Kristopher, this is Michael Lansing, Mr. Witter's private secretary. Mr. Witter would like to see you in his office at the network in an hour—half an hour if you can make it."

"I'll be there," Philip said.

Philip followed Michael Lansing to Witter's office.

"Please go in, Mr. Kristopher."

Philip entered the room. With Witter was another man, dressed in a severe, obviously expensive, dark suit. His face was dour, suspicious. He wore small wire frame glasses. Philip recognized him as Dr. Amos Parr, the Washington socialite physician whose work had brought him into contact with many very influential people.

"Philip, this is Amos Parr."

"Yes," Philip said, "I recognized you. I read your book."

Parr seemed only mildly pleased that he was recognized, seeming in fact to expect it.

"Let's get to it, Charles," he said addressing Witter.

"Philip, I have something of a special assignment."

"I gathered," Philip said. "Does it have anything to do with the Michael Ross murder, and the news blackout on it?"

"We believe, Mr. Kristopher," Parr said, "that Mr. Ross's death was quite natural."

"We?" Philip said.

"A manner of speaking. What I am interested in is not Michael Ross but in you, Mr. Kristopher. Charles tells me that you are the best investigative reporter he has, and the most discreet."

"I can be."

"Good. I would like you to investigate something for me."

"Something or someone, Mr. Parr?"

Parr smiled. "Someone, of course."

Witter broke in. "You must understand, Philip, that your status with the network won't be compromised. This is a private matter."

"I'm sure that if you were able to wipe Michael Ross off the record in just a few hours you'll be able to back me up. I think the question is, who will be compromised if I don't take the assignment?"

"You've come to the point," Parr said. "So shall I."

"We'll ask you to keep a secret," Parr continued, looking

very serious, as though he wanted to suggest menance but couldn't quite bring it off.

Philip smiled. "I'm already keeping a lot of secrets, Dr. Parr," he said, "but I believe I could find room for one more."

"Go ahead, Amos," Witter said. "You've seen his folder, and now you've seen the man. Go ahead and tell him."

Philip watched Parr more closely, waiting for whatever would come next.

"What if I told you, Mr. Kristopher, that a famous politician, I may say a very famous politician, is homosexual?"

"You'd have to tell me the name," Philip said, "and in most cases I doubt I'd be particularly surprised."

"The politician," Parr was saying, with the small grim smile of the inexperienced gambler who really does have the cards after all, "is Magnus Hopkenson."

"No!" said Philip. The word blurted out of him before he could stop it.

Parr laughed, a grating sound, and said, "So you can be surprised, after all."

"I had no idea," Philip said, adjusting his mind to this astonishing new reality. "I suppose you . . . have . . . personal knowledge of this?"

Again Parr's unexpected and harsh laugh sounded. "You mean," he said, "have I gone to bed with him?"

"I suppose that's what I mean, yes."

"At one point in life," Parr said, "we were lovers. I don't know who his lover might be at the moment, he may not have one. But his preferences will not have changed."

Philip looked from Parr to Witter, who was looking nervous.

To Parr, Philip said, "You're telling me this, but you want it kept secret."

"There are many secrets, Mr. Kristopher," Parr said.

"Yes, Dr. Parr, there are, and before we go on, what's yours?"

Parr was obviously thrown off guard. "I don't see what . . ."

Philip interrupted him: "What I see is that a young man who worked for Hopkenson was killed in compromising circumstances. Suddenly a lot of very long strings are pulled and a lot of potential noise is silenced. Now you come to town and tell me that this same Hopkenson is homosexual. It was only early this morning that I brought the information into this office and already I seem to be—indirectly I have to say—involved in some sort of collusion to cover up the news. That is difficult to take, gentlemen. *You* should understand that, Chuck. Now what I want to know, before we go any further, is what is going on. I don't take the job unless I have your trust—and *the full story.*"

"All right," Parr said. "You're right. There is a lot going on. You are correct in assuming that we have managed the news. We are powerful men, Mr. Kristopher, and we have powerful friends. It is important to us, and we believe, to the country, that Magnus Hopkenson should be elected. And this secret, you will have to agree, might prevent that. But the significant point is that somebody either knows or suspects the truth."

"How do you know?" Philip asked.

"Several days ago," Parr explained, "I was interviewed by a man named Walter Bray. This Bray is obviously a private investigator, though he passed himself off as a reporter wanting an interview about a commission I'm chairing. But after we had been talking for a while, I realized that he was asking questions about Magnus, not about me. Needless to say, I had to admit that I knew Magnus, that's a matter of record. But nevertheless, I had the feeling that this Bray had something, maybe just a hunch or a rumor. He didn't seem to know if he was looking for something going on now, or something from the past. But he seemed determined to dig something up."

"Did you tell him anything?" Philip asked.

"Only what he could find out in the records. But what I am telling *you* is that Magnus and I were close—we were lovers. It ended suddenly, bitterly, and we are no longer friends. Nevertheless, I admire him, respect him and the country needs him. Thus I will do everything I can, as will my colleagues, to insure his safety and his election."

"I take it you and your friends can do a very great deal."

"Candidly, we can."

"Then why do you need me?"

"Candidly again, you have to do the dirty work. None of us must be—can be—associated with this. And Magnus Hopkenson must never know. That's why we need you. Oh, by the way, I suppose I must ask. Do you have any feelings about homosexuality, Mr. Kristopher?"

Philip smiled. "We're not talking about sex, Dr. Parr, we're talking about power. I thought you knew that."

3.

The speaker raised his hands in an embracing gesture.

"We used to be outside the system, or if we were in it, it was only because we kept ourselves hidden. But now we don't hide, and we are no longer outsiders. We are part of the system now; we've let them see us, and they know who we are."

The large crowd cheered and whistled, stamping their feet. Randy Asher acknowledged the applause. Above him the banner of the National Coalition for Gay People stretched across the stage of the Felt Forum. Row upon row of gay people, members of the coalition, which was meeting here in its biannual convention, extended beyond the lighted podium. Asher stood at the speakers rostrum, his arms raised, the light catching his dark hair. His dark blue suit and conservative tie made him look like a successful candidate for public office, which, it was rumored, he might be in the next election. Behind him on the dais sat various men and women, among them Deputy Mayor Alfredo Rivera, Human Rights Commissioner Neider, and Suffragan Bishop Frederick Witherspoon of the Episcopal Diocese. Also on the dais were Andrew Holroyd, logistics head for the NCGP, Timothy Haley, the coalition's chief strategist, and Margot Canby, its co-director.

The cheering died down and Asher continued.

"I have been privileged to be the co-director of NCGP for four years now," he said, "and in those years I have seen a lot happen, a lot that has materially affected my life and yours. Who would have believed ten years ago that we would be here in the Felt Forum? I say to you that next year we'll be in Madison Square Garden itself."

Before the cheers could begin he raised his arms again, the spotlights shining on his handsome face, thin from the intense energy he put into his job, bright from the exhilaration of his speaking.

"We have seen the coalition grow, and we have seen the gay movement join hands with other rights movements and we have here tonight representatives from the Gay Black Caucus and from the Gay Coalitions within the United Labor Unions."

Asher was leaning out over the podium now, and his voice had dropped to a low and urgent note.

"But even though we have won victories, there have been defeats. We have indeed come out of the ghetto, but there are forces trying to drive us back. The conservative press has mounted what amounts to a crusade against what they call "The Homosexual Problem." And in the smaller cities, and in the larger ones, too, gay people who have enjoyed the last few years of comparative peace are suffering, and badly. Gay bars are being burned, gay people are being attacked.

"We have representatives in the unions and in the black and women's movements and in education; yet school boards in small towns across the country are trying ways, legal and extralegal, to dismiss teachers who are suspected of being gay.

"My friends, there is a lot to do, and we must not delude ourselves that the millenium is at hand. It is not, and there is a lot of damned hard work that calls to us all.

"And another thing," and here his voice became lower than ever, solemn. The crowd was hushed. "We must not forget that while Anita Bryant may have brought about, through her crusade, changes which ultimately were for the good, that now there is another force loose upon us. Bryant propelled us in the seventies to a place of national recognition. But now, we have to face Jennings, who has taken up where Bryant left off, and in him we have an opponent who is appealing to the Right in ways Bryant never did. We may be portrayed as fun-loving, harmless people on the television networks, but to the supporters of Jennings, we are still children of the devil and a clear and present danger to them all. I do not mean to sound like a rabble-rouser, but the danger is clear to us, too.

"Let us now all vow to be one people, for despite the defeats, despite the violence, despite the setbacks along the way, the path is open for us at last, and we are soon to grasp our golden fleece. And what the last years have brought is a chance now to do it not from outside but from within. Next week, I can now announce to you all, I will be meeting with Magnus Hopkenson, who will be, if we can help, our next president."

The crowd cheered again. Many rose to their feet applauding. Asher raised his arms to quiet them. He continued.

"I will be meeting, I say, with our next president, and I hope to go to him and say that we are all with him, that we can deliver the gay vote. I will tell him that twenty million gay people can't be wrong, and I will tell him that if he will be for us, we will not be against him, and who can be against us?

"My sisters and brothers, gay women and men, we stand now at the threshold of the new life. This election year will ratify what we have for years been working toward. Give me your mandate to take to Washington. Give me your faith and your hope. Give me the torch."

The crowd rose, cheering.

Indeed Randy Asher was worthy of the emotion. He had, in the years since the close of the seventies, moved determinedly and actively from his job as media director for the mayor of New York into the city and the national organization of the coalition. He was elected its co-director and he had become, in a way that no other gay spokesman had ever become, a nationally recognized leader for gay people. Before that time the gay movement had been fragmented, with small groups here, small civic organizations, collegiate groups, religious organizations. The coalition had begun in New York and had, under Asher's leadership, expanded the national thrust it had developed before he was its director. It was the coalition that had begun to bring to gay people a sense of national identity, the sense they were not just gay New Yorkers or San Franciscans or Bostonians, but gay Americans. It was said that Randy Asher, if he had the organization in back of him and the money, could seriously run for president.

Later that night in their apartment, a tired but jubilant Randy Asher sat over a late night cup of coffee with Tim Haley. He and Tim had been lovers for four years now, ever since Tim had come to New York for graduate work. Since they met, Tim had made himself invaluable to Randy as an aide. Somehow, rightly, they had drifted into intimacy, and had decided, two years before, to live together.

"You know kid"—Tim always called Randy 'kid' though Randy was older than Tim by five years—"you put the fear of God in them tonight."

Randy nodded. "I hope it will do some good."

"If Hopkenson meets with you," Tim went on, "he'll be close to endorsing the Gay Rights Bill in Congress."

"Don't be too hopeful," Randy said. "After all, meeting with me is good politics, but he doesn't have to endorse anything. He knows there's a gay vote out there, but what do you bet there won't be a lot of press coverage."

"Then we have to see that there is," Tim said. "And pressure him."

"I don't think Magnus Hopkenson is too susceptible to pressure," Randy mused. "He really is his own man. But he's also a very smart man and he knows just how the wind blows. I think he's fair, and honest, and I think he probably does believe in civil rights, but he won't make a grandstand play."

Tim poured more coffee and got up and came around the table, putting his hand on Randy's shoulder. Randy reached back and laid his hand on top of Tim's.

"Thanks for being there tonight. It always helps," Randy said.

Tim kissed him and went back to his seat.

"I wish Michael could have been there," Tim said. "Without him, we've lost a contact with Hopkenson."

Randy nodded, not speaking.

"That was hard, wasn't it?" Tim said.

"Michael and I went to school together. I'd known him a long time."

"It was a shock," Tim said. "I didn't know him well, but he was sharp. You know, there are rumors going around that it was violent."

"The paper said it was his heart."

"He was pretty young for that," Tim said.

"I know," Randy agreed.

"A friend of mine," Tim said, "insists that he didn't die in his apartment. He says he saw Michael at the baths the night it happened and that late that night there was a lot of police activity there."

"Michael was pretty careful," Randy said.

"You mean he wasn't out?"

"Yes and no," Randy said. "It wasn't generally known at Hopkenson headquarters that he was gay. Michael kept his private life quiet."

"I think there's something strange about it," Tim insisted.

"You're always looking for plots around every corner," Randy said. "Come on, let's go to bed."

"No," Tim said, "I mean it. Don't you think it's odd that there hasn't been any news coverage to speak of?"

"Well, yes, I guess so," Randy said. "But what's there to say?"

"What's to say," Tim said, "is that a prominent member of the Hopkenson staff was killed in a gay bath. Wh that's the kind of story that the *News* or *Post* thrives on."

"But Timmy," Randy said, "all that is only rumor. All you've got is some street gossip."

"There have been others," Tim said stubbornly

"Other what?"

"Other gay murders. Tony Marrazano, Lenny Goodman, Harvey Milk, all politicians."

Randy paused for a moment. "Okay, you're right. those people are dead. And they were gay and in politi What does that give you?"

Tim got up and began pacing around the room.

"What it gives me is that in the last few years three gay politicians have been murdered, men who were active and up front. Now, Michael Ross, who was in an important position and who was gay—whether it was known by people on the street it was still no secret to hundreds of people—is now dead. The papers say—insist even, that it was a heart attack. But he was twenty-nine and in good health. On top of this there is a lot of talk that it was murder and there is no—I repeat *no* investigation of these rumors."

"Have you checked that?"

"Well, no, but . . ."

"You check that," Randy said. "If you can come up with something from the precinct, then maybe, just maybe, I might take you seriously on this. But I'm willing to bet you won't get far. They always stonewall things down there, you know that."

"But there's something else," Tim said.

"You know, I'm tired and really want to crawl in bed

with you," Randy said, coming over to Tim and pulling him toward the bedroom.

"Please listen," Tim said.

Randy was struck by his serious tone.

"Just suppose it's true that there is someone gunning for gay politicians," Tim said.

"If its true, then whoever got Michael was trying to harm Hopkenson. Right?"

"Okay." Randy said. "It's a big if, but I can see that."

Tim went on. "If someone were trying to harm Hopkenson, then they wouldn't want Michael's death covered up if it happened at the baths. Would they?"

"Okay, okay," Randy said. "Get to it."

"But there is some evidence that it has been covered up. And whoever did the cover up must be trying to protect Hopkenson. And whoever killed Michael . . ."

"If he was killed," Randy interjected.

". . . is trying to hurt Hopkenson," Tim said triumphantly.

"It makes sense, if you're right," Randy agreed.

"Then what it comes to is that there is a big war going on out there and we ought to know who's doing the fighting because we're right in the middle of it."

"I agree," Randy said. "If you are right, we should investigate this. But I don't see how that puts us in the middle between these two mysterious forces you think are out there. I'll go along with some digging around, but where are we at risk?"

"Randy, don't you see?" Tim said urgently. "If someone killed Michael Ross because he was a gay politician who supported Hopkenson, then after what you said tonight, they'll be out to get you. Randy, you're a target, and I'm scared."

4.

Walter Bray, partner in Confidential Research Associates, took another sip of Scotch, and slid the file folder back into the pile on his desk. The circle of light revealed a desk top littered with folders, stacks of papers and magazines, telephone books from around the country, road maps, biographical atlases and street maps of major cities. Three large Rolodex wheels occupied one corner next to a three-button telephone. The silence was broken only by the shuffling of papers and the occasional clink of ice in the glass.

Bray glanced at the clock; it was nearly midnight, and he was tired. He wanted to be in the office early tomorrow, but he had to review these cases, decide which to go forward with, who to assign to them, and recommend lines of action. He picked up the next one, studied it briefly and wrote across the front: "Return to client, decline assignment." While he was sure the *Post* was on to something, the question of influence-peddling by presidential relatives was exactly the kind of case Confidential Research Associates preferred to avoid; not because they feared to tangle with the mighty, but because they determinedly kept out of the bright light of publicity, and the *Post*'s allegations, if true and provable, would provide plenty of publicity for all. Bray would rather keep away from it; especially with something like the Hopkenson file in front of him.

The Hopkenson file. He pulled out the next folder and leafed through its pages. On top was the abstract of the official campaign biography. Underneath this was the dossier on Hopkenson's friends and those who had been close to him during the course of his career. Among these were friends from college, from the army, staff members from Hopkenson's days with Senator Rideau, members of Hopkenson's own staff while he was a congressman, and then later as a senator. There was a file on Hopkenson's medical history, a copy of the FBI's file, a financial statement and microfilm of the senator's financial transactions over the last ten years. Underneath all this was the file on Miriam Hopkenson, the senator's wife. But what did it add up to? Lots of facts, but no color. Many pieces of information, but nothing that gave him the lead to what he wanted. At least nothing that was apparent now.

Bray had amassed this material in the last several weeks, working as fast as he could. He had been approached to do the background work on Magnus Hopkenson, a not unusual request for Confidential Research Associates. He had done private files on many candidates and would-be candidates, on corporate executives, on anyone who was or might be in the public eye or who might touch some other influential person in some way.

Often his clients were large corporations needing information that would place them in good bargaining positions. Sometimes the inquiries were more delicate, like the major record company that needed the facts about an auto accident; an accident in which one of their major singers, whose voice thrilled millions of teenagers and who was beyond caring on cocaine, had walked away from the scene, leaving two dead. Usually what the clients wanted was every detail, every piece of gossip, every nuance or innuendo which when put together by skilled lawyers might get them off a hook or put someone else on one.

But with the Hopkenson case it was different. The client was very specific. He wanted only one thing. He wanted it quickly, the money didn't matter, and secrecy was essential. The client wanted to know what Magnus Hopkenson did in bed and with whom. It was made clear that if it were discovered Hopkenson did it with one-hundred-dollar-a-night call girls, or the bored wives of senatorial aides, the information would be of no use or interest. But if it were established that Magnus Hopkenson did or had ever done it with men, then the investigation would be considered a success.

The assignment had been brought to the office by a young man, vaguely Latin in looks, very businesslike and explicit. He had set conditions: Bray must make no attempt to identify the client. All reports were to be made to a "Mr. Smith" who would phone every three days to arrange to pick up a cassette tape detailing Bray's progress. Bray had been intrigued by it all, taking on the case at least as much for the mystery of the client as for the mystery of Hopkenson's sexual bent.

So far, he had compiled a thick dossier. But nothing seemed clear, and nothing had turned up. Bray's staff was tracing army connections, checking out college friends, but Hopkenson's life seemed blameless, even boring. Bray's impression was of a man who had no sex life at all.

But Bray was intrigued by two things. First, if someone was willing to shell out so much money to search for something that was proving so elusive, then there just might be something to be found out. Second, there were those interviews. He had personally spoken with Senator Louis Rideau and Dr. Amos Parr, Rideau being the senator from Hopkenson's home state, and Parr a college friend of Hopkenson's who was not, apparently, close to the senator now. However, Rideau had been Hopkenson's guide and mentor on the thorny trails of political life.

During the interviews both men had seemed open and

casual, in their very different ways, and it wasn't until afterward, in going over the transcripts of the tapes he'd made, that Bray noticed the anomaly. While Senator Rideau and Dr. Parr had known Hopkenson at different times in the man's life and career, and while their answers on all other subjects reflected this difference as well as the differences in the two interviewees' own lives and personalities, on the subject of homosexuality as it related to Magnus Hopkenson there had been a startling unanimity. Bland, smooth, casual, uninfluenced answers, matching one another almost word for word: Magnus Hopkenson was a champion of *all* minority groups, Senator Rideau had explained, but he himself had never discussed homosexuals in particular with Hopkenson. Of course Magnus Hopkenson would have to seek the votes of many different minorities, Dr. Parr had pointed out, but he had no memory of ever having discussed homosexuality with Hopkenson.

There was something there. Now Bray had to get it in focus. He put down the file and rubbed his eyes. The clock read one-thirty; he had to be up at seven. He closed the file and put it in his desk, locked securely inside the center drawer, underneath a thin, false bottom. Turning off the light, he made his way to his bedroom, shedding clothes as he went. In his room he looked out the large window at the gleaming lights of Washington, over toward the government buildings in the distance. He knew that what he had in his drawer was potentially the most explosive document this country had yet seen. He recalled the clumsy burglars who had broken into this same huge complex a few years ago, even while he was living here, asleep many floors above; clumsy burglars whose ineptitude had brought down a government and sent a king into exile, and had made a man's name an epithet for dishonesty. What would the name Magnus Hopkenson mean on the lips of Americans in years to come if what Walter Bray suspected was true?

April 2   *7:20* A.M.

Bray heard the clock chime, but it wouldn't stop; it kept on ringing, ringing. Slowly he realized it was not a clock, but the phone next to his bed. He struggled up out of sleep, seeing light against the closed draperies. Groggily he reached for the phone.

"Lo."

"Walt, it's George. Are you awake?"

Bray felt jumpy, the remnants of dreams still in his head. "What time is it?" he asked. "Did I oversleep?"

"It's seven-thirty. But, Walt . . ."

"Seven-thirty. Jesus, I wanted to be in by eight."

"Walter," George said, his voice hurried and tense, "listen, the office was broken into last night."

Walter Bray was suddenly awake.

"Broken into. Robbery, money, what?"

"I don't know yet," George answered. "I'm having the photo system stills developed now, and the tapes analyzed."

"Okay. I'll be right there. Don't call the law, don't do anything."

April 2   *8:30* A.M.

George Farrell waited in Bray's office, with a spare cup of coffee. "You look like hell", he said.

"Good," Bray said. "Tell me about it."

"Drink coffee a minute," Farrell said. "The guy's long gone." George Farrell, a burly, worried-looking man of about fifty, was one of Bray's two partners in Confidential Research Associates. He specialized in industrial espionage, in both committing it and guarding against it, and in general plant and office security. It was he who had designed the sophisticated security system that protected the offices, and which had been breached last night.

While Bray sipped at very bad, very hot coffee, Farrell said, "They knew what they wanted—or he knew what he wanted, I should say—and he knew how to get in and just where to look."

"What did he get?"

"I don't think anything, judging by the sensor films," Farrell said, holding out a sheaf of pictures. "Look," he said, almost apologetically, "even with our security system, a really good man—and this is a really good man—could get in. I mean, he did. But I've got him on film, and it looks to me like he was stymied. But I'll tell you one thing. He didn't break in, he got in because he knew how. That broken window is only a cover. He knew how to cancel the magnetic lock and he knew how to negate the sonic alarm, and he knew about the cameras. Look."

Bray picked up the pictures. They had been taken by one of Farrell's more ingenious devices, a system of heat-activated cameras that when switched on were activated by the heat of anything as warm or warmer than a human body. They were set to take photos every thirty seconds. And they'd worked, but all they showed was a tall, slim man who had come prepared. He was wearing Playtex gloves and the kind of glasses-nose-and-mustache for sale in novelty stores that effectively hide the face. Bray could see from the sequence of photos that the intruder had moved directly from the rear janitor's entrance, across the central office, past the secretaries' desks and files, directly to Bray's office, where other cameras had picked up the intruder as he came in, as he bent over Bray's desk, as he jimmied the lock on the file drawer, as he pulled out various files, looked through them and then carefully put them back. He apparently took no photos, and from a quick check of his desk, Bray knew nothing was missing. The next-to-the-last photo showed the man looking up, directly into the camera, his arms on his hips in an attitude of apparent annoyance.

"Didn't get what he wanted," Bray said. He put the attache case containing the Hopkenson file on his desk. He knew what the intruder had been after. "Listen, George," he said, "make copies of all these, and especially that full-face shot. Maybe someone on the staff will recognize him despite the mask. See if you can get some enlargements of anything in the photos that might be traced."

"I know what to do, Walt," George Farrell gently reminded him.

"Sorry, George, I know you do. And listen, it wasn't your fault that he got through. He knew something."

"Damn right it wasn't my fault," George said. "Nobody, but nobody, could have broken into that system cold. But let me tell you something, anybody who could negate that lock has had some special training, and that kind of training is pretty hard to come by. I know almost everyone who might know how to do it, and sooner or later, I can find out who gave him the info—got me?"

"Got ya," Bray said. "Got ya."

George Farrell went out, and Monte Dillon, who had been standing in the background, said, "Listen, Walt, do you know what they wanted?"

"Sure I know, Monte, they wanted the Hopkenson file. They didn't get it because I took it home last night. And our mysterious 'Mr. Smith' is going to call this afternoon—I think maybe he'd better not know about our break-in."

"Unless our intruder is on 'Mr. Smith's' payroll," George suggested.

"Then he already knows," Bray said. "Do we have anything on Hopkenson?"

"One potential. A fellow named Hugh Tilden. A few

years ago he worked at Defense, some small position, nothing significant, but with some security clearance. He was there about five years, led an impeccable life until one day, boom, he got busted in a YMCA men's room trying to grope a vice squad cop. It was all kept very quiet. He 'resigned,' left the city, and maybe went to San Francisco, maybe not."

"What's the connection?"

"Two years before coming to Defense, he was a junior staffer with Senator Rideau, during his second campaign. Hopkenson was also there, just about to run for the junior post."

"Anything connecting the two?"

"No." With his thin, worried-looking smile, Monte said, "Like always, Hopkenson was Mr. Clean, and this Tilden guy was pretty discreet, too. For the life of me, given his record, I don't know how he managed to get busted in the john. It wasn't like him."

Bray thought. Then he said: "Maybe it was a setup. Those things do happen. Remember Walter Jenkins?"

"Yeah, could be. I'll see what I can do on that angle. I've got more."

"Okay. More."

"More is Tilden's ex-roommate. Name of Aleister St. Pierre."

"Sounds phony," Bray said with a grin.

"It is. His real name is Marvin Goodman; he's been around the gay life for a few years, sometimes a dancer, sometimes a model, but mostly a call boy. Now he's getting a little long in the tooth. At one time, according to this source, Tilden was involved with someone big on The Hill. Don't know who. That's how this St. Pierre got into it."

"So that's how I'll start my day," Bray said. "With an Aleister St. Pierre. Give me the address."

The address was not Georgetown. Bray walked up a short flight of stairs to the foyer of the five-story apartment building and looked over the buzzers. Most of the names, scrawled in pen or typed on cards, were last names only. The few full names were male. Among them was one in script: *Aleister St. Pierre.* Bray pushed the buzzer and after a short time a voice responded.

"My name is Anthony Bradlee," Bray said, speaking loudly into the speaker grill. "I'm from the Gay Worker's Alliance. I wonder if I might speak to you."

"Will it take long?" the voice from the intercom asked.

"It's about Hugh Tilden."

There was a moment of silence; then the buzzer sounded. Bray pushed open the door and went into the lobby, where elegance, cheaply attempted but unsuccessful, dictated the decor. He summoned the elevator and rode up to the third floor.

The door of 310 stood ajar, held by a chain lock. Bray knocked. From behind the door the voice said, sounding as metallic as it had over the intercom, "If you don't mind, I'd like some identification."

Bray pulled out the detective license bearing the name Anthony Bradlee, carrying the official stamp of the Washington police, and held it near the opening in the door. An eye studied it, after a pause the door shut, the chain dropped, and the door swung open.

"Come in."

A young man, though not as young as he wanted to look, stood near the door, holding a glass and cigarette. His hair and mustache were dark. He was dressed in tight jeans, a plaid shirt, heavy construction boots and wool socks. A gold chain hung around his neck and a gold ID bracelet circled his wrist. Despite the lumberjack look, the way he stood and held his glass belied the super-macho image he was trying to convey. The slight slackness in the skin of his neck and the puffiness under the eyes suggested that age and maybe too much booze were taking their toll.

The young man motioned Bray to a chair, one of two covered with grey tweed, which with a TV set, stereo and sofa bed was the only furniture in the room. The place looked temporary, an encampment far from home.

"Not much, is it?" the young man said. "But who has time to pick out nice things. You know what I mean?" Hurrying on, with a kind of nervous, dismissive shrug, he said, "So tell me, what's this about the Gay Worker's Alliance? I've never heard of them."

Bray said, "The GWA is a small group of gay activists who . . ."

St. Pierre interrupted him: "You're not going to tell me you're gay, baby."

Bray blinked. "No, I'm not gay, but I've been hired because I'm good and because I'm sympathetic to the cause they believe in."

The young man raised one eyebrow. "I see," he said.

"At any rate," Bray went on, "the GWA is doing a study on people who were dismissed from government positions because of their homosexuality and one of our cases is Hugh Tilden. I have your name as an old friend of his."

"And just how did you get my name?" St. Pierre said.

"I really can't reveal my sources," Bray told him, "but I can assure you everything we do is in the strictest confidence, nothing you say will be made public. It's all background material and you won't be identified by name, only by code number, in my report."

"Ummmmmm," St. Pierre said. "Well, ask me the questions, and I'll try not to lie."

"Do you know where Hugh Tilden is now?"

"Not a clue. He disappeared from my life, oh, a while ago, and I haven't heard a thing for a long time."

"Were you close?"

"Close? Do you mean were we lovers? That's a laugh. No, we were definitely not lovers. Let's just say we were in the same line of work."

"I see, and what was that?"

Archly, St. Pierre said, "Oh, I have my secrets, too, Mr. Bradlee."

"Yes, I see," Bray said, writing in his book. "What did Tilden do after his dismissal from the Defense Department?"

"I told you, he left town, but not before he borrowed nearly five hundred from me, and never paid it back, the bitch. That's the last time I'll see any of that money."

"What do you think of the circumstances of Tilden's dismissal?"

"Circumstances?"

"Yes, his arrest."

"You mean his getting caught in a tearoom." St. Pierre became knowing and confidential. "Listen, honey," he said, "Hughie Tilden liked sex, but one thing I know, he would not do it in a tearoom. No, you can tell your GWA Hugh Tilden was set up for that one, but don't ask me any more, because I don't know any more about it."

"Set up? Why? By whom?"

"Sorry, but that's all I know."

Bray was sure St. Pierre was lying, but he continued the questioning, asking about Tilden's life, his other friends. He came up with next to nothing, one or two names, but as St. Pierre talked, his evasiveness gave way to loquaciousness and his natural desire to gossip began to give Bray a pretty clear picture of the life St. Pierre led.

"This one's off the record, Mr. St. Pierre," Bray finally said, "but you say you have known some, shall we say, important people who are gay?"

There was a long silence, then St. Pierre smiled. "I get it," he said, "you're not here for Hugh Tilden, are you? You want more than that."

"Okay," Bray said. "Let's level with each other. I know what you do and I know you get paid for it. I am interested in Hugh Tilden, but I'm interested in a few more things as well."

"You want the big names, don't you," St. Pierre said.

"They wouldn't hurt," Bray responded.

"They wouldn't be free either," St. Pierre told him.

"Money's not a problem. You have names?"

St. Pierre looked at him with narrowed eyes. "I could rattle your teeth loose if I wanted to."

Bray thought for a moment. "I'll give you five hundred."

"Make it fifteen hundred."

"Fifteen hundred? One thousand."

"Big names cost big money," St. Pierre pointed out.

"Okay," Bray said. "Fifteen hundred. But only if the names are worth it and if you've got some proof."

"What do you want, pubic hair?"

"No, just some facts; enough to hold up under my client's scrutiny."

"Your client's . . . ?"

"I ask no more questions, you get no more answers," Bray said. "I'll be back at four o'clock with the money, in cash."

St. Pierre held out his hand as Bray rose to leave. "Mr. Bradlee," he asked, "is *that* your real name?"

"No, Mr. St. Pierre," Bray said. "Is *that* yours?"

Bray felt his anger rise as he left the building. Little fairy, he thought. No, that wasn't it, the guy was just plain nasty. He'd seen that type in straight people as well, lonely, desperate, always looking to cut someone down, to make a deal, a quick buck. Part of human nature, he decided.

He crossed the sidewalk to his car, climbed in, and, as he was looking in the rearview mirror, he saw a figure walking swiftly the other way. The man stopped for a moment, half turned back toward the car, and then walked on.

"That's him," Bray said aloud. "Jesus Christ, that's him."

There it was, the same half-profile he had seen in one of the photos, made distinctive by the curly black hair framing the face, black curly hair that had not been hidden by the false face the intruder had worn. The same posture, the same stance.

Bray sat still a second, wondering if the guy realized he'd been seen. But he kept on walking and got into a green Pinto parked up the block.

Bray started his car and pulled out, hoping the tail would follow him. He switched on the radio, using the voice intercom so he would not be seen picking up a mike.

"This is Bray," he said, when Kathy in the office responded to his call. "Tell Monte I've got our intruder on my tail. He's in a two-door green Pinto, seventy-four or five. I think he'll follow. I'll come down Sixteenth Street. You can pick him up at Scott Circle. I'll take it all the way around and go out Massachusetts westward. Then I'll drop him, and you see where he goes."

"Right."

Bray nosed his car into the traffic, watching the other car pull out and keep a discreet distance behind. Nervy bastard, Bray thought. He made his way over to Sixteenth Street and headed south, keeping the green Pinto in his rearview mirror at all times.

After a quarter of an hour he switched on the radio again: "Monte, I'm crossing Q Street."

"I'm in the Circle already," Monte answered, "going around and around."

Bray entered Scott Circle, made a complete circuit once, passing Monte's gray Ford idling in the inside lane, and said, "It's the green Pinto, about three cars back." Then he made the turn onto Massachusetts, going toward Dupont Circle, one long block ahead. If he didn't unload the tail at Dupont Circle he'd take him up around the Naval Observatory and get rid of him there.

From the radio came Monte's voice, sounding uncertain: "Walt? I don't see him."

Bray frowned at the mirror. "He was right there, in sight."

Then Bray got it. "Shit," he said. "Last night that motherfucker copied off our wavelength and just spent the half-hour listening in."

5.

Philip parked the Pinto beneath a large elm tree. Across the street, at 3497 P Street, was Parr's house, a four-story clapboard building, gray with white trim, built, Philip guessed, in the early part of the last century. It stood on the corner, fronting on P Street. The main house extended along the small alley, and an extension, obviously of later vintage, ran almost to the next corner.

Philip crossed the street and went through the iron gate, up the steps and to the door, where there was a large brass knocker in the shape of a hand cut off at the wrist. A small plaque surmounted a buzzer set discreetly in the side of the door frame: *Amos C. R. Parr, M.D.* Philip lifted the heavy knocker and rapped four times. A sharp voice said:

"Mr. Kristopher?"

Philip couldn't see the hidden intercom." That's right," he said in the general direction of the voice.

Almost immediately the door opened. Inside stood a dark-haired young man dressed in dark trousers, black tie and white coat. "Please come in," he said with a French accent. "Mr. Parr is expecting you."

"Je vous remercie," Philip responded.

The man smiled. "Eh bien," he said, but did not continue in French. "If you will come with me, Dr. Parr will meet you in the library."

"Thank you." Philip followed the young man along a dark, heavily carpeted hall. Aside from a large pier glass mirror, the hall had no furniture, but was lined with portraits of dour-faced women and balding benign men, severe clerics or prosperous businessmen.

The young man held the door open. "May I get you a drink, sir?"

"No, thank you," Philip said and went into the library.

"Dr. Parr will be with you in a moment." The young man bowed and quietly closed the door.

The room was bathed in sunlight, slanting across the large double desk in the center of the room, its top embossed in tooled green leather, the drawers heavy with ornamental woodcarving. On the desk stood ranks of pictures, silver-framed mementos of the life of Amos Parr. Here were pictures of Parr shaking hands with Nixon, dining with Johnson, walking with Kennedy, golfing with Eisenhower. Here were pictures of Parr with groups of senators, with UN diplomats. Philip recognized Nelson Beverwyck with Parr together on the steps of Blueshores, Beverwyck's Virginia estate. There were framed photographs of many famous men, signed with scrawls, with flourishes, with illegible signatures: photos of Robert Kennedy, of Gore Vidal, of Leonard Bernstein, of Carson Blake, of Cardinal Castillo, of David Lillienthal, of Felix Frantfurter, of Kinsey and Ellis.

Philip wondered why such a man as Parr who moved so prominently in the halls of power should want to involve himself in such a potentially dangerous situation. What did he have to gain? Or to lose?

The door opened and Amos Parr came in, followed by the butler. "Good morning, Philip. I may call you Philip?"

Philip nodded. He sensed that Parr was trying for an informality that he felt necessary but which he disliked.

"Now, a drink?"

"No thanks."

"Well, you'll certainly have some breakfast. Leon, bring us something to the morning room. We'll be down in a few minutes. You will have breakfast?" he asked again, as Leon departed.

"Yes, that would be fine," Philip said.

Parr crossed the room and motioned Philip to a chair. "Let's get down to it. What do you have for me?"

"You're right about Hopkenson," Philip said.

"Right, what do you mean?" Parr said sharply. "Of course I'm right."

"I mean," Philip said, "that he keeps a low profile. No hint of anything improper or damaging."

"I told you that," Parr said. "That's why we have to find out what they've got."

"What I've got is this," Philip said, taking out the small leather notebook he used to make jottings to himself.

He told Parr about starting to investigate other candidates who might oppose Hopkenson either in the primaries or at the convention.

"I've done some checking on the security men who work for Samuels from New York, Good from California and Sung of Hawaii. I want to find out what they've been doing, especially if they made any moves of a covert nature toward our man."

He then mentioned some names in the business sector who might be thought of as dangerous to Hopkenson.

"I've started a file on all of them," he said, "especially Randolph and Symington."

"Good," Parr said. "You've started a lot; have you found anything?"

"I've found Walter Bray," Philip said. "He runs Confidential Research Associates."

"Private detectives?"

"More sophisticated. He's big time, well-funded. He's got good contacts, top-notch security systems."

"What do we do about him?"

"Nothing now."

"Why not?" Parr asked.

"If I move too fast, I'll endanger the whole thing. We don't want to risk exposure through impatience. I don't know enough yet. And I think he knows who I am."

"He saw Parr react with alarm to the suggestion.

"You mean by name?" Parr said.

Parr had gotten up and was pacing back and forth through the slanting beam of sunlight.

"No, by sight."

"But how?" Parr said, etching a line of anxiety across the floor.

"From the photos."

"Photos? What photos? Now, look here, Kristopher, first you tell me you don't know anything and now you say the man you're hired to investigate knows more about you than you do about him."

"That's not what I said," Philip patiently explained. He told Parr about the foray into Bray's office, about the encounter with Bray that morning.

"I see," said Parr, not mollified. "And just what did you learn in Walter Bray's office?"

Philip did not answer for a moment. Rising, he went over to the desk, where he picked up a picture of Parr standing with Magnus Hopkenson on the steps of the Capitol.

"Mr. Parr," he said, holding the photograph, "I don't care whether or not Bray finds out anything about Magnus Hopkenson, but apparently you do. You've hired me. I'm doing what I can."

Parr's face had drained of its color. He grasped the back of the chair tightly. "Go on," he said.

"Okay, I didn't find much in the office," Philip continued. "The file folder on Hopkenson wasn't there."

"How do you know there is one?"

"There was a cross reference to it in the master list in Bray's file. And there are interview tapes, one with you, another with Senator Rideau. There was also a rough case sheet on someone named Hugh Tilden. Do you know him?"

"Is that important?"

"I think so," Philip said.

"In fact, I do, but it's been . . ."

"Yes, years. I know," Philip said. "That's in Bray's file, too."

"Oh my God," Parr said, and sank into the chair.

"That's not all," Philip went on. "What about St. Pierre?"

"Oh yes, Aleister," Parr said dejectedly.

"You know him?"

"Yes! How did you get *his* name?"

"The case sheet on Tilden. It has three cross references: Parr, St. Pierre, and Hopkenson. Who is this St. Pierre?"

"Just a little two-bit whore," Parr said savagely.

"I thought so," Philip observed, more to himself than Parr. "The interesting thing . . ." he continued.

"What now?" Parr said, seemingly fearful of more revelations.

"The interesting thing," Philip went on, "is that on none of the sheets is the client's line filled in. They're all blank."

"I don't understand."

"I don't think Bray knows who he's working for," Philip told him.

There was a discreet knock on the door.

"Yes," Parr said.

The door opened. "I've made coffee and breakfast, sir, if you're ready."

Philip followed Parr out of the library and down the hall to the back stairs. "This house has been in my family for many generations," Parr was saying. "My great grandfather built it, my grandparents lived in it; I was born here, I have inherited it. Unlike my predecessors, however, I will not be leaving it to . . . anyone at all."

"That's too bad," Philip said sincerely.

"Yes, it is."

They reached the bottom of the stairs and entered the small breakfast room that looked out onto a brick patio, shaded with cherry trees.

"Of course," Parr continued, "perhaps I will find some deserving young man, and then . . ." He left the sentence unfinished.

"And then?" Philip asked him.

"And then perhaps I won't," Parr said. "Perhaps I won't," he said again, almost to himself.

Philip was moved by the loneliness in the man's tone. For a moment, Parr had let down his guard, dropped the haughty exterior. Philip liked him better for it. Parr motioned him to a seat at the breakfast table.

"I hope you find that young man," Philip said gently.

Parr looked at him intently for a moment. Then: "No matter if I don't. I've had, I have, a full life. I have memories, and still a few dreams. Being alone isn't quite as much of a sin as the movie magazines suggest. I'll survive."

"Yes," Philip said, "I think you will. I'm sure of it."

As if recovering himself, Parr said, "Let's go on. We have work to do."

At that moment Leon brought in breakfast. Philip wondered if he was Parr's deserving young man. Over ham and eggs, croissants and coffee, Philip outlined what he needed from Parr.

"I need someone who can get to Walter Bray. Someone who knows security or has contacts in the intelligence network, and who is big enough that he can't be touched. Do you know anyone?"

Parr thought for a moment. "Must he be a friend of mine?"

"Not important, but he will have to be someone you can go to with a reasonable story, or at least put me in contact with reasonably."

"I do know someone," Parr finally said, "but surely you're not going to tell him what's going on?"

"Who is it?"

"I could put you in touch with Otis Ferguson. I don't know him well, but we know some people in common. He's a retired army general, military intelligence. I haven't seen him for a couple of years. I hear he's a bit odd, but I think he might be your man."

"To answer your question," Philip said, "I won't tell him what's going on, but I will have to bring in Bray. If you'll set it up and tell him that I'm working for you, doing some investigation for a report on the ethics of private investigators for a report you're doing, I think we could find out what I need."

"I'm not sure if I'm clear. Just what do you need?"

"I need access to Bray's files. Someone like Ferguson, if he's what you say, could find a way to get me in without Bray suspecting. I've broken in once, I can't do it again."

"All right," Parr said. "He owes me a favor for a little situation I managed for him a few years ago. I think I could well collect on that now."

"Should I ask what the situation was?" Philip asked.

"I don't think so," Parr replied with a smile. "Let me go and make a call."

Parr left Philip alone. What a curious man, Philip thought. He had begun to understand Parr more now. He stood at the hub of a circle of the very great and the very rich. Himself holding no particular office, but holding instead many strings that he very artfully pulled. His manner was often arrogant, aristocratic. But as Philip got to know him, it was clear that Parr *was* an aristocrat, and a man of great ability. Philip was sorry he was alone.

"Pardon me sir," Leon said, softly entering. "Will there be anything else, more coffee?"

"No, Leon, thank you," Philip said. Then, as an afterthought, "Leon, have you worked for Dr. Parr for a long time?"

"For some time, sir."

"Does he treat you well?"

A slight smile crossed Leon's handsome face. "Very well, sir."

"Leon," Philip said. "I hope you're properly grateful."

"I don't understand, Mr. Kristopher."

"Oh, I think you do, Leon, I think you do. I don't know you, and I probably don't much like you. But just a word: If I should ever learn that you've taken advantage of Dr. Parr, I'll see to it that you won't be happy about it."

Leon looked as though he had been struck. "Why sir, I don't . . ."

"I think you understand quite well," Philip said. "Don't forget."

"Well," Parr said, coming back into the room, "I think it's all arranged. "Oh, Leon, thank you, that will be all, you can have the rest of the day off."

Philip could tell by Parr's tone that his guess was not far off.

"Thank you sir," Leon said, and with a dark look at Philip, left the room.

"I've called Ferguson. He was curious, but I reminded him that we had a debt. He expects you. Be careful though, he's smart, and very hard."

"I think I can handle him. After all," Philip said with a smile, "you're not easy to handle yourself."

"Now," Philip continued, "I've got to ask one more thing. Louis Rideau?"

"Rideau. Ah yes, King Louis," Parr said. "He's another story."

"Do you know him?"

"Everyone knows Louis Rideau, and nobody knows him."

"He is in Bray's file," Philip said.

"Of course. He is—was—Magnus's mentor. He brought Magnus up through the ranks. They've largely parted company now, though not with any open hostility. He would surely be in any file on Hopkenson."

Philip continued, "Bray interviewed him. That's why I can't. Too many interviewers, too many questions. He's a supporter of Hopkenson, I suppose."

"Yes," Parr said, "I suppose. He is in public, at least."

"Yet," Philip said, "he is also quietly backing Billy Jennings and has been lending his name, discreetly, to other right wing causes. There's a contradiction there."

"So some have noticed," Parr said sarcastically.

"This needs finesse," Parr finally said. "I think Douglas Haley could be of some help here. They are old law cronies. Served on many legal committees together. They battle a lot, and like many others, Haley has drawn away from Rideau in the past few years, but there is probably no one who would be a better contact."

"Could you get him for me?" Philip asked.

"You don't 'get' Judge Douglas Haley," Parr said. "Presidents have been known to stand at his door."

"Yes, no doubt true," Philip said, "but right now, I have some other doors to open and my time is more important than his. I need to see him, tomorrow afternoon."

April 2   11:15 A.M.

Aleister listened at the door until he was sure his visitor had gotten into the elevator.

Well, he thought, how about that? Maybe that bitch

Hughie will do me some good after all. At least I'll get some of the money back—after all these years.

He crossed to the mirror and examined his face.

Not bad, he thought, not bad. Got to start the gym again though, this stomach is getting a little loose. Maybe I'll cut down on the booze. Fifteen hundred bucks. I could do a lot with that. Some new clothes, a trip to New York, maybe even Fire Island. Fire Island, hell, I could go down to Key West or even Puerto Rico, get a little real action.

He opened another button on his shirt, letting it hang loose to reveal his chest. Hiking up his pants, he ran his fingers through his hair, and with a last look in the mirror crossed to the phone. He perched on the edge of the sofa and pulled the small princess phone toward him.

Damn things, he thought, too small. Nelly little phone.

He realized his hands were sweaty and he felt a nervous lump in his throat. He hadn't called this number in quite awhile, and he had been told never to call it before 5 P.M. But this was important; fifteen hundred bucks was a lot of money but it was peanuts compared to what was available—if he would just make one call.

He stared at the phone, got up, went back to the mirror, back to the phone and then in a sudden rush leaped on it, grabbed the receiver and punched out the familiar, forbidden number. It rang once, twice, three times. A click. A voice.

"Hello, this is Aleister. Is *he* in?"

A pause. A click. Another click.

Aleister, peevishly: "Well, tell him to call me back, it's important—What? I can't tell you. Just tell him I'll be talking to someone else at four this afternoon and I'll want *him* to tell me what to say."

He hung up.

"When they don't want you they think they can brush you off. Those people are all alike," he muttered, brooding at the phone, then crossing the room again, starting to smile.

Aleister felt a sense of elation he hadn't known in a long time. Maybe things would get better now. Maybe he wouldn't have to rely on "modeling" and turning tricks to get by. Shit, he thought, the last modeling job he had was stripping and doing simulated jerk-off at the Ganymede Male Playhouse, a cheap porn flick in Maryland. Some modeling that. He got seventy-five bucks and lots of old men who wanted to suck him off. He shuddered and went into the kitchen to make a pot of coffee, skimping a bit on the last measure of coffee, out of habit.

If I play this thing right, he thought, I won't have to be so damn careful with coffee again, or put up with blow jobs from horny Sunday school teachers and married creeps afraid to admit they like boys better than their wives. No more raunchy bumps and grinds, and no more rich old men who take everything you've got and then push you out the back door with fifty lousy bucks.

"Listen, honey," he said aloud to himself, "this is your chance. Go for the big money. What you've got to say could really do some harm, and they'll pay to keep you quiet, and pay big."

He poured boiling water over the coffee, made a quick pirouette to the fridge and, humming to himself, pulled out its only contents, a loaf of bread, a jar of mayonnaise and a half-finished can of tuna. Oh, yes, he thought, San Juan here I come.

From the other room he heard the phone ringing.

"Oh my God," he said aloud. "It's him."

He dropped the tuna on the table and rushed into the living room and toward the phone, now on its third ring.

"Jesuuus," he said, "what am I going to say? Calm, baby, be calm. Remember it's strictly business."

He seated himself on the sofa, picked up the phone and, with his head tossed back, said in his most level and businesslike voice: "Aleister St. Pierre."

Without preliminary the caller said: "I assume you have a good reason for this call."

"Yes, yes I do," Aleister said. His heart beat painfully.

"I don't have much time. You disobeyed by using this number. Let's have it, I'm leaving for The Hill in five minutes."

Aleister tried to focus, to make his explanation clear and precise, the way he was expected to. "This morning," he said, "well, this morning about nine o'clock . . . ."

"Get to the point, I don't care *when*, tell me *what*."

"Someone was asking questions," Aleister blurted.

"What kind of questions?"

"About Hughie Tilden."

"And?"

"He wanted names."

"What kind of names?"

"People I'd . . . I'd known."

"I see. What did you tell him?"

Aleister was frightened now. It wasn't going as smoothly as he'd thought it would.

"Nothing, really, I didn't tell him anything. I mean, well I told him it would cost money. I really need the money. It's getting harder now . . . ."

"Now that you're getting older," said the unsympathetic voice. "Who was this man? Police?"

"He said he was an investigator for the GWA."

"What's that?"

"A gay . . . ."

"Never mind. What was his name?"

"He said his name was Bradlee, but I'm sure it's a fake. I think . . . ."

"What did you tell him?"

Aleister couldn't lie. The voice was too insistent. Too powerful. "Nothing," he said in anguish. "But he's coming back at four o'clock, with fifteen hundred dollars. I know that's not much to you, but it's a lot for me. If you . . . if you . . ." His voice trailed off weakly.

"If I what?" the voice said evenly.

"If you could see your way clear to . . ."

"To come up with a better price?"

There was a pause. Aleister simply couldn't speak.

The voice said, "I'm putting you on hold."

The phone clicked. Aleister stifled an urge to hang up, to run away, but waited, his stomach tied in a sick hard knot. What was he going to do? Had he made a mistake calling like this? Suppose he . . .

The phone clicked again. "Are you there?"

"I'm here," he said weakly.

"I'm sending a car for you. Maybe we need to talk. After all, we haven't talked in some time."

Aleister felt a rush of hope. "You mean it?"

"Of course," the voice answered, kinder now.

"And you think maybe we could work something out?" Aleister rushed on, relief sweeping over him. "I mean I really need it. You know what I mean?"

"I know what you mean. I'm glad you phoned, you should have done it before. It'll be good to see you. The car will be there in half an hour."

"I can't tell you," Aleister started.

"Don't. See you soon." The phone clicked into silence. Aleister stood with the receiver in his hand. He was trembling.

"My God," he said aloud. "He's going to see me; he's going to help me."

He put the phone down and realized he had to get ready. He leaped up. He had to look nice for this, really nice. What should he wear? He ran to his room and started pulling things out of drawers.

He looked at himself in the mirror. Got to shave, he thought. Clothes. What to wear? He looked at several pairs of jeans. No, jeans weren't right. Something more formal, subdued.

Oh, God, get hold of yourself, he thought. Shave first. He went into the bathroom and turned on the water. He washed his face in the warm water, lathered it up with Vitamin E soap. He wanted his face to tingle, to look young. He lathered his cheeks and carefully scraped off the two-day growth of beard.

"Damn," he said, as he nicked himself. His hand was trembling. He felt he needed a drink to calm down. He went into the kitchen and poured a straight Scotch, downed it, poured another and took it back to the bathroom, feeling the welcome glow come over him.

He finished shaving, patted his face with Eau Sauvage and ran a comb through his hair. That looked good, he thought, maybe just a quick shampoo. No, not enough time.

He hurried into the bedroom, carrying the Scotch.

Now for the clothes, he thought. He took out one pair of slacks, then another, and finally settled on a tight-fitting pair of gray flannels. When he slipped into them, they were a little tighter around the waist than he remembered.

He took another gulp of Scotch. With the money he could rejoin the gym, and get his body back in shape. He selected a dove gray shirt and a maroon sweater. Good. But the sweater wasn't right. Maroon was too preppy, he decided. He needed a more mature look. Brown. He picked up the brown cashmere sweater that Mark had left behind last month. Yes, that was it. He had always been going to call Mark and return it, but somehow he never had. And cashmere was good for today, he thought. It looked rich. He didn't want to seem too desperate.

But I am desperate, he thought. Maybe today would make it all right. He raised his glass to his reflection in the mirror. "To today," he said. He knew he was frightened.

He pulled on the sweater. It was good. Soft, elegant, but

it made a clean statement. He brushed his hair again and let it fall down over his forehead in a way that took a couple of years off. He wanted to look mature, experienced, but not too old.

The voice on the phone: *"Since you've gotten older."* The remark still stung.

He looked at the effect in the mirror. Yes, it was good. He was ready. He hurried into the kitchen. One more drink, he thought, just to calm my nerves. He poured the drink. What if he won't give me any money, he suddenly thought. No, he will, another voice countered. I know too much. He needs me. He needs me to keep quiet. And I could help him a lot, if he'd just give me the chance. He never really gave me a chance, even back then.

But now I've got a second chance. He brightened at the notion. Yes, and he had to be very calm and play the cards right. The reason it hadn't worked before was that he'd let his emotions get the better of him. He had to be cool, very cool. No one liked a faggot who couldn't control himself. He walked into the living room, trying to compose himself into a semblance of calm. He tried to imagine what the meeting would be like. *He* would no doubt be brusque. Aleister would be reserved, but not distant, warm without being affectionate. Men like that needed warmth, but they didn't like too much demonstration of affection. But he had to be forgiving. He knew what was important.

He sat down, wondering what he ought to say, deciding it would be best just to extend his hand, give a firm handshake and say, "Nice to see you again." Yes, that was it, keep it simple. He said it aloud in the empty room: "Nice to see you again."

The sharp summons of the doorbell startled him. Jumping up, he ran to the intercom button, pushed it and said, "I'll be right down." He grabbed his best leather jacket from the hook, looked about in panic for a moment, dropped the jacket on the chair and ran into the bedroom to pull a corduroy sport

coat out of the closet, yanking the other two coats off the rack
as he did so. He went out, grabbed his keys from the table and
pulled the door shut, forgetting to lock it, and leaving it ajar in
his haste. He took the stairs down, not wanting to wait for the
elevator. At the bottom he stopped, waited a second to get his
breath and then walked nonchalantly out the front door.

The car was waiting, the long black limousine, shining,
parked in the No Parking zone with all the arrogance of the
rich. The license plate had no rental numbers on it, just four
letters.

Aleister went to the car and the driver got out, nodding
formally to him as he held the door. "Good day, Mr. St.
Pierre."

"Oh, hello, how are you? It's nice to see you again, it's
been so . . ."

"If you'd get in, sir, we have to be going," the driver said,
interrupting him.

"Why, yes, of course."

Calm down, he thought, don't go gabbing off to the
driver. Be calm, baby, be calm. Who knows, this may not be
the last time you'll be riding in a car like this, maybe even this
car. After all, he did say he'd been neglecting me, and that's
for sure.

He sat back in the cushioned gray luxury of the car as it
majestically moved away from the curb, down the street and
away toward the circle. Aleister noticed the bar had been
thoughtfully opened; a bucket of ice was provided and a bottle
of Chivas Regal stood ready and inviting. He picked up the
heavy-bottomed crystal glass, poured a little Scotch, sipped it
slowly. This was the life, a lot better than he had ever known.

After a few blocks he knocked on the glass between him
and the driver.

"Yes, sir." The driver's voice came over the intercom.

"Where are we to meet?" Aleister said, hoping he
sounded bored and used to riding in limousines.

"My instructions are to drive you out to the country."

Of course, Aleister thought, clever man. They couldn't very well meet in the city, too many people would recognize them. They'd probably get together at the country place. He'd never been there, but he knew it was only a short drive into Virginia. He wondered idly why they hadn't traveled out together. Too risky, he decided. He had to remember who he was dealing with.

The city gradually disappeared as the green of the country increased. Aleister settled back and poured himself another Scotch. Sometime later, when the big car lurched off the main road he comfortably decided he'd been right. This was certainly the country place.

The sign read *All City Wrecking*.

Aleister stared at it.

He realized he'd had a little too much Scotch.

"Hey, what is this?" he yelled, suddenly panicked. He knocked on the glass partition. The driver didn't answer.

He grabbed for the door. It was locked.

The car abruptly stopped but before Aleister could do anything, the electric locks sprang up and two men appeared, one on each side of the car.

"My God, who are you?" he shrieked.

No one answered him. One of the men threw open the door and in one swift gesture grabbed Aleister by the collar and dragged him from the car. The breath was knocked out of him as he landed with a jolt on the ground. He tried to scream again, but quick hands covered his mouth. He saw the flash of metal but when his throat was cut he felt no pain. Only the terror.

His wallet, watch, rings and I.D. were stripped by the same expert hands. Now the pain closed in, but it was brief and he knew only the final darkness as the big car, in its hasty passing, insured that any identification of the body would be impossible.

6.

A stand of pines broke the horizon as Philip nosed the car along the winding Virginia road. He had been driving for an hour through the green country, passing a few houses now and then, big houses, set back at the end of long tree-lined lanes. The road headed up a long hill toward a stand of woods. Off to the right, a few hundred yards farther on, was the sign he was looking for, telling him to turn off the main road into a smaller one, which would lead, if his directions were right, to Faraway, the home of Brigadier General Otis Ferguson.

Around him rolled the moneyed Virginia hills, whose owners were descended from English proprietors and whose names were like a roll call of the men who had made the country great, as the history books all too often said. The turnoff was a two-laned narrow country road that used to be red dirt before it had been haphazardly paved. It was lined as far as he could see with white rail fencing, as bright as if the painter had just departed.

About half a mile head, Philip saw what he was looking for. The white rail fence was pierced with a simple gate, standing open, and a gravel road led into pine trees similar to those he had seen before. Beside the gate, a discreet sign read *Faraway*. He turned into the lane and drove through trees which soon closed in to become tall elms and oaks, trees that had grown here when other presidents reigned in Washington and other names were on the tongues of men. The old trees provided a shady covered road and when they suddenly ended and he drove into the open, the contrast was dramatic, as no doubt had been intended. The lane had turned into a wide drive that went around in a large majestic circle. Standing at the far side of the circle was Faraway, the great house that Otis Ferguson's great-grandfather had built of solid stone and slate, its elegant facade pierced by long gleaming windows. The wings on either side of the house, built by Ferguson's father, stretched out formally, folding the main building in an elegant embrace. He steered around the circular drive and pulled to a stop in front of the house.

As he got out of the car, the front door opened and a young man came toward him, apparently having seen Philip drive up. He appeared to be at attention as he walked.

"May I help you, sir?" he asked politely.

"Yes, I'm Philip Kristopher. I have an appointment with General Ferguson."

The young man took a small notebook from the pocket of his starched, tight uniform and consulted it. "Yes, at 1100 hours," he agreed. "The general is at the stables. He asked me to take you there."

Without waiting for Philip to reply, he turned and walked toward the far wing of the house. Philip followed, striding to catch up.

At a door at the far end, the marine paused and turned to Philip. "If you'll wait here just a moment, sir," he said, holding up a restraining hand, "I'll find out if the general is ready to see you."

He went through the door. Through the window Philip could see a small room, containing only a desk and a telephone. The marine picked up the phone, said a few words and returned. "This way, sir," he said, and once again walked away without waiting.

They walked in silence through a formal garden laid out on one side of the house, crossed a brick path, walked through a break in a hedge and toward a stand of trees behind which Philip could see some barns and stables.

"The general has quite a place here," he said, hoping to coax the young man into conversation.

"Yes, he does, sir," the marine replied.

"You work here for long?" Philip asked.

"Yes, sir. I'm assigned to the general."

They walked on through the trees. Philip could see the young man wasn't going to provide much information, but he thought it strange that the general should have as a private attendant a marine enlisted man. "Just how big is the general's farm?" he said.

"I'm not exactly sure, sir."

"He raises horses?"

"Yes, sir, horses."

"I see," Philip said. "Do you like horses?"

"The stables are just over there, sir," the marine said with an edge of irritation in his voice. "If you'll come with me, I think the general is in the smithy."

They walked over a wide, graveled work area, lined on two sides by white-painted low-roofed stable buildings. From them the smell and sound of horses was evident. Off to the right, Philip could hear the clanging of metal on metal. As they approached, through the large open door, Philip could see a scene out of Currier and Ives. The blacksmith in his leather apron, the bay horse with one foot up, a group of men watching the progress, sparks flying as the smith shaped the metal shoe over the fiery forge. Aside from the smith there were four men present, two in uniform, one in work clothes. The fourth, who Philip took to be the general, was wearing an open-necked red plaid shirt, tan riding breeches and black boots.

The young marine strode briskly up to the door, snapped a smart salute and said, "Sir. Mr. Kristopher."

The man in the boots turned, nodded to the marine, but did not return the salute. He waved Philip in and turned back. Philip went into the low shed.

"Threw a shoe," Ferguson said without preamble, nodding at the horse. "Ever been on a horse when they throw a shoe? Damndest thing."

Not waiting for Philip to answer, he said, "So, you're Philip Kristopher. I've heard good things about you."

"Thank you, General."

The smith, who had paused in his work when Philip entered, started hammering again. The reverberations prevented further conversation. Philip noted that under his leather apron the smith, too, wore a uniform. The other uniformed men, like the attendant, who had left upon completing his errand, were young, trim, and dressed in uniforms that looked as if they were made of iron. The one man not in uniform was somewhat older and held a clipboard. He looked like an overseer or manager. Philip was not introduced.

When the smith had stopped, Ferguson turned to Philip. "Well, we can't stay here all day. You ride?"

"Yes, sir, I do."

"Good. Randy," he said, turning to one of the uniformed men, "bring out Irma and Little Docket."

"Yes, General," the young man said.

"Come on, let's get out in the sun," the general said. "Too nice a day to be in here."

Philip followed the general out of the shoeing shed. As he followed he noted Ferguson's upright carriage, his muscular back. He was about six foot, Philip figured, and in very good shape for a man his age. Once in the sun, Philip could better see his face; broad, regular, with a square nose and deep-set eyes. The lines around the eyes were etched and harsh, as if he had been squinting into the sun for years. His mouth was firm, almost set. Philip was sure Otis Ferguson had made all his decisions about the nature of things many years ago. His system was closed. Philip knew he would have to tread carefully.

They had been waiting only a few minutes when the general turned to the other young man who was hovering at a respectful distance. "Go see where those horses are," he commanded. "I don't have all day."

"Yes, sir."

"On the double," Ferguson barked.

The young man threw a quick but correct salute and hurried toward the other end of the stables.

"You've got to keep them on their toes, or else they go soft," Ferguson said.

"I guess that's right," Philip said.

"You ever in the service, Mr. Kristopher?" the general asked, curling his lips around Philip's name.

"Not on active duty, sir, but I was connected with Special Services during the war."

"The army," the general said. "Not like the corps, not the tradition."

The two enlisted men came running up, leading the horses.

"Careful with those horses, goddamn it," the general said. "They're worth more than you two will be any day. Here, Mr. Kristopher, choose your mount. I suggest Irma, the bay."

"Fine with me, sir."

They mounted and the general looked down from his horse at the two enlisted men, who were standing at attention as if on parade. He spurred his horse. "Come on, Mr. Kristopher. I'll show you some country."

They rode past the stables and out over the wide Virginia fields, the horses at a canter. After a time they slowed and came to a stop on the crest of a hill. Below them they could see the farm buildings and the main house rising up behind the trees.

"It's beautiful," Philip said.

"Yes, it is," Ferguson said simply, but Philip heard a depth of feeling in his tone.

"You've been here a long time, haven't you, sir?"

"Since the beginning," the general said. "Before there was a government in Washington, we were here."

"It must give you a lot of satisfaction to know that, General."

"You're damn right it does. A lot," he said with some vehemence.

"How long is it?"

"We had this land from the king, back in the seventeenth century, and we kept it through the Revolution. My great-grandfather built that house, my grandfather started the stud farm. My father added to it."

"And you're carrying on?"

"I'm carrying on. Fergusons are always going to own this land. That's what they say in this country, Mr. Kristopher, two things are sure, taxes, and that there'll be Fergusons at Faraway."

"It's an impressive heritage, General."

"Yes, we need more like it in this country today. Too many things are run by the upstarts and the Johnny-come-latelies for my blood."

"You may be right," Philip said, noncommittally.

"Of course, I'm right. Why look at Congress, full of types who would have been shopkeepers in my granddaddy's time. And the services aren't much better. It's only in the corps and the navy where you can find real men, and gentlemen."

Philip realized this was a favorite subject with the general.

"What about you, Kristopher, where do you hail from? New York, isn't it? English name?"

"New York, that's right, General. I work for the network. Investigative reporting."

"That's what I hear. Where'd you go to school?"

"Princeton, that's where I got into journalism. I work for Chuck Witter now."

"Princeton, eh, good. Sent my son to Princeton, then to Harvard. You married, Mr. Kristopher?"

Philip was determined to keep away from his own background. "Not at the moment, General."

The general seem satisfied with Philip's answers. Philip sensed he had risen a notch or two in the other man's eyes.

"So what are you investigating, or more to the point, why are you here to see me?" Ferguson said, in a sudden pointed about-face. "I'm sure you're not here to learn about Ferguson family history."

"No, I'm not," Philip said, deciding to be just as direct. "I need something."

"And you think I can get it for you."

"I hope so, at least Amos Parr and I hope so."

"Yes, Amos Parr," the general said. Philip sensed a certain reservation in the general's tone. "How well do you know Amos, Mr. Kristopher?"

"I know him just enough to have accepted this asign-ment, General."

The general smiled. "I can see you're a cut above some of the men I have around me, Mr. Kristopher. What do you want?"

"I know, General, you're familiar with the intelligence community. I expect you know Walter Bray?"

"Yes, I know Walter Bray. I've met him; I don't know him well, but I've had occasion to use him."

"Good. I need access to his files."

The general raised his eyebrows. "Why don't you break in, Mr. Kristopher? We've all done that kind of thing at one time or another."

"That wouldn't be quite legal, General, would it. Nor too useful."

"I see, you want continued access. Someone on the inside."

Philip admired the general's sense of his purpose. "That's it," he said. "I can give assurances that the material I might find would never cause trouble for whoever might provide it. I can give absolute assurance."

"There's no such thing as absolute assurance," Ferguson said. "What's going on?"

Philip smiled. "If I were to tell you, sir, it would lessen my control over the situation *and* weaken my absolute assurance."

The general gave Philip a look of irritation, but grudgingly said, "Yes, you're right."

The two men sat in silence for a moment, the horses restlessly pawing the ground. Then the general said, "Interesting." He pulled on the reins of his horse and without another word wheeled around and started at a gallop back toward the stables.

Philip followed the marine orderly into a large sunny parlor.

"May I get you a drink, sir?" the young man asked.

"Yes, Scotch, thank you."

The orderly produced a Scotch and left the room. Philip was pleased with the morning's work; the general had promised to make a telephone call and had gone to do so. Philip was also pleased with the reluctant acceptance he had seemed to engender in the stiff old man.

"Well, hello. Who are you?" a light, edgy voice cut into his thoughts. He looked up and saw a young man, tall, with auburn hair and a direct glance, standing in the doorway. He wore a classic riding outfit and carried a riding crop. His eyes were green and knowing. Next to him stood a young man with short blond hair, in the uniform of a navy ensign. He stood one step away, his eyes hooded.

"I'm Philip Kristopher. I'm waiting for General Ferguson." He stood up and moved toward them.

"Waiting for daddy? He'll come when he's ready. I'm Michael Ferguson."

Philip decided to nip further questioning. "I'm here on some private business with your father. Nothing of much interest, I'm afraid."

"God knows that's probably true around here," he said.

"What's probably true around here?" Ferguson's voice boomed from the door.

Startled, the two men turned. "Nothing, father, nothing."

"You've met Mr. Kristopher, haven't you, Michael?" the general was saying. "Good. Now if you'll excuse me a moment, I want a few words with Mr. Kristopher, then we'll go in to lunch." He took Philip by the arm and led him across to the French windows that stood open to the brick terrace.

"Now," Ferguson went on, "I have a name for you." He gave Philip an envelope. "Her name is Alice Copley, her number is in here. She's a secretary at Bray's office and she and her husband owe me a favor. Call her. She expects you."

"Thank you, General."

"But one thing. It must be very clear that nothing you use will be harmful to Walter Bray or the agency. You'll have to convince her of that."

"I can," Philip said.

7.

Monte Dillon looked at his watch. He had been sitting in his car about a half a block from St. Pierre's apartment building for nearly half an hour. During that time he had seen only three people coming and going. One was a woman of about sixty, who, from the string shopping bag and purse clutched under her arm, was going out to do some shopping.

Someone who must have been the building superintendent came out a few minutes later, swept the walk, pulled in the garbage cans sprawled on the edge of the sidewalk, and went back inside. And now a young man in his thirties arrived dressed in jeans and sneakers and a Lacoste shirt. He was carrying an armload of groceries and a full laundry bag. He looked to be in a hurry.

Earlier this morning Dillon had been assigned by Bray to relieve the man put on the building yesterday, when St. Pierre failed to show up for the promised payoff. St. Pierre still hadn't returned, and the time had come to find out why.

Satisfied that there was no one to be seen or to see, Dillon got out of the car after checking the street for a sign of the Pinto or any other car that might jar his interest. He crossed the street and entered the building. At the door, the young man with the groceries was juggling his laundry bag and groceries.

"Let me help you," Dillon offered.

"Thanks," the young man said, handing Dillon the groceries. He dug in his pocket and came up with a key ring with two keys, opened the door and took the bag from Dillon. Dillon followed him inside.

"You visiting someone here?" the young man asked.

"No, building inspector," Dillon said and headed toward the stairs since it was clear that the young many was going for the elevator. "Got to check the cellar for leaks," he threw over his shoulder as he started down the stairs, which obviously lead to the cellar. He continued down until he heard the elevator stop, the door open and close. He counted to twenty and then hurried up the stairs and took the flights to Aleister's floor.

He knocked on the apartment door. No answer. He knocked again. He tried the door. It was locked. He took out his kit and, checking the lock, inserted one, then another needle-thin pick into the lock. After a few seconds he heard the satisfying click of the tumbler, and the lock opened. A thin plastic card sprung the lower lock and he cautiously pushed the door.

Inside there was silence. He noticed that the overhead light was on, and that various clothes were strewn over the chair. A half-finished drink sat on the top of the TV next to a plate with an untouched tuna sandwich. He could see from where he was that the kitchen too was empty. A quick look into the bedroom discovered the same.

Where the hell is that guy, he wondered as he stood in the bedroom door. He decided to do a quick search before Aleister got back from wherever he had gone. He would start in the bedroom.

The room was small, and contained only a double bed covered with a plaid throw cover, a dresser of the kind that had round wooden knobs and was painted with coats of pine-colored enamel. One or two pictures, both cheap prints of sculptures by Michelangelo, hung on the wall. On the dresser there were three framed photographs. One showed Aleister in what Dillon assumed must be some sort of resumé shot. He was much younger, and Dillon could see why he had been successful in his work. He had tough good looks that the years had softened and blunted, that poverty had made petulant. The others were of Aleister with other people. One showed Aleister with another young man, both in bathing suits on a beach in front of an ocean. It could have been anyplace. The other young man was about Aleister's age, dark haired and smiling. Dillon wondered if it might be Hugh Tilden.

He opened the drawers, being careful not to disturb anything. The top drawer had nothing but shirts, the middle drawer the same, clothes, underwear, some socks. The bottom drawer was heavy when he pulled it out. Inside were magazines. Dillon looked them over. *Tomorrow's Man*, *Real Men*, *Numbers*, *Honcho*. This was apparently Aleister's library. There was nothing else.

There's got to be something else, he thought.

He went to the closet. Inside, a few sport coats, some jeans carefully pressed and hung on hangers, three pairs of shoes, a laundry bag bulging with what he presumed to be dirty laundry. On the top shelf there were books: *High School Sex Stud*, *Truckers*. Dillon was amused to see *Our Lady of the Flowers* mixed in with what were obviously porno books. He had a flash that Aleister's life had been like his books, limited, lonely, mostly trash and now and then a moment, perhaps, of glory. Dillon almost liked him.

Stuffed in next to a copy of *The City and the Pillar* he saw a tattered manila envelope. He pulled it out and went over to the window to study it.

Inside he found a sheaf of papers, some letters, other single sheets with a few notes on them. He leafed through them quickly. One of them was a yellow legal pad. On it was a list of names.

Is this the list? he wondered. He looked at his watch. It was four-thirty. He slipped the list into his pocket. As he went out of the bedroom, he glanced toward the kitchen, but he wasn't prepared for the blurry figure that came hurtling at him, nor was he ready for the impact of the blow to the side of his head. He crumpled, slipped down, without seeing who hit him. As he slipped into the darkness, he felt hands searching him, felt papers being pulled from his pocket, and then the darkness closed in. He did not hear the single shot fired, which killed him.

April 3   2:30 P.M.

Philip sat waiting at the bar of the Blue Fox. The bar was on a side street of Constitution Avenue, but a long way from the center city. The afternoon crowd at the Blue Fox was, Philip suspected, the morning crowd as well. A querulous couple sat at one end of the bar, three solitary drinkers were spaced between them and where Philip sat. The bartender looked like he wasn't against joining them now and again. The bar was silent, except for the talkative couple. Dust hung in the air. It was warm. Philip nursed a beer.

He glanced at his watch. It was after two.

Just as he was about to order another, a woman, alone, came in and went to one of the tables. Philip noticed that there was no sign of recognition by the bartender. It was good she hadn't chosen a place where she was known. She looked like she had described herself over the phone:

"Look, Mr. Kristopher," she had said, "you'll know who I am, I'll be the only gal there with a little class and lots of red hair."

She was right. There was lots of red hair, falling down over her shoulders, framing her face which was made up of angles and planes: A nose that would have been sharp if it had been a little longer, lips that would have been sexy if they were a little fuller, eyes that looked surprised rather than seductive. It wasn't all quite right and yet it was the little touch of class that made her attractive. When put all together, it seemed somehow to work.

He realized she was looking his way and that she had recognized him as he had her. She didn't smile, just cocked her head a little. He got up and went over to her table.

"Hi," he said. "Like a drink?"

"Hi, yourself, and yes, if you're buying and if you're Philip Kristopher."

"I am if you're Alice Copley."

"Good," she said. "Vodka martini."

After he got her drink, he sat down opposite her in the booth.

"I guess the general told you what I want," he said.

"Suppose you tell me again," she replied.

Philip outlined his need for access to Bray's files, for copies of his active cases.

"You know if I do this I'm putting my job on the line," she said.

"I know," he replied, counting on what he thought was true, "but I understand that the general once put himself on the line for you, right?"

He thought a quick shadow of pain crossed her face. She said nothing, instead took a sip of her drink and lighted a cigarette. After a moment she spoke.

"I owe everything to Otis Ferguson," she said huskily. "There's no way around that."

"But," she went on, "I don't like doing this, I don't like it at all. Is anyone going to get hurt?"

"I promise you Miss Copley—"

"Mrs.," she said, "and call me Alice."

"Alice, no one is going to get hurt, I promise you."

"Will this make trouble for me or my husband?"

"Not if you keep it to yourself," Philip said. "Not even the general knows why I need this material."

"Do I get to know why?"

"No," Philip said. "Another drink?"

"I see," she said thoughtfully. "Look, Mr. Kristopher, I'm doing this because I've got to. I owe it. But I've got to be sure nothing will happen to me or mine."

"Mrs. . . . Alice, all I can tell you is that I need access to Bray's files, and that the material will be known only to me, shown to no one else, that no one will know where I got it from. That's the best I can do. But I can say that sooner or later, it'll be worth your while."

"You mean money, Mr. Kristopher?"

"I mean money, Mrs. Copley."

She let out a long breath; the smoke from her cigarette wreathed around her head.

"Okay," she said.

"Good," Philip replied. "When can I have the material?"

"You can have it right now. I've already got some in my apartment."

"You mean you knew you were going to say yes?"

"No," she said, "I wanted to get a look at you first. You've got good eyes. I believe you." She smiled a radiant smile that transformed her face. She *was* beautiful; the years had been kind. Philip was glad.

"Okay, let's not waste time," she was saying. "We've got to go back to my place. Look, Mr. Kristopher, here's five bucks. I may look a little like a hustler, but I'm not one. Pay the check." She ostentatiously handed Philip the money.

She let herself into the apartment, Philip following behind.

The door opened directly into the living room. Philip was ready for the large television with the lace cover and statue of the virgin; he was ready for the green sofa shot through with gold thread and the armchair to match. But he wasn't ready for the man in the wheelchair.

"Philip, this is my husband, Ted."

"Hello," Philip said, uncertain what to do.

The man sat in the chair, covered with an afghan that Philip was sure Alice had crocheted herself. One of his arms was clearly paralyzed; his chest was sunken, his legs apparently useless. He nodded his head and raised his left arm slightly.

But his eyes were fierce. The man was physically incapacitated, but the eyes showed an awareness and intelligence, and helpless rage.

"Ted, Mr. Kristopher is from Otis; you remember I told you he called," Alice said, putting her hand on the man's shoulder. "I said I'd help him."

Ted nodded his head vigorously in affirmation.

"Otis helped Ted when no one else would," Alice said. "He got him a disability pension and cut through the red tape with the hospital. Ted used to be in the Marines. He was Otis' first lieutenant in the war. Otis has been a friend to us all these years. He still comes to see Ted now and then."

Philip could see why Alice Copley felt duty-bound to help.

"Sit down," Alice said. "I'll get what I have for you."

She disappeared into another room. Philip sat uncomfortably, not knowing whether to talk or ignore the man. He decided to chance talking.

"Thanks for putting up with me, Mr. Copley," he said. "Mrs. Copley has been a great help."

The man nodded. Philip suddenly had the frightening knowledge that no one had called him "Mr. Copley" for a long, long time.

"I won't stay too long, sir," Philip said, wondering as he said it whether he ought instead to stay longer.

"Here they are," Alice said, coming into the room. She

carried a brown case bulging with several manila file folders. She handed it to him.

"Anything you want especially?"

"No, I'd just like to look at them all," he said. He leafed through the files, catching names as he went. Parr, Rose, St. Pierre, Thomson. "Good," he said.

Alice nodded. The man in the wheelchair watched intently.

"I guess I'd better be going," Philip said, rising.

"Wouldn't you like some coffee first?" Alice said, reaching out to restrain him. Philip felt a sudden powerful desire projected his way.

He glanced at the man in the chair. The hooded eyes watched.

He looked back at Alice. Her eyes were pleading.

"Not now," he said. "Maybe another time." He looked directly at her.

She said nothing. A little class, Philip thought, but not a lot. He realized that she had made a pass at him in front of her husband. He knew that the man in the chair missed nothing. He wanted to get out of the stuffy apartment. And then he thought: The *war*, she had said. Then he knew what it was she was talking about. She had been nursing the man in that wheel chair for over thirty years! He understood the pleading in her eyes.

At the door he took her hand, holding it a bit tighter than perhaps he should.

"You've been very helpful," he said.

She returned the pressure on his hand.

"Please call," she said.

"I will."

April 3   6:00 P.M.

Philip sat in his car and leafed through the files. He pulled out the one marked, St. Pierre, Aleister, scanned it quickly and glanced at his watch: 6 P.M.

He would make a quick swing past. Maybe he could talk to this St. Pierre. He knew that he was part of the puzzle and apparently an important part, though unlike the other files there were no notations on the case sheet, just the address. Philip knew now that it was to Aleister's place that he had followed Bray.

He parked the car around the corner, got out and walked toward the building. Cars moved slowly down the block since it was one of the main arteries that fed out of the city. Workers were returning home. There were a lot of people round. He went to the building and looked for the buzzer. He pushed it. There was no answer. He tried again. Nothing. He tried the front door. It was locked. He didn't want to take a chance at picking the lock; someone might come home from work. He went out of the lobby and into the street. The building was one of a row of square detached five-story apartment buildings, brick, built in the thirties. They were connected by chain link fences that closed narrow concrete alleys that ran between them. Some had gates, others not. The fence between this building and the next had a gate.

Philip looked quickly around. There was no one in sight and he quickly slipped through the gate and back to the rear of the building. At the back was another long concrete alley, separating the rear of this building from the rear of other buildings like it on the next street. Each building had a rear door and a hatchway to the cellar. The hatchways were heavy. The one he wanted had a tungsten lock. But the cellar door had a simple lock, the kind he could force with a credit card. He took out the strip of plastic and gently turned the handle before slipping the card between the jamb and the door. But the door opened easily. It was unlocked. Inside he could hear noises. He slipped in and realized he was in an entry way that led to the cellar on one side and up the stairs on the other. The noises came from the cellar. The super must be down there. He gently closed the door and slipped up the stairs.

He decided not to take the elevator and he hurried up to the third floor. The door of 310 was ajar. He knocked softly. No answer. He pushed open the door and went in. The room was in a shambles. Whoever had done it had left nothing unsearched. Drawers were pulled out, chairs, the sofa, torn. Philip went into the other room, the bedroom. That too was torn apart, ransacked. On a dresser there were piles of books. Lying on the bed was a manila folder, full of papers. Philip looked through them: letters, an insurance policy, but nothing that seemed to be of help. If there was anything, Philip decided, it was gone.

He went back into the living room. There was a tuna fish sandwich on the top of the TV. The bread was stale. At least a day old. Whoever made it made it yesterday and had not been back. Whoever had turned over the apartment must have done it recently, perhaps today, earlier. Philip had a feeling that St. Pierre might not be coming back again, and he also had a feeling that Walter Bray had gotten here before him. Had Walter Bray also gotten to St. Pierre? The question was easily answered, when, in the kitchen, he came across the body of a man who he recognized as a partner of Walter Bray, though now Bray had a partner no longer.

8.

Tim stood outside the Falcon. The spring night was exciting, and up and down the strip, that long street that runs next to the river from Christopher to Twenty-third Street, gay men paraded, cruised, stood in groups or walked alone, meeting eyes here and there, sizing up likely prospects for a night, an hour, or a few minutes of sex. Across the street, near the piers, figures hidden in darkness lounged outside abandoned hulks of the old docks. Some simply stood, others wandered among the cars parked there. From time to time someone would get into a car, or clamber up in the back of a truck or disappear into one of the darkened buildings. From the bars, music sounded, offering a mixed accompaniment to the dance of the streets. This was the world that had seen the death of Michael Ross. Tim had come to find out what he could about that death.

He had just come from inside the Falcon, a leather bar filled with bearded men in tight jeans and leather jackets, sporting the paraphernalia of motorcycles and Madison Avenue macho. Tim knew many of the men there, and knew that the roughness and costume hid many sweet hearts and kind natures. But in the bar, the ritual was played out to the fullest, the fantasy was the life.

The Falcon was the fourth bar he had hit that night. In

the others—Stud Farm, Country Boys, Nightwatch—he had asked the same question: What have your heard about Michael Ross? Most didn't know the name. A few recognized the photo that Tim had gotten from the coalition files. But few knew more than they had heard on the news, which was very little.

Ross apparently had few friends. Tim had checked him out as far as he could. There was no lover. No roommate. He had worked hard at his job, but no one at Hopkenson campaign headquarters had been his intimate. He was apparently well liked and spent long hours, but when his day's work was done, he vanished into his own world. Tim was surprised to learn that even at campaign headquarters, it was assumed that Michael had died of natural causes. No one questioned that. Tim was increasingly puzzled by this, and he was certain that someone, somehow, had covered up the real facts about Ross's death. So little was known about him that when Tim came to add it up, Michael Ross was not so much a mystery as a blank.

At one bar, a man recognized his face.

"Oh, yeah, that one. I knew him for about two hours. Met him at the baths. Good sex, not much of a talker, but then who talks in the baths? Don't think his name was Michael though. Dead? Too bad, he was a nice kid." And the man turned back to his drink.

Much of the evening had been spent like that. If Michael Ross had spent any time on the strip, he had been noticed by few and made little impression. So far, there was nothing to support Tim's supposition that Ross's death was other than what the papers said, save that it seemed suspicious that there was so little coverage.

Earlier that day he had gone to the baths where Ross was supposed to have died. There he drew a blank. The owners were unavailable. The boy at the desk claimed—and Tim believed him—to know nothing. When Tim asked to see Treat

Watkins, the towel boy who had told him the rumor in the first place, he was told that he no longer worked there and had left no address.

Frustrated, Tim had then called on his old friend Sandy Markham. Markham was a columist for the *Voice*. Among other things, he wrote its gay column and was a good source for every kind of news and inside information.

"Sure I heard the stories," Sandy said. "But you know this town, every time someone sneezes there are rumors. Believe me, every gay death is not a gay murder. I mean, I did a piece on this a few months ago and I'm not about to say there isn't a lot of unreported queer-bashing going on, but sometimes, people do just die. Look, Timmy, if there was something to it, I would have heard."

"And suppose you didn't?" Tim asked.

"Then try Lenny Donato."

Tim knew who Lenny Donato was, and he was loath to "try" him. Lenny was a minor power on the dockstrip. Rumor had it that he owned half the bars on the strip, other stories had him as front man for the Mafia. His fingers were in every pie it was said, and in order to get anything done down there, Lenny had to be courted, and paid. How much of this was true, no one really knew, or at least cared to comment on. Lenny was a dangerous man, some said; others called him a bastard and others called him worse. What Tim knew was that he certainly dealt drugs and boys, and that he liked to have a series of young and dark-haired Latinos in attendance. Lenny was not liked, indeed was feared, and Tim knew he was a source of information that he would have to try.

"If you see Lenny," Sandy said, "be careful. He's a snake."

Now, standing in front of the Falcon, having asked the question over and over again, with no real answer, he knew he had to hunt Lenny down. It wasn't much of a hunt, since everyone knew that Lenny spent his nights at Peter Pan, a noisy and disreputable bar at the corner of Tenth Street. There, he held court, dispensed favors and heard petitions, arranged for drugs or a boy for the night.

Tim walked toward Peter Pan, catching a few glances as he went. The spring night stirred him, making him wish that he and Randy had made love earlier. But that would happen. Now it was business. Ignoring inviting glances, he headed toward the corner, and entered the bar.

The place was filled, the music loud; the smell of smoke and drugs hung over the room. The bar was packed three deep. Tim shouldered his way in and decided to try his question once more. He motioned for the bartender to give him a beer and when the drink came, he asked:

"Know this guy?" showing the photograph.

"Hard to say; I see lots of people."

"I'm not a cop," Tim said.

"Didn't think you were," the bartender said. "He in trouble?"

"Not now. Do you know him?"

"I've seen him in here. Not lately though. Maybe a week ago."

The bartender turned away.

"Give me another beer," he called to the retreating bartender.

He took the drink and put down a ten.

"Would Lenny know?"

"You'll have to ask," the bartender said, pocketing the ten. "But if I were you, I wouldn't."

"What do you mean?"

"That's all I got to say," the barkeep replied. "Lenny's back there," pointing to the back room.

"Thanks," Tim said and drained his beer. He pushed through the crowd on the dance floor. On it, men whirled and turned to the disco beat. A few hands touched him as he passed through. He moved into the next room, a large, very dark room between the front bar and the rear barroom where Lenny held court. Here there was no dancing. Figures stood against the wall; others were closed in dark embrace. On the wall a porno movie flickered, its light revealing real life enactments of the events on the screen. More hands brushed Tim as he passed, trying to draw him to them, into groups of men. But Tim pushed through and into the rear barroom. Here, men drank. There was no dancing, no sex. Serious business was transacted here. At a table in the far corner, Lenny sat with one of his young Latin boys at his side. Tim went up to the table. He realized he was frightened.

"Lenny?" he said tentatively.

"You know it sugar, what's up?"

"I need to talk to you."

"Anytime sugar, your place or mine," and he smiled lewdly.

Tim felt slimy. "I don't mean that. But I do mean privately." He tried to sound self-possessed.

"You can talk in front of Jorge. He doesn't speak English. What's up kid? You need drugs, want a job? I got a lot of boys on my string, but I could use another. Especially like you. Nice wasp type. Mr. Clean, that's you sugar, Mr. Clean."

"Look, Lenny, I just want to ask a question. About a friend of mine." He took out Michael's picture, and gave it to Lenny.

Lenny studied the picture for a long time. Tim thought he saw something flash across Lenny's face—concern, even fear—but he couldn't be sure. Lenny looked up. He was smiling but his eyes were narrow and hard. He seemed about to say something but thought better of it. He handed the picture back to Tim.

"Never seen him before kid. No one I know."

Outside on the street, Tim added up what he knew. A few had seen Michael. Some had slept with him. Maybe he was in the Peter Pan on the night of his death. Lenny may—or may not—have recognized the photo. Not much.

He glanced at his watch. It was nearly three-thirty. He had to get home. Randy must have been home for a long time now. He was probably asleep. He had gone to a fund-raising dinner party that night. Tim hoped he would still be awake, so they could talk.

He walked up Tenth Street, reached the corner of Greenwich Street, turned north, passed the rows of trucks and turned east again. The street was dark. He was suddenly aware that someone was following him. He felt vaguely annoyed. He didn't feel in the mood to fend off a late-night proposition. He was sure it was a late night cruiser, looking for a trick. He glanced over his shoulder, and saw a man a few yards behind him. He hurried on and became aware of a more dangerous possibility. The street was dark, and muggings were common. He wished he had gone back home by way of the brightly lighted Christopher Street. Without warning, the man started to speed up. Tim started to run toward the lights of Hudson Street, two blocks away. But from around the corner of another building, a second man emerged and barred Tim's way.

A set-up, Tim thought. He tried to dart around the man, but was grabbed and pinioned against the wall, both arms forced high up against the rough brick. A knee was shoved brutally into his groin. The man following approached rapidly. Both men were in leather motorcycle jackets, caps pulled down low over eyes. He couldn't see their faces.

"I don't have much money," Tim said. "Take it."

The two men were silent. Tim struggled. The taller of the two slapped his hand over Tim's mouth, while the other twisted his wrist and exerted more pressure with his knee.

Suddenly he was being spun around, his arm painfully twisted behind his back.

One of they men bent close to him.

"Don't ask so many questions, Mr. Clean," he rasped. Then Tim was pushed violently against the wall, and fell sprawling on the sidewalk. One of the men aimed a kick, and connected. Tim felt dizzy, blackness filmed his eyes. He could just hear his attackers running off into the night.

Randy sat by the bed, looking down into Tim's face, bruised and cut, but not too battered. Randy had been in bed barely half an hour when the doorbell rang. From the intercom he heard his name, faintly called. At the door he found Tim, slumped against the stoop, his clothes torn. He had clearly been beaten.

That night, after a stop at the emergency room of St. Vincent's, Tim, nestled in Randy's arms, said, as he drifted off to sleep:

"I told you someone was trying to scare us."

"I think I'm ready to believe you now," Randy said, and held him close.

The next day the two men awoke late. Over coffee, Tim outlined what happened the night before.

"You tangled with Lenny Donato," Randy said, clearly angry. "You know he's slime, and dangerous."

"I can see that," Tim said, touching his bruised head.

"And you think Lenny knows something about Michael's death?" Randy asked.

"I'm not sure," Tim said. "It's clear he wanted to scare me off, but I don't know if Lenny was trying to scare me because of Michael or because I was asking questions on his turf. I mean if he were really involved, he wouldn't tip his hand by coming to get me or . . ."

"Or leave you alive," Randy said grimly.

"I think," Tim said, "that Lenny has heard street rumors, the same way I have. If he were involved, he would have played it cooler. He's no fool."

"Involved or not," Randy said, "it's all over the strip that you've been asking questions. We don't have the muscle to do any more snooping, so I want you to stay out. If something is going on, I don't want you hurt."

"I agree," Tim said. "But what can we do?"

"I think we drop the Michael Ross investigation for now, at least. We can't lose sight of the fact that it's not Michael's death we're investigating. What we are trying to find out is if someone is trying to smear Hopkenson. If someone is, that's a danger not only to Hopkenson, but to us. Look, Lenny Donato may be big on Christopher Street, but he's not big enough to try to unseat a potential president."

"But there may be someone who is," Tim said.

"Yes, there may be someone who is."

"And the place to look," Tim said, "is at the Billy Jennings rally next week. If there's a campaign to get Hopkenson, we might learn something there."

"I'm not sure how much we'll learn, but you're right, the Jennings rally has to be our target. All I hear is that he is going to use this rally to make a major antigay statement. Jennings has been sweeping through the South, drawing bigger and bigger crowds. He's pushing legislation in Congress against gays. He's the real danger."

"You don't think he engineered the Michael Ross murder, do you?"

"I don't know," Randy said. "He's unscrupulous. All I know is that if this rally succeeds, he's heading for New York. So we've got to make our presence known in a big way. I've arranged for buses to take protestors to the rally, but we need a lot of telephone work to get them filled. That's what I'd like you to do."

Tim nodded agreement. "Do you know," he asked, "if Louis Rideau is going to speak at the rally? That's what I'd heard."

"I've heard it too, though Jennings hasn't made it public yet. But I think it's true."

"If he is, then that will be the first time Rideau has been on a platform with Jennings. It must mean that Rideau sees Jennings as becoming a real force."

"But it also means that if Jennings corrals Rideau, and the coalition doesn't respond, he'll march right to New York."

"So we've got to mount a big demonstration . . ."

"And," Randy continued, "come off as a very large, very unified and strong political force. I'm going to promise Hopkenson I can deliver a gay vote, for the first time nationally, and I've got to have something to back me up."

Tim sat, watching Randy as he talked animatedly about the plans for the rally. They made plans to contact all the major gay groups, to circulate leaflets, and organize even at such short notice, a big march. Tim knew that now, with the strong organization that Randy had built in the coalition, that it would be possible to draw a large and impressive number of marchers to picket the rally.

"You know," Tim said, "there's only one more thing."

"What?" Randy said scribbing notes.

"Put down that pencil," Tim said, getting up and crossing to the other side of the table. "We have some unfinished business of our own." He bent down and pulled Randy up to him, "I need some affection," he said.

Randy smiled. Taking Tim's hand, he said, "Follow me, I think I know just the thing."

The two men went into the bedroom and Randy pulled Tim into the bed, nuzzling his neck as he started to unbutton his shirt. Tim lay back, a mischievous smile on his face. Randy pulled off the shirt, and Tim rolled across the bed and ran to the other side, his naked chest shining in the dim bedroom light. Randy ran after him and the two tumbled in a heap on the floor, laughing. Tim kissed Randy, holding him on the floor.

Their play was interrupted by the ringing of the phone.
"Oh shit," Randy said.

"Don't answer it. The machine will pick it up," Tim said.

The phone rang once again, a third time, and then the click of the answering machine on the bedside table indicated that the caller was listening to Randy's recorded message. The tone sounded, and they could hear the rasping harsh breath coming out of the machine speaker. Then the voice, muffled with a handkerchief over the receiver, said:

"If you don't want us to finish the job, back off. Queers are easy to kill."

The phone clicked and the long wail of the dial tone punctuated the silence.

Tim's face was white; Randy's set, and hard.

"I guess you're right," he said finally. "We're going to war."

9.

Douglas Haley squirmed in the hard wooden chair trying to make himself comfortable. The seat seemed too short and the back had a hard wooden ridge that cut into the spine. On his left, to make matters worse, was a large woman whose chair was much too close to his and who kept jabbing her elbow into his ribs. She smelled of Lily-of-the-Valley, a scent Haley detested. His wife wore it constantly. On his right was a thin and sanctimonious young man who kept trying to press some sort of leaflet on him and who Haley, with equal industry, was trying to ignore.

He had been sitting in the hall now for over half an hour. The crowd was noisy, though not raucous, and various functionaries every now and again would rush up or down the aisle, carrying books, sheaves of paper or official clipboards, looking businesslike and purposive. The hall was nearly filled, mostly, Haley could see, with middle-aged men who it seemed all wore blue suits, and women who surely must be their wives. They all seemed to have flowered hats, and many of them clutched Bibles.

But, Haley noticed, the crowd was not universally middle-aged. There was a scattering of young people as well, and the choir on the stage, dressed in flowing white robes with blue collars, was entirely made up of bright-faced youngsters who seemed to smile as they sang, though they were drowned out now and again by the overeager organist who would often give a full crescendo just when the choir was singing softly. Haley thought to himself that this was the first time he had heard an electric organ in years.

The woman next to him was once again trying to claim more territory for herself, and Haley was determined as well to remain sovereign of his. In back of him, someone was nattering incessantly, and the woman turned, her elbow making more inroads into his ribs, to answer her neighbor.

"Madam, please," Haley said in exasperation. But she simply turned back with a glare and didn't move.

"Perhaps, sir," the young man said, "you'd like to change seats. Then we might have more room."

Haley thought about that for a second. If he did that, then he would have given the young man a toehold into his privacy. He decided to suffer. Surely the rally couldn't last long.

"No thank you," he said stiffly.

Haley felt uncomfortable and out of place. He had never attended a Fundamentalist rally before, and he had never dreamed that he would be at a Billy Jennings rally, but it was, he had found, the only way to see Louis Rideau.

And he was irritated at being here, irritated at what he felt was the high-handed way that Philip Kristopher had treated him, demanding that he, Douglas Haley, fly to Washington to have a conference. Of course, he refused. But Amos, who was unaccountably genial about Kristopher, insisted also. When they finally met, he wasn't at all sure what Kristopher wanted. Louis Rideau had been a friend, a mentor, almost a father to Hopkenson. Just what did Kristopher want him to do, accuse the man of . . . of what?

"Just read between the lines, Judge," Kristopher had said. He suggested that Haley infer to Rideau that Haley might be interested in some possible favors "should there be a Hopkenson Administration."

Reluctantly, Haley agreed. But he felt he was going too far. He didn't agree with Rideau, didn't favor his increasingly rightist conservative policies, but he was a senator and a respected man. Haley liked to bargain, to play the politics of power, but now he felt like a spy who didn't know what information he was supposed to find.

After he had spoken to Kristopher, Haley returned to his hotel and got on the phone to the senator's Washington office. He asked for an appointment but he was told that Rideau was not in the Capitol and would not return for a week, but that he had speaking engagements in Minnesota, two of them, one in Maryland, and another at the end of the week, in the Sports Arena in Hershey, Pennsylvania.

Haley decided not to attempt to go through Rideau's staff to make an appointment, rather he decided that the best thing to do would be to try to confront Rideau in person at one of the points where he would be speaking. Minnesota was out of the question. Rideau was speaking at a party fundraiser that night in Maryland. But Friday night, Haley learned, he would be the main speaker at the Billy Jennings rally in Pennsylvania. That would have to be the place.

Haley arranged for a plane the next day and for a car rental once he got there. By seven, Friday night, he was sitting in the arena waiting for the rally to begin.

The choir had ceased, and the organist, left to himself, had literally let all the stops out and was playing a spirited and largely improvised version of "Nearer My God to Thee." Around the perimeter of the hall, uniformed policemen had quietly slipped in. It occurred to Haley that indeed there might be trouble. He had forgotten that possibility.

"Sir," he heard the young man saying. He turned to him.

"Yes?" he replied, brusquely he hoped.

"I wonder if you'd like to see some of our literature?"

"No, I don't think so," he said, making no attempt to take the two pamphlets the young man was pushing toward him.

"It's the Lord's word," he said. Something in the earnestness of his neighbor decided the judge that the simplest thing to do would be to take the things and that, once done, would probably insure his being left alone.

"Well, thank you," he said, taking one of the pamphlets.

"Bless you," the young man said, and, as Haley had hoped, subsided into contented silence and became rapt with the playing of the organist, who, Haley realized, had apparently never learned the principle of pianissimo.

He glanced idly at the pamphlets. In red letters on the cover the headline proclaimed: "The Sin of Sodom: Here and Now." A drawing of two glowing angels wrathfully pointing at a group of cowering men adorned the cover. Behind the angels stood someone who Haley supposed to be Lot. The men, groveling at the angels' feet were vividly drawn with obvious eye make-up and lipstick. One of them, even though struck down by the Avenging Angel, was kissing another.

Haley opened the pamphlet. On the inside in Gothic script the legend read: "Thou shalt not lie with mankind as with womankind, it is an abomination."

Haley's eye traveled quickly down the page. More Biblical quotations, more drawings and several paragraphs which he assumed to be more of the same kind of thing.

He had turned the page when from the side of the hall there was a noise of running feet. He looked and saw many of the police moving toward the stage. Shouts sounded, and some screams. He heard chairs being overturned. Out of the confusion there became evident a rhythmic beat and then the beat became words. "Say-it-loud-gay-and-proud. Say-it-loud-gay-and-proud." He rose with the others, the large woman nearly pushing him down, and saw a group of young men and women. The group had forced its way near the foot of the stage.

"Of course, I should have expected this," he said to himself. At every Billy Jennins rally, groups of gay activists had come to heckle. Haley looked toward the area of disturbance. He felt irritated that on the night he had chosen to come there to do important work that these unwashed young things had chosen to come as well. He was suspicious of such demonstrators and the noisy barbarism they stood for. He had never heard Billy Jennings speak, but he didn't think that he could be as repulsive as his criticism made out. But, he had to admit, the pamphlet he held was the crudest kind of propaganda.

As the commotion grew louder, Haley found himself curiously ambivalent. He distrusted and suspected the single-minded political lobbying of the gay activists, with their tactics which seemed aimed at shocking and flaunting their sexuality and their seeming indifference to the general values of American society. They were, he felt, often their own worst enemies. And yet, because of his own life and choices, he could not sympathize with what Jennings stood for, even though he was in some ways representative of his own people. Douglas Haley came from the old stock that Jennings represented, and it was the very values he preached that had been instilled into him since childhood. But in one area he had chosen to march differently from his forebears.

He began to see some order in the confusion. The police had contained the group of demonstrators. Though too far away to see their faces, to his surprise, they looked respectable, even decent young men and women. The men were neatly dressed in suits, the women in sweaters and skirts. They had somehow produced signs and a banner which they were brandishing. The banner said "God Loves Us Too." They were standing, with arms linked, the banner in their midst, chanting. The police had ringed them around by now. On the outside stood members of the crowd, looks of disbelief and anger on their faces.

The group of young people, to Haley's eyes, seemed respectable. And there was something—a determination— that caught him. He was reminded of paintings of the Christian martyrs. Now the crowd had started to try to shout them down. The incessant beat of "Say-It-Loud-Gay-And-Proud" was interrupted with hurled epithets. "Sinner!" "Queer!" Haley sensed that the crowd was turning ugly. At that moment, the organist, apparently signaled, outdid himself, and even more loudly than before played a fanfare and broke into "The Star-Spangled Banner." The crowd, distracted by this and used to silence when the anthem was played, became quieter. A few voices took up the verse, and then others. The woman next to him picked it up in a high quavering soprano.

Haley glanced down at the pamphlet in his hands. At the end, in letters which the artist had tried to make look like tongues of flame, was written: "If a man lie with mankind, they shall surely be put to death. Hear the Word of the Lord."

As the anthem finished, the attention of the crowd began to shift to the group of young people who were still circled by the police, but at that moment the hall went dark and a burst of light illuminated the stage. The organ sounded the opening chords of "The Battle Hymn of the Republic," and a figure dressed in white and carrying a white Bible appeared. Wave after wave of applause washed over the arena. The woman on his left was vigorously applauding and shouting something. The young man was applauding too and staring with almost beatific attention at the figure of Billy Jennings standing on the podium. A clever lighting man had bathed him in a pink and golden glow. Haley did not applaud. He glanced at the group of young people. They stood silent. They had dipped their banner as if at a funeral.

The man on the stage raised his arms in a wide gesture. The applause gradually died away.

"My friends," he said. The voice was husky and intimate.

"My friends and fellow Christians," his voice gained strength.

"Tonight we are here to witness the great work of the Lord. I am not going to speak long tonight, because we have with us a great crusader for righteousness and I know he is the man you have come to hear. But tonight, here in front of you I want to reaffirm my cause to you all. Now you know that there are many people both in the press and in the world who are trying to discredit me and say that I am up here for publicity or even money. But I know that I don't have to prove myself to you good people."

There was applause. The woman next to him shouted, "God bless you, Billy."

"You know why I am here," he continued. "I am here for the same reasons that you are here, to save our country, our religion, our children and our God-given way of life. We all know there are forces trying to stamp out the things we love, and we know that these forces are strong and organized and that they have money, hidden money that none of us could ever match. But the one thing they don't have, and you know the people I am talking about as well as I, the one thing they don't have is God and His Holy Bible."

He held up the white Bible for all to see.

"Now these people who have chosen to walk in the shadow of Satan rather than with God, these people who have chosen to disobey the word of God itself, are arrayed against us. But the word of God is clear. He destroyed Sodom and Gomorrah for their sins. And he says in the New Testament that "neither idolators nor effeminites nor abusers of themselves with mankind shall inherit the kingdom of heaven." And he further says in Leviticus that what they do is an abomination. Do you hear that? An abomination." His voice had risen to full pitch and power.

"You're an abomination, Billy. Come off it," someone yelled.

"God loves all people, straight and gay," another shout echoed.

"Yes, yes, that's true," Jennings said, picking up with professional ease the taunt from the group. "He does love all people. He loves homosexual people, too, and I never said he didn't. But he doesn't love what you *do* and what you want. He doesn't love 'abusers of men with men,' he doesn't love 'the effeminate.' It's in god's Holy Word." Here he held up the Bible again.

"He doesn't love bigots either," another voice shouted.

"If you call being true to God's Holy Word bigotry," he shouted back, "then I am proud to be a bigot."

The crowd cheered. Haley was amazed at the pandemonium, surprised at the vehemence in Jennings' tone, moved at the bravery of the small group of young people who were fighting back. He didn't know what to do. He wanted to do something, but he stood still. The woman next to him stared suspiciously at him. Jennings spoke again.

"Yes," he said. "I'm proud to be a bigot in the cause of righteousness because in the eyes of God those who would molest our children, those who would strike down the sacred family, those who want to undermine the American Way itself do not deserve any better."

The crowd once again yelled its approval. The shouts of the group of gay people were lost in the general chaos. The police ringed them more tightly. Some of the crowd had started to move toward them. From the stage Jennings saw what was happening.

He spoke into the microphone and his voice was strong, commanding.

"Christians, brothers and sisters," he said. "Listen to me."

All movement stopped.

"Listen to me. I want all of you to stop for a moment. Tonight we are here to witness the power of the Lord. And the Lord has sent us a great man to speak to us. But he has also sent us these young people who are standing there, ringed in by the police just as they are ringed in by their own sin and unhappiness. But they can be saved. And my friends, God will save them. I know he will. Maybe we can save them tonight. Maybe we can be present at a miracle."

"Amen," someone shouted. It was the boy on Haley's right.

"We don't want your God, if he hates us," someone from the circle shouted.

"There, you see, you see!" Jennings said triumphantly.

"There you hear the voice of Satan, but I am sure that it is not the voice of that poor misguided young woman. It is her sin that has so confused her. But, my dear," he said, and his voice became low, husky with emotion. "God will protect you. He can save you. Just come to him and repent.

"Friends, Christians, brothers and sisters," he called, "fall on your knees and pray with me, pray that the good God in his mercy will take this dreadful affliction from these young men and women and show them the error of their ways and the viciousness of their sin. Oh, the Lord *will* have mercy on the unrighteousness.

"I want you all to pray with me that those young people, those young Americans, standing right there, will come up to this stage right now and confess their love for Jesus Christ."

"Amen," someone shouted.

"Jesus loves them, all of them, it's what they do that he doesn't love. I know hundreds of reformed homosexual people who have given up their vice and come before the throne of God, and he has saved them. And it can happen here tonight. I know it." He had raised his hands high in the air. "Do you hear me?" he cried, his voice full, imploring, earnest. "Do you young people hear me? Come up now and be saved. Jesus will forgive you and save you." As he spoke, he sank to his knees, arms outstretched.

The crowd looked at the group of young people who throughout this had stood silent. Listening. Haley felt the tension and the rage and was struck by the power of the confrontation between Jennings and the group of young women and men. The hall was silent. Heeding Jennings' continued call, one by one people fell to their knees. The young man on his right, the woman on his left. People all around him. The entire front of the hall was on their knees. On the stage Billy Jennings had begun to pray. Soon Haley was standing alone in his row. All around him men and women were on their knees. Around the still standing circle of young people the audience was kneeling.

"Pray for them," Billy Jennings was saying. The organist began, softly this time, to play "Rock of Ages."

"Oh God in heaven, take these poor sinners to thy bosom," Jennings prayed, emotionally sighing the words into the microphone. "Take them and heal them and forgive them of their terrible ills. Make them whole again."

As he prayed, still more people fell to their knees. The circle of gay people drew in upon themselves. Haley watched them exchange uncertain glances, but as Jennings' prayers continued he saw the faces of the tight little circle become infused with a common purpose.

The police nervously drew in around the group, but rather than threatening gestures, the young people, quietly at first and then with greater resonance, began to sing.

"We shall overcome," a few timid voices began.

"We shall overcome," other stronger voices joined them.

"We shall overcome someday," the entire group was singing now.

"Oh Lord, heal them of their wickedness," Billy Jennings prayed.

"Gays shall overcome, someday," the voices were strong now, with pride and purpose, changing the lyric slightly, meaningfully. When they had finished their song they began to move, pressed on either side by the police, who were, it was clear, herding them toward the door. Jennings' prayers were now intense, and the audience responded with massed "alleluias" and "amens."

"Oh Lord, smite them in their wickedness," he was saying.

"Say it loud," the gays chanted.

"Cleanse them of their iniquity," he called.

"Gay and Proud!" It was a chant no longer, but a shout of defiance. The police pushed them now toward the center doors.

"You can't stamp us out, Billy," one young man shouted.

"We are *your* children," the voice of a young woman pierced the tension of the hall.

"Oh Lord, call down thy wrath," Jennings pleaded.

"Proud! Proud! Proud! Gay and Proud." The words became a marching beat. As the group of young people marched up the aisle, shepherded by the police toward the doors, Haley realized he was standing nearly alone.

He felt his heart twist within him, and his eyes fill with tears. But he knew that the time was not now, and as the marching legion passed, he sank to his knees and buried his face in his hands.

"Amen," the woman next to him said. Haley looked up. He realized the rally was finished. He had sat through it all; through Jennings' introduction of Rideau, through Rideau's speech, even through the eventual expulsion by the police of the young demonstrators and the thunderous singing of the "Battle Hymn of the Republic." Shaken, he had endured it all. Jennings had spoken again, Rideau had come to the stage. His speech was moderate, calm, rational. In measured tones, the cadences of the statesman that he seemed to be, Rideau spoke about a middle path. But as he listened, Haley realized that Rideau's speech was different from Jennings only because it lacked the extreme fire and the high passion of Jennings' commitment. While Jennings stirred up his listeners with visions of Sodom and of the dangers of homosexual sin, Rideau did not speak of sin at all. He conjured up no days of judgment, no destruction of the cities of the plain. He did not speak about the word of God. Instead in his judicious manner he spoke of the Constitutional law upon which this country was founded, but he noted that it was the basic unit of the American family which the Constitution was written to protect. He spoke of the equality in the eyes of the law of all men, but noted that those who disrupted the smooth and ordered workings of the established social system did not deserve the protection which the law offered. He spoke of the inalienable right of all men to the equal possession of jobs, housing and accommodation, but pointed out that certain beliefs and practices had always been inimical to the best interests of a democratic society, and that one of the foundation stones upon which our society was built, having its origin in English common law itself, was the right of the free use of private property. He asserted that he stood for every man's right to use such property as he saw fit. He noted that while all men deserved equal access to housing, that if the conditions of moral uprightness, trustworthiness and usefulness to society were not met, that it was not only a property owner's right but indeed his duty to make distinctions between those he would provide housing for and those he would not. He further went on to say that while the free enterprise system was intended to provide jobs and education for all men, the very structure of our society was, and had been for two hundred years, based upon the premise that our teachers would be morally as well as socially responsible people and that jobs—all jobs—were finally intended to further the moral intentions of the nation. And if, he said, we could not trust our education and our educators, then who can we trust?

As he listened, Haley realized that Rideau had never once

mentioned the word homosexual; he never once leveled an attack on gay people nor sided with Jennings' opposition to them. His speech seemed to be a model of moderate discourse. Yet as he listened, Haley could see that Rideau's respectability masked a more subtle and therefore more dangerous demagoguery. His arguments were insidious: stripped of their Jeffersonian tones they advocated equality for the middle class and the propertied, but not for those who had nothing. They defended the right of all men to have jobs and housing, as long as they did not deviate from the standards of the majority. His arguments defended the American Way, but that American Way was, he subtly made clear, the exclusive province of the Christian, the middle American, the white and the heterosexual. And at the end, he raised the dreadful spectre that those who deviated from the American Way might find themselves facing severe punishment. He said: "In conclusion, my friends, tonight, privileged as I am to stand upon this stage speaking to this dedicated group of Americans, my heart is heavy with the knowledge that all is not well in this great land of ours. We are all here tonight dedicated to the principles which have shaped our nation and which with the help of Divine Wisdom will guide it, I have no doubt, in the future. But from all sides those principles are under attack, by those who, perhaps through no fault of their own, have chosen to seek another road than that down which most of us have chosen to walk. Abraham Lincoln once said that God must have loved the little man, because he made so many of us. And the wisdom of that great man should guide us all tonight. We are many, we are legion, and it is all of us, the little men, who have made our nation great and who will continue to make it great. And if it is necessary to fight for our right, to fight for our right to be free against those who would question that right, against those who would insidiously infiltrate the very basic institutions of our nation: our churches, our schools, our homes, the minds of our sons and daughters, then fight we must. We have something, God given, that is worth fighting for. I do not call upon you to rise up in wrath. The days of Holy Wars are gone, but I call upon you to look around you, to see the enemy if he is here, and to use those tools which our great nation has given us. One nation, indivisible, the pledge says. We must be indivisible in our battle. Go to your governors, go to your legislators, go to your city councils, go to your president and above all go to your voting booth and cast your vote for decency, and for yourselves. Thank you."

The crowd rose, thunderously applauding. Haley rose with it. He looked dully out across the multitude that filled the huge auditorium, at the white-robed choir on stage, at Jennings now standing with his hand in Rideau's, arms raised, at Rideau, serious, dressed in senatorial blue, his gray hair cut short, his small gray mustache trimmed and military. Haley wondered, for a moment, what the point of it all was. Yet as the applause surged around him, as the heavy woman next to him now aroused to near hysteria shouted and applauded, as the young man on his other side seemed about to embrace him in his ecstasy, Haley knew without question that his mission to protect Hopkenson was the most important thing he had ever done. That it involved Rideau was an irony not lost upon him. Douglas Haley was not sure where he stood, but of one thing he was sure. Tonight he had seen the fire in young men's eyes, and had seen the forces which would try to extinguish that flame. He had heard the pride in young men's voices, and had heard the tongues which would try to silence those voices and shout down that pride. But most of all he had heard something in Rideau's speech that he, Judge Douglas Haley, who had sworn to uphold his nation's Constitution, could not stand idly by and sanction. He had heard a man declare that equality was for some, not all, that the law and its justice excluded those who did not dress the same, live the same, or love the same. Against that, Douglas Haley knew, if against nothing else, he had to fight.

Haley pushed his way against the crowd, down toward the platform. He wanted to get to Rideau, but he also wanted to avoid anyone seeing them together. Rideau had gone off stage with Billy Jennings. Haley ducked across an empty aisle and toward a side door that seemed to lead backstage. Once in the shelter of the door, he took a card from his pocket and scribbled a note on it. Then he went through the door. It opened into a long corridor. At the end of the corridor he could see the backstage area. He heard voices, among them the excited voice of Jennings. The pop of flashbulbs punctuated the babble of tongues.

He hurried down the hall. The room behind the stage was crowded with people, all of them clustering around Rideau and Jennings. Haley edged through the crowd and across the room. A group of young men and women, chorus members, were standing on the edge of the crowd. He took one of them aside.

"Young man," he said, "could you see that Senator Rideau gets this note?"

He looked surprised, but caught up in the general enthusiasm, he agreed. Haley watched the young man push through the crowd toward the senator. People around Rideau were congratulating him on the speech. Snatches of conversation floated above the crowd.

"Fine speech, senator," a man in clerical garb said.

"Good to have you with us," another man, dressed in a dark suit with what looked from where he stood like an American Legion button in the lapel, said to Rideau, pumping his hand.

"You really gave it to the queers," a young woman chortled.

"I speak for all men, as I must," the senator said gravely.

A diplomat even off-stage, Haley thought.

A reporter took a picture of the two, and another, notebook in hand, asked:

"Does this signal the beginning of a nationwide crusade against gays, senator?"

"I am not the leader of the crusades," Rideau responded. "I simply fight for justice in my own way."

"How about you, Reverend Jennings?" the reporter pressed. "Now that you have Senator Rideau, are you going to press for legislation against homosexuals?"

Billy Jennings glanced at the senator, who imperceptibly frowned. "I will do what the Lord asks me," he said. The young man to whom he had entrusted the note had managed to get up to the senator. He held out the note. Rideau took it, glanced at it, and turned to see from where it came. Haley made sure that Rideau saw him. He had written that he needed to see Rideau and that he would wait for him outside, in his car, in the North Parking Lot, when he could get free. He knew that though he had not seen Rideau personally for some time that his summons would not go unheeded. Satisfied that Rideau would soon follow, he slipped out of the room and down the hall to an exit. He left the building and walked toward the parking lot. He found his car, got in and settled down to wait.

The parking lot was so filled with people streaming out of the arena that Haley feared Rideau would not find him. Near the entrance, he could still hear the now-muffled chanting of the demonstrators whose disruption of the rally had so disturbed him. He did not know what to think or feel about these young people, and he knew that he must not let his own interior turmoil surface when he talked to Rideau. Louis Rideau was a cool and impenetrable man, sure of himself and used to wielding power. His face betrayed only what he wanted seen, and his manner seldom gave a clue as to what he really felt. Haley too was master of that manner, and he knew he had to confront Rideau tonight from a position of strength, yet without revealing anything about the real purpose of his being there.

The real purpose. Just why was he there, in fact? Philip had said to listen, to see what he could discover. What he had discovered was that Louis Rideau was speaking on a Billy Jennings platform. This was not entirely surprising, since Rideau was essentially conservative. His politics had veered away from Hopkenson in the last several years. Hopkenson was the candidate of the center, Rideau the statesman of the moderate Right. Haley was not sure that Rideau did in fact countenance the extreme conservatism of Jennings, but he knew that if there was political value in it, Rideau would find a way to use it. The alignment was clear: Rideau, despite his deferences, would work for Hopkenson, the party candidate, against the president whose bankrupt policy and lackluster administration was serving the country badly. Jennings would work for Hopkenson, not because he was politically support-ing Hopkenson's far more liberal attitude, but because the president was no longer useful to him. Presumably Jennings felt that by currying favor with Rideau, he could count on using that favor with Hopkenson, whose ties with Rideau were still strong, if strained. And it was surely clear to both men that Hopkenson had a very strong chance to win. The polls gave Hopkenson a substantial edge because he represent-ed what most of the nation wanted: neither a too conservative nor a too liberal stance.

What was most clear to Haley was that the election of Magnus Hopkenson was a reasonable certainty; a certainty, that is, unless the small fact which he and the others possessed became known. He thought back on that fated telephone call when he learned that Magnus Hopkenson had a secret, and a past. Amos Parr's words still echoed: "Magnus Hopkenson and I were lovers." But it was in the distant past, Haley thought; yet someone was investigating Magnus Hopkenson, and might find the secret. The investigation of candidates for any office had become routine. He had himself run various investigations on candidates for office. In fact, he had once, very quietly pursued certain inquiries about Jack Kennedy, inquiries which he had found substantiated much rumor and Boston gossip, and which he, as a supporter of the young president, had helped, as Bobby was fond of saying, to "render harmless.'

What could be found out about Magnus Hopkenson now? Parr insisted that since that time, Hopkenson had been absolute in his discretion. Consider young Kennedy; *he* got elected, Haley reflected. Or Adlai Stevenson, he thought. Haley knew that Stevenson had led a life which did not shy away from being "sexually irregular." Though he, like Hopkenson, was absolutely discreet. And now that J. Edgar Hoover was dead, it was common knowledge that his life, which included no women, had been oriented, in a painful and hidden way, toward that homosexuality which he professed to despise. The fact was that nothing about this did come out. Kennedy's infidelities, Stevenson's past, Hoover's predelictions, none of this had in fact surfaced at the time. But if information about Hopkenson did surface, if someone found it and used it, it could—it would—end the candidacy. People might accept it in a mayor, even in a senator, but for a president to have a hidden homosexual past, this would never be forgiven by an electorate for whom sex, of any kind, was still the worst of sins, and homosexuality the most unforgiveable.

It seemed probable to Haley that Hopkenson's past was not known to Jennings. It was clear what Jennings felt about the subject, and Haley doubted that Jennings, who was mounting, it appeared, a full-scale crusade against homosexuals, could ever support Hopkenson if he knew that Hopkenson had such an affiliation. As to Rideau, Haley did not know. Rideau was a private man, but he *had* been Hopkenson's mentor. Surely he would know everything there was to know about Magnus. But, what was there to know about Rideau?

What his tastes were, Haley was not sure. Rideau was married and had two daughters. His marriage, like that of so many others in public life, was a combination of political usefulness and, perhaps, real affection. His wife, Catherine Brandt, was from an old family, with ties to other families in the state. She had campaigned long with Rideau, and though formal and rather stiff, seemed to be a useful asset to his political life. His private life was kept very quiet and without publicity. What Rideau felt, Haley was not sure. But he suspected that from Louis Rideau, such a thing would receive no condemnation. His professional dealings with Rideau had left him with the impression that the senator rarely condemned; he only asked about the political value of an event, an action, a piece of information. If he knew of Hopkenson's past, he would not condemn Hopkenson for it. He would only ask, "How dangerous is it?"

And that, of course, was the question. How dangerous was this information? If it were found out, who could use it against the candidate? One answer, clearly, was the opposition. But what Haley needed to know was if Rideau and Jennings knew. If they did know, would they withdraw support from Hopkenson? Loss of Jennings' support would be significant, since his following was large. But loss of Rideau's support would be catastrophic, since it would signal a major rift in the party, indeed, might signal that Rideau himself would run. All of this was imponderable, even unknowable now. From his public stance, Haley could see that Rideau supported Hopkenson, but his remarks tonight were not the kind of thing that Hopkenson could endorse. Haley knew that he needed to talk to Rideau, to get a sense of what he could perceive behind the mask.

Out of the crowd one of the young men who was with Rideau and Jennings came toward the car.

"Mr. Haley?" he inquired. Haley was irritated that he did not call him Judge.

"Yes, I'm Judge Haley."

"Could you come with me, The Reverend Jennings can see you now."

"I didn't come to . . ." he started to say, but decided he didn't want this anonymous functionary to know anything. He followed the young man. From a distance he could hear the chanting of the demonstrators outside the arena. They went through the door, down a corridor and into a small dressing room at the back of the stage.

"Mr. Haley, sir," the young man said as he knocked.

"Come in," a voice boomed.

"Go right in, sir." The door was opened for him and Haley went in. Seated in a chair was Jennings, looking tired.

"Well, Judge Haley, what a pleasure." He rose, holding out his hand and the weariness vanished and the public personality took its place, genial, engaging, intimate.

"I'm glad to see that you were here to witness tonight Judge. We need men like you in our great crusade." He looked at Haley with clear, cold eyes.

"I'm afraid there has been some mistake," Haley said. "I really wasn't expecting . . ."

"To see me. Oh no, I know, I know, but Louis couldn't stay, had to make a plane back to Washington you know. Busy man. So he asked me to give you his best."

Haley was furious, but he controlled himself, and said levelly:

"I was expecting to see the senator, not you, Mr. Jennings."

"I guess that we don't always get what we want in this vale of tears, Judge. But if you have some message for the senator, why I will be very happy to get it to him. After all, he and I are on the same team. We're both fighting for righteousness."

"Mr. Jennings . . ."

"My friends call me Billy," he said heartily.

"Mr. Jennings," Haley continued, "I don't think we really have much to say to one another, so if you will excuse me, I think I'll go."

"Why Judge, before you go, I hope you'll agree to share a platform with me sometime. Consider: Senator Rideau and Judge Douglas Haley. Why, these are names to conjure with, and I am sure we all want to see Magnus Hopkenson elected."

"Mr. Jennings, I have to say, at the risk of offending you, that while I very much want to see Magnus Hopkenson elected, I doubt that he will be grateful for your support, and I must tell you that you will not likely ever have mine. Now good-bye."

Haley started to leave, but Jennings reached out to restrain him.

"Mr. Haley, the apostles have said that whosoever is for the Lord is for the right, and we here, in God's People, are certainly for the Lord. And they also said that whosoever is not with us must surely be against us. Surely you're not against us?"

Haley felt his temper rising. After the demonstration in the arena, his emotions were close to the surface. He knew he must be politic in his answers.

"I'm for justice, like everyone is, Mr. Jennings."

"Oh, well, that is good to hear, Judge, so good to hear. You know, the world is in a sorry state today, so many people trying to undo the Lord's work, trying to undermine this great country of ours, trying to destroy the sacred family and all it stands for. Why, Judge, you wouldn't believe how many people everyday try to fight against the work the Lord has prepared for me to walk in. Why those young people out there tonight. Oh, good folk if they only had the word of God, but now, damned, Judge, damned sinners all of them, perverts, the Lord knows that. Why Judge, they're the kind of people who are trying to destroy everything that men like you and the good senator have worked to build, everything that my people, God's People, believe in. I expect you agree."

Haley had heard enough. He turned and walked toward the door. As his hand grasped the knob, Jennings said:

"Oh, yes, I almost forgot, Judge. The senator did say something, right out of the scriptures it was, too. Now what was it? That dear good man is always quoting the good book. Oh, yes, he said to you, "Watchman, beware of the night." Now what do you suppose that means?"

Haley stopped and looked squarely at Jennings, but the bland and smiling face did not change. He stood there, his hand out, waiting for Haley to shake it.

"I believe, Reverend," Haley said, "that the correct quotation is "Watchman, what of the night?""

"Ah, perhaps it is, perhaps it is, Judge," Jennings said, smiling blandly. "I'm glad to see that you too are up on the Good Book. Can't rely on that blessed text enough, can we?" He held out his hand again.

"Sure am glad to meet you at last, Judge. I really hope we can count on you in the good fight. You know what they say about the wages of sin."

Haley had heard enough. Without shaking hands, he turned and left the room.

As he hurried toward his car, he was disturbed and puzzled by what he had heard. Why had Rideau avoided him? Why the implied threat? He got into his car. He must contact Philip as soon as he got back to Boston, and let him know about this. But had Rideau threatened him, he wondered? *Could* he have said "Beware of the night"? Or was it Jennings himself who was threatening? "The wages of sin are surely death." Haley knew that quotation also.

But his thoughts were interrupted by the pressing crowds in front of his car as he edged toward the exit. The red light of police cars inscribed irridescent circles in the night, and he saw that the demonstrators were still circling, handing out leaflets to the departing crowds. Here and there the hordes of Jennings supporters made menacing gestures toward them. As he approched the gate he looked at the young people, but the policeman directing traffic hurried him on with an impatient wave. He could see their faces now, young faces, serious, dedicated, angry, marching against the bigotry they had encountered tonight.

One after another the line of marchers passed his car. He felt a wave of admiration for them, of identification. He wished, half-wished, he could be there with them. But he was sure he never could, feared he never would. Behind the rolled up windows of his car he felt sealed off from these young men and women, sealed off by age and by time, by years of repression and hiding, by other mores and other manners. These young people were carrying a torch he had never dared to light.

He felt tears well up, as they had risen earlier in the hall. The line of marchers passed him one by one, but it was on only one face that his gaze was suddenly riveted. Unexpectedly haloed in the headlights, marching with the others, his face serious with their united purpose, his eyes lighted by their mutual anger, blind to everyone around him save his cause, marched his son, his only son, Timothy. Timothy with whom he had shared little, whom he barely knew, and who, despite the silence between them, he desperately loved. One by one the marchers passed him by, and his son was lost in the line, one among a hundred. Haley blindly nosed his car into the street and fled into the alien night.

10.

As he drove through the darkening streets, Walter Bray felt the clutch of anxiety in his stomach, anxiety and sick sorrow. He did not fear the encounter to come, that was part of the job. But he feared he might give way, if just for one moment, give way to tears and to rage. In his heart, he had always been prepared for death. In the army, in Korea, he had known it. When he was a cop he had walked with it. And it was part of the job now. When Fred Tompkins died, gunned down on the McIntosh case, Bray had handled the loss, finally, even accepted it. But the loss of Monte was harder to bear, impossible, he feared.

Monte Dillon was not just a partner; he was Bray's closest friend. He and Monte had built the agency together, and in so doing built lives together as well. When Walter was married, Monte was best man, as Walter was for Monte when the time came. He had stood godfather to Monte's daughter, and Monte had stood by him during those terrible months when it became clear that Jessica was not going to survive the ravages of cancer. Monte and Helene had made a second family for Walter Bray, a place to go when the loss was too keen. But now Walter had to be the comforter. He would have to comfort Helene and try to explain the inexplicable, try to make sense to her of the fact that her husband had been gunned down by a stranger in the seedy apartment of a cheap callboy. How could he tell her why? All he could say was that it happened and there was no reason. No explanation could comfort or explain, and the reasons only proved that the world everyday went a little more insane.

And what were the reasons, Bray asked himself. Someone, a client he didn't know, wanted to find out if a prominent politician who happened to be a likely choice for the next president had ever slept with boys. Why the hell was it so important what the man might have done thirty years ago? Why had it led to all this: to Monte dead, to his own life broken now by sorrow and by loss. And more: his office ransacked by someone obviously not a two-bit burglar, but instead by someone who was as interested in Hopkenson's past as Bray's client, and who very much wanted the identity of that client.

Did he want it enough to kill for it? Was the man caught in Monte's camera Monte's killer? Could Bray have inadvertently caused Monte's death when this same man overheard him and Monte on their CB frequency? And what about St. Pierre, the worm who was the cause of it all? It was his list of names that Walter wanted. It was his list that he sent Monte to try to find in St. Pierre's empty apartment. But an apartment not quite empty, because someone else was there looking, too. And that someone was too quick for Monte, had gunned him down, silently, efficiently. Killed him for a list of queers, Bray thought bitterly. Was the same man who he had glimpsed outside St. Pierre's apartment waiting to kill St. Pierre as well? Who was he? The question hammered home, repeating over and over a litany of pain.

Bray searched every inch of the past hours: his talk with St. Pierre, leaving the building, getting into the car, realizing, too late, who was following him. Then he lost him. That's when he must have gone back to St. Pierre, threatened him, and killed him.

But no, that didn't work. If he had gotten the list, then Monte would be still alive. No, St. Pierre wasn't there when the stranger got back. He must have called someone. Or another possibility. Maybe the stranger didn't know about St. Pierre. Maybe he was just following me, Bray realized. If that were the case, if the tail was not after St. Pierre, didn't even know about St. Pierre—and how could he since Bray had that file at home—then he was tailing me. St. Pierre must have skipped town, or worse. He had a feeling it was worse.

The few pieces of the puzzle whirled in his head as he drove toward the destination. Only one thing was clear. Monte was dead and Bray intended to find out who killed him. He tried to control the rage he felt rising, knew he must control it. Anger made dead men, and he was sure that whoever killed Monte would try to kill him, too, once it was clear that he was still searching for whatever was to be found about Magnus Hopkenson. He had a job to do, and rage would not get it done in the quiet and efficient way Bray liked. No passion, no drama, just quiet, careful work, missing nothing, checking everything, believing nothing until it was proved. This was how Walter Bray and Monte had always worked and this was how he was going to work now. The job he had was to find out who killed his friend. And the man who killed his friend was probably the same man who was trying to find out the secret that might lie at the heart of Magnus Hopkenson's life.

Bray nosed his car onto the down ramp of the parking garage four blocks from the Pentagon as the instructions he had gotten from "Mr. Smith's" young messenger had told him to do. Tonight he was to hand over to "Smith" in person the result, on tape, of the investigation thus far. Smith wanted to meet Bray, it was explained, to see if he was "comfortable" with the investigator. Well, Walter Bray sure as hell wanted to find out who his "client" was. That afternoon he had put on the tape all the information he had about St. Pierre, about the missing Hugh Tilden. Later he had added that St. Pierre was also missing and that Monte was dead. He also mentioned that he had interviewed Amos Parr and Senator Rideau, that neither man responded to his questions about homosexuality. In fact, their very lack of response was what had bothered him most. But, the upshot was that in all the investigating done thus far, there was no hint that Magnus Hopkenson had anything in his past that might damage him. The last information on the tape was about the list. Or, as he put it: "The presumed list, since in fact when I talked with St. Pierre, he only indicated that he had names, not a "list" of names. To secure these names, presumably of men who had used his services or those of his friends, among them perhaps Hugh Tilden, I promised him fifteen hundred dollars. I told him I would be back at four that afternoon with the money. I returned, but St. Pierre was gone. I left Monte Dillon on stake out, with instructions to call in. When Monte didn't call, I went back, and found him, a bullet through his temple, the apartment ransacked, St. Pierre's things scattered and torn. I can only presume that Monte was searching the apartment when someone, perhaps St. Pierre, though I think that unlikely, found him there and killed him, either because Monte had found what we wanted, namely, the list, or simply to keep him quiet. There are suspects: first, St. Pierre himself; second, a stranger who appears to be the same one on the film of the burglary of my office; or a possible and unknown third party. I discount St. Pierre because I do not believe that he could kill an experienced agent like Monte Dillon. I also believe that St. Pierre himself may be dead. The stranger is a mystery. I have no clue as to his identity, but his motives are reasonably clear. He wants what I—we—want, information about Magnus Hopkenson, and one other thing, information about who is investigating Magnus Hopkenson, namely my client, you Mr. Smith. So far as I know, he has neither. As to a third party, this is only conjecture. But it is possible that the "mysterious stranger" may not have known about St. Pierre at all, but may have only been tailing me. If that is so, then St. Pierre was taken away and/or killed by someone else, who may also be the killer or killers of Monte Dillon. As you see, Mr. Smith, my information is sketchy at best. There are dead men, but not much else. I intend to pursue the investigation with further examination of contacts of Hopkenson, among them deeper probing into Amos Parr, and Senator Rideau's connections with Hopkenson. If you have any suggestions, most especially about the whereabouts of Hugh Tilden, who I am actively seeking, I would be grateful."

Bray patted the small cassette in his right pocket and drove down into the garage to the D Level and followed the numbered signs to Bay 34. As he had been instructed, he pulled in to wait, killing the lights and the engine. The garage was dimly lighted. Bray didn't like the situation much. Only a few cars were parked this far down, and none near him. He loosened the .38 in his holster and slumped down in the seat while trying to keep watch through the side and rear-view mirrors. He was satisfied that he could pretty well see the large area of the garage in back of him. His right was protected by the wall of the bay, his nose by the wall which he pulled up to. The vulnerable spots were left, and the rear. He checked his watch. Five to nine. Smith's boy had said nine sharp. The garage was silent, except for the occasional boom of an engine four floors up, and the hum of the city which was more felt than heard this far below.

Out of the corner of the side mirror, he thought he saw lights. He inched up in his seat. Yes, coming slowly, silently down the far ramp was a large Cadillac limousine. Tinted windows kept him from seeing who was inside. The car cruised toward him. Bray turned the ignition and stepped on the brake lights three times as he had been told to do. The big car slowed, pulled past him, stopped and reversed, backing into the space until the rear passenger door was opposite his own driver's seat. Behind the tinted glass, Bray could just make out a figure hunched near the window, wearing, apparently, a cap of some kind pulled down low. Through the side mirror he could just see the chauffeur's back, only a silhouette through the glass partition, also tinted, that separated the driver from the passenger. The car stopped, but Bray could hear the engine softly running. Nosed out like that, the big car could leap away in a second, long before Bray could turn around to follow. He felt a moment of irration at being outmanuevered.

Bray started to get out of the car, but the figure in the back raised his hand in a signal to remain where he was. The window of the limo rolled quietly and smoothly down and the figure sat up. Bray realized with a start that there was no face, only darkness and two deep eye sockets. Once the chill had passed, Bray saw that the eerie visage was only a ski mask. Without a word, the figure handed a small black box out of the window. Bray opened his window and took the box. It was a small walkie-talkie. The limousine window slid shut. A voice, disguised in some electronic way cooly observed:

"There, Mr. Bray, with this we can speak intimately and safely without the necessity of being physically close. I can also record our conversation so that no one will be embarrassed by forgetting details at some later date. Shall we get down to it?"

"Yes, let's," Bray replied.

"What have you got for me?"

Bray pulled the cassette out of his pocket.

"It's all here," holding up the tape.

"Efficient."

"Thanks," Bray said. "Now what?"

"I suppose I ought to apologize for the secrecy, this mask, the meeting, but it would be best not to reveal myself to you."

"At the moment?" Bray tried.

"If at all," Smith countered.

"I don't much like not knowing who I'm working for."

"I wouldn't either, in your position, Mr. Bray, but it is impossible to have it any other way."

"Suppose I don't go on?"

"An understandable threat, but I know, as you must, that there is too much at stake. I know that your office was burglarized—"

Bray stifled an exclamation.

"How do I know that? I am not without resources, and you are not the only conduit of information I have."

"Then do you know who did it?"

"No, Walter—may I call you Walter—?"

"No, Mr. Smith, I think we ought to continue our formality," Bray said coldly.

"Very well. No, I do not know who it is, except that it is quite clear, to me at least, that whoever it is is after the same thing you are, and wanted to find out what you know. Did he?"

"No, he didn't. The only thing he could have found was the name of one of my contacts, who I think is now dead, probaby killed, though not certainly killed, by whoever broke into my office."

"I see. I suspect you must realize that this is not just an ordinary hunt for scandal, Mr. Bray. One man is possibly dead, and . . ."

"And another certainly dead," Bray cut in, feeling the pain and the anger.

"And that is why you won't quit," Smith said.

Bray suppressed a flash of rage at the cool presumption of the man's tone, but knew he was right.

"Yes, you're right," he finally said. "Now, tell me what you want and why you want it."

"I've told you in my written instructions," Smith said, this time with a trace of his own irritation. "My client is a very wealthy man, and as is not uncommon among men of his influence, he intends to support the presidential candidate. This investment, as it were, must, like all his investments, be sound and without risk. Therefore he would like to know what there might be in the life of the candidate which would put his investment at risk. It's that simple."

"Mr. Smith," he said, emphasizing the name with sarcasm, "one man, possibly two, have been killed because of this 'investment.'"

"I'm not here to debate this with you, Mr. Bray," Smith said coldly. "You are being exceptionally well paid to pursue this. Either you do it or you don't. However . . ."

Bray sensed there was distinct menace in Smith's unfinished sentence.

"However, what, Mr. Smith?"

"Let us say, Mr. Bray, that my client has power in many areas and that if you do not help us to do what we have to do, then it may become increasingly difficult for you to do what you have been doing."

"Another little murder?"

"No, Bray, that's not uh . . . our style. We can be far more subtle and far more effective. And by the way, I assure you that we are not responsible for your man's death. It ought to be obvious to you that if you find out who killed your partner then you will also be very close to finding out what we need to know."

Bray nodded in agreement, then:

"What will you do if you find out Hopkenson has, shall we say, an irregular past? Blackmail him?"

Smith paused a moment. "Hardly, Mr. Bray, hardly. You can certainly know that we, my client, wants nothing more than for the candidate to be elected. It doesn't matter what he might have done, or in fact what he is. All we are concerned about is what can be learned about the past, and it seems evident, does it not, that someone, someplace, is trying to find out what can be learned. Presumably it will be useful to find out who."

"And stop them?" Bray said.

"We'll handle that," Smith replied.

"All right, now let me talk," Bray said. "First of all, you're right. I'll go on with this, and if there's anything to be found out, you'll have it, but I think it's a dirty business. Second, something has been added to this. When I took on this assignment, when I agreed to do this without meeting the client, when I started dealing with your messenger boy, I was looking for scandal. I was trying to find facts. You wanted to know if your man had ever slept with boys. Not unusual, lots of people come to us trying to ferret out sexual peccadilloes. And your object is a potential president which makes the case a little out of the ordinary. But now it's changed, your investigation has caused two murders. We're not looking for some teenage sexplay now, we're looking for real grown-up murderers who don't seem to have many qualms about who they kill. Has it occured to you, Mr. Smith, that by stirring up this hornet's nest you have not only gotten a couple of people killed but that there may be more: maybe you, maybe your client, maybe even Magus Hopkenson."

Bray realized that his words had risen above a whisper that the conversation had been conducted in until now. The silence after he finished seemed accusing and heavy. Finally Smith broke it.

"I know," he said simply. "I know, and it can't be helped. I'm sorry to have to say that, Bray, but it can't be helped. Magnus Hopkenson must be elected. If someone is trying to unearth something in his past to use against him, then we have to know this and stop it. I cannot tell you how vital this is. We are prepared to offer you whatever you need to continue. But our conditions must be met. You will not know who I am, who we are. And once you have discovered either an irregularity—your word I believe—in the candidate's background, or whoever is also delving into this, you must then do nothing."

"Nothing?" Bray exploded.

"If you make any attempt to use the information against Hopkenson, or to avenge your partner, or do anything other than what I have outlined, I can assure you, Mr. Bray, that the consequences will be extremely swift and extremely unpleasant. Now, please hand me the tapes of your progress until now. I will add them to this conversation we have just had. We will not meet again except under the most pressing circumstances. I will give you a private number which you can call if you absolutely need to be in touch with me, but it must be used with great discretion, though all conversations will be scrambled. Is there anything else?"

Bray shook his head, and handed the tapes and the black box through the window, and received the number.

"Mr. Bray," Smith said, "I hope you realize I am protecting you as well as myself by not letting you meet my client. It would be very dangerous for you to know him, and would serve, you must believe me, no useful purpose."

The limousine pulled quietly away. Through the window Bray could see that its license was covered, and that the occupants were only shadows.

11.

As the plane slipped in over Boston, Haley knew he must act quickly. The uncertainties of the evening before nagged him. He was not sure yet why Rideau had avoided him, but it was clear that the senator knew he was there. Haley was not used to being snubbed, his name was powerful and he found it strange that a man, even one as influential as Rideau, should take the chance of alienating him. Even more disturbing was his meeting with Jennings, whose cool arrogance and smug assurance was especially irritating. But most troubling of all was the message preached by them both at the rally, a message that Judge Haley could not accept. Why should Rideau, a man who, heretofore, had not associated himself with such exrtremists, now court someone like Jennings? But Haley had been long enough in the political arena to know that rivals quickly became allies if necessity demanded.

Rideau, Haley knew, was a man who relished the uses of power. His stance had always been statesmanlike, but his record did not always reflect the appearance. While opposing the present administration, he had nevertheless supported them in key voting as often as he had opposed them, and it was clear that in the last few years his politics had become more conservative. Yet he remained an announced supporter of Hopkenson. It seemed clear that since Jennings' disaffection with the president had increased, Rideau wanted to capitalize on that dissatisfaction and rally Jennings and his people to Hopkenson's side, even though Hopkenson could hardly approve of Jennings' extreme conservative program.

The politics, Haley thought, were, though devious, clear enough, and no stranger than the many compromises and small betrayals of principle that were the everyday stuff of political battle. But what remained mysterious was Rideau's unwillingness to see him, sending Jennings in his place as an emmissary, though an emmissary whose arrogance and closed mind was hardly suitable for the conduct of any serious negotiation.

The plane had landed. It was nearly noon. He would have to get to his home and call Philip to report on what had happened. But first there was another call to make.

Last night, glowing in the headlights, Haley had seen his son, marching bravely against Jennings and his kind. How could he deny that son any longer? How could he allow them to remain separated? How could he perpetuate the pointless argument which had divided them? The cause was a product of Timothy's youth and Haley's own inability to show the love he deeply felt. He had so much wanted Tim to follow him into the law, to be like him, that when the boy was not like him, he could not accept it. Haley couldn't allow this to go on any longer. He had to approach his son and tell him that he loved him, and that whatever he did and whatever he was, made no difference to that love.

Whatever he was. Yes, that was where it all lay. His son was a homosexual, gay they called it now. When Tim had first told him, Haley had refused to listen. He was haunted by what it might mean for Tim, because he knew what such things had meant for him. His own past clouded the possibilities of Tim's future; his own fears and the pain of remembrance came between the two, and he would not, could not accept it. He angrily refused to hear Tim saying that the world was different and that he was proud of himself and his sexuality. But most of all, Haley was driven to cold anger because he could not tell his son that he understood far better than Tim could know. He was ashamed that his son had the courage to face him and to be honest and that he, Judge Douglas Haley, who had confronted the great of the nation with his own high principles, could not share with his only son the fact that he too had once known what it meant to love men, to love a man, but that he had suppressed those feelings, and denied them, assumed a mantle which was not his, hidden his desires, and never, since he had married, acted on them.

Haley knew he had been been blinded by his love for Tim, and his fear that to be openly gay would deprive Tim of a life. He recalled what the discovery of homosexuality had meant to many he had known. To some it meant ruin, loss of job and family, and to others the discovery had lead to disgrace and sometimes to death. To Haley's attempt to explain to his son that such a life would place him under stigma and opprobrium, Tim had angrily insisted that the world had changed.

"Haven't you heard of Stonewall? Don't you know what's going on in the world? Gay people can have a life now. We don't have to be afraid anymore."

But Haley wouldn't, couldn't, listen. What had he to do with that life, with those lives? He had been married for nearly forty years. In Boston he had been reared in a family where sex was never discussed. His life had been laid out for him. Harvard at eighteen, on to law school, a marriage with the proper woman from a proper family. Practice in his father's firm, inheritance, and then the gathering of power and wealth, until he had become a judge. But more than that, he had become one of the power brokers, one of those men whose place in life was not in the public eye, but whose influence extended across the nation and into the highest places. All of this he had achieved by dint of hard work, discipline and, he knew, denial. He had not loved Anna Peabody Milligan when he married her, even in those days, now decades ago, when such matches were not always arranged with love in mind.

Anna brought to his life the needed wife, family connections of great value, and wealth in her own right. Together, they were a formidable team, and became, as time and fortune aided them, among the first of Boston's great families. Eventually, it became clear that they must have children. The first, a daughter, died young. The death was terrible and its consequences were disastrous. Anna blamed him, irrationally, for their daughter's death. They became cold, she estranged and distant, he concentrating on the life of power. They met at dinner and continued to present themselves to the world as united, but in reality their life was gone, and they had become strangers to one another, in the great house on Louisberg Square.

But as with all the events of their lives, duty became insistent. Family talked. Grandmother Haley asked why there were no more children. Haley knew that love would not provide them with another child, but dynasty demanded one. And so, one night, dutifully, coldly, they spent some time with one another and conceived a child. A son.

Timothy was born, and there was proper and dutiful rejoicing since there was now an heir to the great fortune which had been inevitably growing to await him. But Haley could feel no warmth for the boy. He was the product of necessity rather than of passion or love, an acquisition, another piece of rare furniture needed to round out the appearance of things. In due course everything was done for him, everything given him, save intimacy, save love.

Finally, as if she had decided her part had been played, Anna announced to Haley that from now on they would separate. She would live in the family home in Florida. There would, of course, be no divorce, no public notice of the event. Timothy would receive the best education, a job in the firm, and visit them separately.

Haley agreed, and without asking, Timothy's life was prepared for him to live it. Harvard, law school, and a berth in the firm were assumed. But assumptions are seldom enough and lives do not always fit the patterns cut for them. And so Timothy Haley one day returned from a summer in Europe to tell his father he had chosen a different life. There would be no Harvard, no law, no law firm.

"And don't look around for some proper Bostonian daughter for me to marry. I won't do it."

"Timothy," Haley said, "I don't understand any of this. You say you want to go to New York, that you want to work there, but you don't know what you want to do. Timothy, you have so much here, why . . ."

"Why, Dad? Perhaps because there is so much, and none of it's mine."

"It will all . . ."

"I know, it will all be mine someday if I play the game; do what I don't want to do, learn what I don't want to learn, and live a lie."

"A lie? But . . ."

"Dad, I'm not stupid. I know what your life has been like. I fly to Florida to see my mother. I fly to Boston to see my father. They don't see each other. I don't want that. I see you, *when* I see you, working ten hours a day, wheeling and dealing with people who are hardly better than criminals. I don't want that. I have a life of my own, and I intend to live it."

"Then live it," Haley said angrily. "But you'll be back. What will happen if you go to New York and get some job at which you make nothing? What will your career be? Who will you marry? None of this is decided."

"Dad, I'm eighteen years old, nothing has to be decided now."

"When I was twenty . . ."

"I know, when you were twenty you were already bought and harnessed to the rest of your life. I won't be."

"You can say that now, but if you meet a girl, how will you live, how will you support her?"

Haley remembered the sudden silence that descended on his son then. The confusion in his eyes and then the straightening of the back, the indrawn breath and the resolve that he seemed to grasp from the air, when, in a low voice, he said:

"Dad, there's something else."

"Well," Haley said with annoyance. "What else can there be?"

"There won't be 'a girl.'"

"What do you mean, of course you'll marry. We . . . you have to."

"No Dad, I already have a friend."

"Well then, who is she? Some New York tramp, no doubt."

"His name is Randy."

"Randy, I . . ."

"Dad, I'm gay."

The rest of the interview remained unclear in Haley's mind. Gay? What was that? But he knew, had in fact always known what it meant to be gay. But he had pushed that knowledge deeper and deeper into his past, denying those feelings for the sake of a life, rejecting them, supressing them when they arose. He heard no more that Timothy said. He did not know what he said in return. He remembered only fear, and anger, and a sudden overwhelming love for the son he barely knew who now seemed to be declaring a dreadful independence. But that love, born out of the shocking realization that what his son had declared himself to be was what Haley dared not face in himself, born out of a desperate desire to be as courageous at this late date as his young son was now, that love was smothered by emotions so irrational that the words which followed upon them were equally irrational. They were words which forbade the young man to return, words which banished him, exiled him, and destroyed any chance, at that moment, for father and son to reach out to one another, words which only succeeded in driving Haley deeper into his own hidden life and driving Timothy desperately away.

But now, Haley felt, that must all be undone. He would have to do it, he would have to be the one to reach out. But when he saw his son last night, marching against the hatred and bigotry which Jennings stood for, he knew his son was a man and deserved a father. He would call him. He would tell him. He would describe his own life, tell his son about how he, too, when young, had loved another young man. How they had touched and held each other, determined always to be there one for the other.

He wanted to describe how, when he was seventeen, he began to know that he wasn't like other boys. But he wanted to tell Tim how hard it was then to grapple with such a realization. What anguish it brought, what terror, and what despair, for there was no hope then. People like that were sick, insane, criminals, doomed to vicious lives of perversion, or so the doctors and lawyers and the priests insisted. "I'd rather have my son dead then queer." That was the opinion of his father when the young son of another prominent Boston family was caught in a raid on an establishment that catered to "such people."

Haley wanted to tell Tim that such things, such pressures, had driven he and his friend apart. And that when it became clear that if he were to act on his secret desires or to pursue them, his life would be ruined like the life of the young man whose prominent family had sent him to a home for the criminally insane. He wanted to tell Tim that it was his own friend, the young man who might have been his lover, who was incarcerated there. He wanted to tell Tim of the shame and guilt he felt when he let his friend go, abandoned him,

him, did not defend him, disowned acquaintance with him, betrayed him, like Judas, denied him, like Peter.

But now the chance had come, a chance made more appealing by certain changes in Haley's life, changes which even at this late date, allowed him to look with favor on the world which he had once rejected. The ferment that had always simmered within had been fueled by the change in society itself, a change which Haley knew about, but which he had largely tried to ignore. That his son was gay he knew. That his son was leading a life which seemed productive and happy he half-suspected, since there was communication between them only through what he heard from his estranged wife. But changes had happened in his own life as well, nothing so dramatic as his son's—he almost said 'flaunting'— but meant 'acceptance' and proud awareness of his homosexuality.

For Haley it was quiet awareness of his own real nature. This had come about because he had gradually been made aware of the fact that one of his oldest friends, Amos Parr, was himself homosexual. He had known Amos since college days, and kept infrequently in contact with him. Parr had remained unmarried, Haley knew, but he thought little of that, since Parr was a busy doctor as well as a man of considerable influence in Washington politics. The two men spoke once in a while, saw each other when one or the other was in Washington or Boston, brought together by politics and business. But one time, a year after Timothy had left home, seemingly forever, Haley was in Washington. There, he encountered Parr at a party fundraiser, and was invited to Parr's home for dinner the following night.

"It'll just be the two of us, Douglas," Parr had said, "if you can bear my conversation."

"I'll look forward to it, we haven't had time to talk for years."

The next night Haley found himself at the table in Parr's

Georgetown home. After an excellent dinner, the two men, mellowed by wine and some old brandy, sat silently reflective.

Parr's butler, a Frenchman named Leon, poured more brandy for the judge. Haley could not help noticing how handsome the young man was. His senses sharpened by what he had been going through during the last year, thinking about his son, his awareness of the seemingly constant manifestations of gay people in the world around him, he began idly to wonder about Parr himself. The man lived alone, attended by a handsome butler. Elegant, sophisticated, worldly, Parr seemed to be publicly at ease, never at a loss for words or for a quip. But his private life was itself shrouded and unknown.

The conversation was subdued. Then Parr asked Haley about his own life, a question which Haley found surprising, since it seemed unlike the discreet Parr to make such a probing query. Haley, warmed by brandy, and feeling the need to talk, confirmed what Parr suspected. Yes, he was separated from his wife. No, his son was not in law school. He had gone to New York, to ah, find himself.

Finally, Haley found himself talking a great deal, more than he intended, and then:

"Amos, you're a doctor, do you ever deal with, well, with abnormal psychology?"

"Abnormal?" Parr said. "I'm afraid Douglas that that word isn't used much now. There may be variations from norms, but such a phrase is, well, somewhat dated."

"I see, I guess I mean . . ."

"Do you mean insane?" Parr asked.

"No, Amos, I mean . . ." he wanted to say it. He felt he needed to talk to someone about this. He wanted to ask Parr about homosexuality and about his own culpability in it. Had he made his son gay?

Commanding his courage, he said: "I mean homosexual. Have you ever dealt with that?"

Parr looked at him, strangely Haley thought, and then with a wry smile:

"Yes, Douglas, I deal with it every day."

"I don't follow . . ."

"Ah Douglas, we have known each other for years, yet never really been friends," Parr said. "Never really had a serious nor certainly an intimate talk."

"No," Haley said, wondering why Parr seemingly changed the subject.

"Yet," Parr went on, "certainly you must have wondered, from time to time, about me, about my life, perhaps as I have wondered, from time to time, about yours?"

Haley felt himself stiffen. He wanted to shrink back, not deal with the direction the talk was taking.

"I must admit Amos," he said, emboldened by the other man's candor, and seeing a way into the subject, "I must admit I have wondered why . . ."

"Why I never married."

"Yes, Amos. Why not?"

"I don't think you would have asked me about the, as you put it, abnormal, if our conversation were not going to lead into, shall we say, uncharted, or at least for you, I think undiscussed areas. I will be direct with you Douglas, and for a reason. I am homosexual. The young people call it gay these days, which is, I suspect, better than what it was called in my own memory, don't you agree?"

Haley absorbed Parr's acknowledgement, more with curiosity than with surprise. After all, all the signs were there, and now the signs pointed in an expected direction.

"Why do you tell me this, Amos?"

Parr looked at Haley with a cutting glance.

"Why did you ask me, Douglas?"

The two men were silent for a moment, and then Haley, bolder still, almost relieved:

"Amos, I cannot say I am entirely surprised by what

you've told me. Would it surprise you if I said that I was—once—not unlike you?"

"I have made my fortune by never being surprised," Parr said with a smile. "I can only say that I would be, ah, pleased."

"Pleased?"

"Yes, Douglas, pleased. You see—indeed I suspect you know—being like we are in the world in which we both move would, even in times such as these, which claim enlighten-ment, be a distinct disadvantage."

"Yes, Amos," Haley replied, "that is why I have never acted on what I have felt, why I have simply put the whole thing out of my life, until now."

"I understand, Douglas. Many wouldn't. Many who carry the banner of what has come to be called sexual freedom consider staying, as I think they say, in the closet, a kind of moral cowardice. But . . ."

"But," Haley interrupted eagerly, "it's not. What would have been the point of it, if I had declared myself, followed my inclinations? What good could I have done, what service could I have been to the world?"

"Yes, indeed, Douglas, what would have been the point, after all, to throw away a life, as we would have had to throw it away, for some very dubious gain. But now, Douglas, times are different. I do not believe that they are different enough for men like us ever to, how do they put it, 'come out.' But they have changed, and young men and women, more open than we, have helped them change. I think we could help, too, and in ways which our secretiveness would make even more effective. Perhaps I've had too much brandy, but I feel that after all this time, we are kindred, and there is much, Douglas, that we can do."

"I'm not sure I understand," Haley said, feeling over-whelmed by the revelations.

"I want you to meet one or two friends of mine," Parr said, "and then I think everything will be perfectly clear."

Parr did introduce him to some friends. Douglas Haley discovered that Parr was a member of an informal group of men, all of them powerful, all of them influential, commanding money and resources. And all of them, like himself, like Parr, though hidden, were homosexual.

"Can we ever call ourselves gay?" he asked Nelson Beverwyck one night at dinner, when he was introduced to Charles Witter, the fourth member of the party.

"Does it matter what we call ourselves?" Beverwyck had said. "We all know what we are. None of us is twenty, but to make up for lack of youth we have more than our share of influence. The three of us, Parr, Charles and myself, have for several years been acting in informal concert for our own interests in business and politics. And out of our financial involvement has come a kind of behind-the-scenes support of organizations which themselves support homosexual rights. None of them know who we are, they never know where certain contributions come from, or why certain strings are pulled. You could be of inestimable help to us, Judge, should you care to, shall we say, share our responsibilities."

Working with these men, Haley had developed for himself an understanding of his own life and had come to see that he was wrong to have for so long denied it, at least to himself, indeed especially to himself. His relationship with Beverwyck, Witter and Parr, though circumscribed by the demands of their busy lives, nevertheless became close, intimate, sharing. Together the four men grew into more than friends, and with this friendship grew their power.

Haley could barely wait for the plane to taxi to a stop. He would call the minute he got into the terminal. He hurried to a phone, fumbled in his wallet for the number he always carried with him, the number of the apartment in New York that Tim shared with his friend. After the money was deposited he waited for the ringing to stop, for the familiar voice to answer. Instead he got:

"This is 777-3487. Neither Tim nor Randy are in now. Please leave your name and number when you hear the tone."

Haley thought of hanging up, but no, do it now. When the beep sounded, he said:

"Tim, it's your father. Please call me. I must see you." He paused. He wanted to say it.

"Tim, one more thing. I love you."

As he hung up the phone, he felt a wave of relief, and indeed of joy. He recalled Parr's parting words after dinner on that night when nearly a decade ago they had first discussed the secrets of their lives.

"And so, Douglas, now we have had our little talk, delayed for so many years," Parr had said. "Did you find out what you wanted to know?"

"I wanted to talk about someone else," Haley said, "but I guess I've avoided talking about myself for far too long."

The two men stood at the door of Parr's house.

"Good night, Amos, thanks for this."

"Douglas," Parr said, "call me tomorrow, let's begin to open up some doors. Incidentally, who did you want to talk about?"

Haley looked at Parr. Should he say it? Yes, he could trust this man. He wanted to trust this man.

"My son, Amos. My son. He told me he's gay."

Parr reached out and took Haley's hand, holding it tightly.

"How fortunate you are, Douglas, to have a son who would entrust you with such a precious gift."

12.

"Tim, it's your father. Please call me. I must see you. Tim, one more thing. I love you."

Tim played the recording again, for the fifth time. The voice of his father, curiously strained, hesitant, was unlike the usual confident, somewhat acerbic tone Tim was used to, a voice that always conjured up reactions so mixed that he could never quite identify them. He wanted to hear assurance in the voice, to hear it praise him, and yet he always feared it would not praise, but rather reprimand or lecture him, withholding what he most desired, affection and approval. The last time he had heard that voice it was filled with anger, taut with disapproval and devoid of the tones that Tim most wanted, and so he had fled from it, fled here to New York and to the arms of his lover to begin a life without his father. From that time on his father was created only in the tones of his mother who lived an increasingly isolated and alcoholic life in the great family compound in Sarasota, attended only by a maid and a secretary as self-pitying and ineffectual as his mother had herself become. Since the time, now some years past, when he had declared himself free of the Haley obligations, he had found a life in New York, working with Randy at the alliance and creating for himself a future.

His first reaction was to ignore the call. The pain was still too deep for him to lightly return, to hope that anything could really change between them. Yet the very quality of his father's voice, gentle, almost pleading, caused him to waiver. Finally it was Randy who convinced him.

"Tim, call him." Randy said. "Maybe he really needs you, wants to reconcile. You can't let the chance pass by."

"Yes, but what if it turns out to be the same thing again. What is there to say? He'll never accept me, or us. He made that clear. He's convinced and stubborn, set in his ways."

"And so is his son," Randy said gently. "Tim, do it, you can only gain. If nothing is changed, then at least you've tried. He wants to meet you halfway, and he *has* made the first move. You owe it to him, to yourself."

Tim could see the wisdom of Randy's urging. For years now there was a blank at the center of his life which he knew could only be filled by his father's love. He rarely talked about it, but sometimes, at night, lying next to Randy, the image of his father crept into his thoughts, and he wanted desperately to see him, talk to him, to be a son, to have a father.

"Okay, I'll go, but only if you go, too. If he sees me, he has to see us. He has to know everything."

"Don't you think . . . ?"

"I don't think anything. That's how it has to be. If my father is going to be part of *my* life, then he has to be part of *our* life."

Randy smiled and pulled Tim to him.

"Thanks, lover," he said.

April 6   10:00 P.M.

Philip caught the night flight back to New York, landing at 10:00 P.M. As the taxi took him toward the city, he tried to sum up what he had found out in Washington. First, there was Parr. Essentially a good man, Philip decided. Difficult, but good. He could work with him.

But the others. Ferguson, half mad, Philip suspected: a private army; obsessed with the past. Yet Alice Copley called him a decent man. A mystery there not yet unraveled. But Copley herself. How much could she be trusted? Living with a vegetable of a husband, a lonely life, as obsessed as Ferguson's. What were her motives in, essentially, betraying her boss?

And Bray. What did he know about him? Nothing really, save by reputation. And so where did this leave him? With a number of dead men, no certainty about the killer or why he killed. Dead men tell no tales, Philip thought wryly.

April 7   *9:15* A.M.

As Tim and Randy drove toward Boston, Tim rehearsed over and over again what he would say. How he would introduce Randy to his father.

"Dad, this is Randy, my friend."

"Dad, I want you to meet my lover, Randy."

"Dad, this is Randy Asher, president of the . . ."

Nothing seemed to work.

"What'll I say to him?" he said to Randy.

"Wait, don't try to plan it, let it happen."

"But what about you?"

"I'm a big boy, okay?"

They drove in silence, the tension building in Tim. He wanted it to work, wanted to be able to reclaim his father again.

"Don't you think we ought to call him," Randy said, "let him know?"

"No, he'll be there, he's always home for tea at four, hasn't changed his habits in twenty years. He'll be there, and today Ada is off. Tim could hear his father saying half-jokingly:

"Only day I get some peace and quiet, when that damned woman's away."

He felt a rush of affection, and eagerness.

"No, let's surprise him," he said with a smile.

April 7   *10:00 A.M.*

Haley sat in his study. He had waited for Tim's call all morning, but it did not come. When he called again, the machine picked up, and this time he hung up without answering. Maybe it was all false hope, he thought. But he hoped he was wrong.

He knew he ought to get to work. He could call Philip in New York, tell him what he had found at the Jennings rally, be he had no heart for it now. Perhaps he should call Parr, ask him if he'd done the right thing. He even almost wished Ada was here; silly old woman was always right. She'd raised Tim, knew him as well as anyone. Haley half-suspected that she was in contact with the boy, letting him know all the family secrets. He hoped she was. He glanced at his watch. It was nearly noon. He would go to the club for lunch. No, maybe he would wait a little longer. Perhaps the phone would ring. He wandered from his study, through the hall, into the dining room toward the kitchen. He would eat here. Ada always left something cold in the refrigerator. As he approached the kitchen he heard the kitchen door softly open. He stopped for a moment. Tim always used to come in by the kitchen door. A half-smile lighted his face. He hurried toward the kitchen.

"Tim, Tim, is that you? I knew you'd come."

April 7   *11:45* A.M.

In the office the next morning it was clear to Philip that one answer must lie with Haley. He wondered if he had been able to see Rideau. Where they might have met, when, or even if they had met, Philip did not know. Philip decided not to wait for Haley to call.

"Susan," he said into the intercom, "get me Judge Douglas Haley's office in Boston, please."

The phone buzzed.

"I have Judge Haley's office. But they say he's not in."

Philip glanced at his watch. It was nearly noon.

"Tell them to try to reach him. Leave my name and tell them it's very urgent."

April 7   *4:00* P.M.

It was nearly four when Tim and Randy pulled into the tranquil precinct of Louisberg Square. Tim by now felt eager and elated. They parked the car.

"We'll go around to the back, through the garden and into the kitchen."

Tim unlocked the side gate and went into the flowering garden.

"Maybe I'll go in alone," Tim said. "I'll call you."

"Sure," Randy said. "I think that's right."

Randy watched Tim stride toward the house and disappear inside. He was proud of Tim. Proud that he had the courage to face his father and the decency to try to change what had come between them. He was glad that he and Tim were lovers. After years of being alone, after the usual explorations of the glittering world of gay life, its places and pleasures, after hoping that out of it all would come someone who could be a friend and more, Randy had found Tim, or they had found each other, not in America, but on an island in Greece. It had seemed right even then, the two of them, right that like Grecian heroes they should meet there in that sun-drenched world, on a silver beach next to Homer's wine-dark sea. And it stayed right between them, very right, and very strong.

They were lovers, they were friends, and they were building a life together, working together, growing together. They wanted each other as much as they always had, and love was sweet between them, but now there were deeper feelings, and desire had blossomed into trust and pleasure into love.

He hoped that now, today, Tim would be able to find what he had lost, that solid certainty that he was wanted as a son as well as a lover. Randy knew how important that was, how necessary it had been for him, and how grateful he was to both his father and mother, who had asked him only one question when he told them about himself and about his life.

"Son," his father had asked, "are you happy?"

His answer was simple: "Yes."

"Then we love you, son," his mother said, and he wept in their embrace.

He looked up to see Tim standing on the steps. But he was stopped by his appearance. When he had expected joy he could see only pain, no, not even pain, but horror. His face was drained of color, and he seemed to be trying to speak. Randy ran to him. Tim could only point toward the door, then collapsed, weeping, to the ground.

Randy rushed inside, and saw the slight figure slumped over the kitchen table, hands tied behind his back, blood slowly seeping from the wound in his temple, running in an idle stream over the polished table top and down the table leg to gather in a small brilliant pool on the white tile floor.

13.

"We'll eat in the green dining room, Frederic," Nelson Beverwyck directed his butler. "We will be four."

"Yes, Mr. Beverwyck." The butler left the study. Beverwyck sat in the window embrasure, absently looking out at the line of trees, marching in paired ranks, stretching down to the Sound. He could not grasp it, even though the *Times* lay on the table next to him, its serious headline confirming what he had learned from a shaken Charles Witter early that morning. Douglas Haley was dead. Murdered in his townhouse in Boston. And no amount of manipulation could keep that news from the press.

Chaos surrounded him, Beverwyck felt. He had been willing to cover up the death of Ross to protect the candidate. But now, Haley was dead, his friend, Douglas Haley. Was this, too, a result of their investigation? Witter knew little, save that Haley was found tied up and shot. Witter heard about it from a source at the Boston Police Department

"What was the motive, do we know?" he had asked Witter when he called that morning.

"Don't know. Could have been robbery. Some things were disturbed. It looked like robbery."

"Is this connected with what we're doing?" Beverwyck asked.

"Nothing to show that it is," Witter said.

"And nothing to show that it isn't," Beverwyck countered. "I think we had all better meet. I'll send a helicopter for you and Philip. Get hold of Amos and arrange to have him here by tonight. Tell him what happened."

"Nelson," Witter said, "we know that it is connected, don't we?"

Beverwyck was silent. Then, "Yes, Chuck, I'm afraid that if we had not started to probe into the past, then my friend Douglas would still be alive."

Amos Parr put down the phone and slumped into a chair. His face was white. How could this happen? His first reaction was: Who would do such a thing? Witter didn't know. He had no information save that Douglas Haley had been brutally murdered. Parr thought of Haley's son, who he had never met, but for whose sake he and Douglas had established a close and cordial friendship. He wondered how the boy had been able to take it, finding his father that way. He wondered if Douglas and the boy had ever talked. Certainly he would need someone to talk to now.

He glanced at his watch. It was after eleven. He would have to get ready. There was a plane waiting for him, Witter said, to fly him to New York, and after that, a helicopter to Beverwyck's Long Island estate. The four of them would meet and discuss this terrible thing. It had become all to horrible now, Parr thought. He was sure it was because he had revealed what Magnus and he had vowed never to reveal. Thirty years ago when once they had loved one another, yes, he was not afraid to say it, they had loved—they had also pledged their love would be secret between them, a private possession, held in trust and confidence. And when it was ended, brought to a conclusion because it could not continue and maintain that first rare surge of delight and romance, brought to a conclusion because Magnus Hopkenson saw that a different path lay ahead for him and that a relationship with a man could never be part of it, and concluded too because Amos Parr saw how hopeless it all, finally, was, yet even when it ended, and not without bitterness between them, they still affirmed that pledge.

And to save him, I broke the pledge, Parr thought. It seemed right, at the time, to tell that secret. He was sure it was the past that would put the present at risk. And so he had told them, the others, his closest friends and the only men who had the power to nullify the past, to put the secret to rest. He had to betray his trust, betray his vow to Magnus to save him, and he had done so willingly. But now because of that betrayal, Douglas Haley was dead.

That night, after dinner, the four men discussed the death of Haley. Witter told again what he knew.

"And you've found nothing more since this morning?" Parr asked.

"No. There's nothing. He was shot once. There are no fingerprints. Nothing was taken."

"Do the police have any theories?" Beverwyck asked.

"No," Witter said. "They're putting it down to robbery because they don't have any other apparent reason."

"But," Parr insisted, "we know it wasn't robbery. We know this happened because we have been delving into things we should have kept out of."

"We don't know any such thing," Philip interrupted.

"Do we know why Ross was killed?" Witter asked.

"There are several possibilities," Philip continued.

"First, he and Hopkenson may have been closer than we know."

"That's not likely," Parr said. "Magnus put all that . . ."

"Where sex is concerned, anything is likely," Witter said. "Magnus is still young. And Ross was good-looking. It's all possible."

"Yes," Philip said, "it is. And someone may have known. Ross was, so I have discovered, discreet, but not that careful. People knew him. I've talked to several who did. He was private, but it wouldn't have been impossible for someone to make a link, real or imagined, between him and Hopkenson."

"Therefore, if someone knew, or thought they knew that there was something between Ross and Hopkenson," Parr said, "they might want to get Ross out of the way for Hopkenson's own good."

"Right," Philip said, "and I'm afraid we have to consider that one possible killer might be connected with Hopkenson's own campaign."

"No," Parr said. "How?"

"Suppose Ross got difficult," Philip said. "Threatened Hopkenson with exposure. Perhaps not likely, but it is possible, and I can't afford to ignore the possibilities."

The men were silent for a time, then Philip continued.

"Or, there's this: perhaps Ross was killed in order to embarrass Hopkenson. To tar the candidate with Ross's brush."

"But we prevented that effectively," Witter said.

"Yes, true," Philip said, "but in doing that, you have done one other thing. You have alerted the killer that he is up against someone or some people who are powerful enough to change the news and even silence it. I'm afraid that is why Douglas Haley is dead."

"Why?" Parr asked, his voice low and shocked.

"As a warning to you all. To stop now."

"Then we should stop," Parr said. "End all this."

"If you stop," Philip said levelly, "then you do nothing to avenge Haley and you put Hopkenson in greater danger. Bray's investigation will go on. And it's possible the killer will kill again. Remember, we have no proof that Bray's investigation of Hopkenson is necessarily connected with the killings. We don't really know yet whether the information sought is to be used for or against Hopkenson." Philip went on, "Three, perhaps four men, have been killed for some reason that is still not clear. Is it to hurt or help Magnus Hopkenson? Is it to reveal what we all know, and thus end his candidacy, or is it to do exactly what we are trying to do: insure that no matter what is in the past, or if it can be found, that he will be the next president? That's why we have to go on with the investigation. We have to find the investigator; we have to find the killer."

"And if we don't?" Parr asked. "If we stop?"

"Then all of us are in danger," Beverwyck said.

"Yes," Witter replied, "all. Even Magnus."

"True," Philip said. "Even Magnus Hopkenson might be in danger from someone who kills with such willingness and ease. But I'm afraid gentlemen that it ought to be painfully clear that Magnus Hopkenson stands to lose the most if his secret is revealed. Michael Ross might have been embarrassing to Hopkenson. He's dead. Aleister St. Pierre may have known something about Hopkenson. He's dead. Monte Dillon may have discovered what St. Pierre knew. He's dead. The death of Haley makes it clear that someone is trying to stop us, too. Though we may not want to think so, we cannot ignore the possibility that it might be Hopkenson himself."

14.

April 9   *10:30* A.M.

Philip hefted his bag onto the hotel room bed. He had arrived in Washington after an early morning flight, and he had a lot to do.

From a few well-placed phone calls, he had gotten a very important address, an address which was listed in no directory, unobtainable through normal channels.

He unpacked his bag and hung up the few things he had brought. On the bed, he laid out a pair of stained overalls, blue workshirt, and cap that said *Otis Elevator* across the front.

He started to slip out of his clothes, stripping off his shirt, stepping out of his trousers. He stood in front of the mirror, looking at himself, the tanned, lean body, well muscled, but not massive, hips narrow and legs showing the effects of his regular workouts. He slipped off his shorts and started toward the shower when the phone rang.

"Hello?" he said, wondering who might know he was here.

"Well, hello. How are you?" he said. "How did you know where to find me?"

"Your secret. Okay, I'll guess later. How about this afternoon? Here, around three? Fine."

He hung up, a soft smile flickered across his face, and he

ran his hand down his chest and over his thighs, realizing he had become excited during the conversation.

"Very strange," he said aloud, but he looked forward to the afternoon.

He glanced at his watch and decided to forget about the shower. Instead, he turned to the bed and pulled on the denim overalls, tucked the workshirt into them and put on the cap, pulling it down over his eyes. From his bag he took a clipboard and, giving himself an approving glance in the mirror, walked out the door.

April 9   *1:00 P.M.*

Philip stood across the street from Walter Bray's apartment building. It had taken some work to find out where that mysterious man lived, but Bray wasn't the only one who could pull strings to find the presumably unfindable. Philip kept out of sight of the doorman who stood just inside the entrance. He had found out there were three entrances. The front, a rear service door, and a side door that apparently led into the cellar. He was sure the rear and side were locked and wired. So he strode across the street and up to the front door, swinging the clipboard.

The doorman looked at him suspiciously.

"What's up?" he asked Philip.

"Elevator check." He waved his clipboard.

"First I heard about it," said the doorman.

"First I heard about it was this morning," Philip responded with a smile.

"You got some ID?"

Philip pulled out his wallet. Inside, a card showed his picture and: "Inspector, Otis Elevator."

The doorman studied the card for a while.

"Okay," he said. "Go on. Don't be long."

"Right," Philip smiled, and went in.

He already knew which of the four elevator banks to take.

Once in, he pressed 17, Bray's floor. Seventeen was down the hall. Philip checked the door. No sound. He quickly went to the end of the hall, to the door that led into the service corridor that ran in the rear. There he found what he wanted, the telephone wires running up from below to the apartments on that floor. He opened the box. It was there. The single wire, unlike the others, that must certainly be the power source for the alarm system connected to Bray's apartment. There were two apartments on the floor, and only one wire. Philip pulled a small battery pack from his pocket and neutralized the system without actually shutting it down. If it were connected to Bray's office, no one would know it had been breached. He hurried back to the apartment and skillfully picked one lock, then the other. He was inside.

He wasn't sure what he was looking for. He didn't even know if Bray was likely to keep anything here pertaining to his work. But it was worth a try. He quickly looked in the various rooms. An unmade bed in a messy bedroom. The living room well decorated but unkempt, somewhat dirty. The kitchen rarely used. The study smelling of smoke, with a bottle of whisky on the desk, and a glass half full. The bottle itself with only an ounce or two left. Philip wondered if Bray drank, or was lonely.

The desk top was clean, except for some crumpled papers. The drawers contained writing paper, notebooks, but nothing that seemed helpful. On the desk was a book, a campaign biography of Magnus Hopkenson. Philip leafed through it. It had been read. He checked the Index. Many references to Hopkenson, of course. Rideau had several. Douglas Haley was given a page reference. He flipped through to the section on Hopkenson's early years. He skimmed the pages and then again checked the index. Under *T* there was no mention of Hugh Tilden. And yet many other lesser people were mentioned in that section, presumably as rewards for service. Yet Hugh Tilden, who should have been there, was not. And in Bray's files that he had seen, the name only was there, but no information. Was this it? Philip wondered. Was Hugh Tilden the connection he needed? But if so, what did he connect? Who was he? And more importantly, where was he?

Philip laid the book back down on the desk. And stared at the desk top, wondering just what it might mean. It was a while before he realized that the desk blotter bore the marks of a pen that had left heavy impressions, as if someone had written on paper, and the marks had been incised into the blotter. There were many impressions, from long use, but swimming out of them, written down four times, one over the other in a little column were the initials HT, surrounded by a circle and surrounded with question marks.

"Ah Walter, my friend," Philip thought, "you want to know who he is, too, don't you?"

That was the key. Find Hugh Tilden, Philip suddenly was sure, and the rest would be clear. Find Hugh Tilden, and you would find everything.

On impulse, Philip picked up the campaign biography again and once more turned to the Index. Yes, Amos Parr was there. Chuck Witter was not, nor was he likely to be. Nelson Beverwyck was not listed. He flipped to the page number for Parr. Halfway down the page the single line read: "And then Magnus Hopkenson left college to go on to begin his brilliant career. Among his classmates who were themselves to become famous were Amos Parr and John McCurdy, the latter becoming Archbishop of St. Louis, the former a nationally known surgeon."

"So much for love," Philip thought. He checked the Index again. Yes. He turned to page 43.

"When he was nineteen, Hopkenson enlisted in the army, serving after basic training in a military intelligence unit. He soon became assigned to the staff of the commander, Captain Otis Ferguson, later General Ferguson."

"Ah Magnus, Magnus," Philip wondered, "were you one of the general's young men, too?"

April 9   *3:15 P.M.*

"Come in," Philip said. "You're right on time."

"I like to be."

"Sorry about the room, I just got here from New York this morning."

"Room's no problem."

"Drink?"

The silence was tense.

Philip looked at the boy. He was probably not much more than twenty, twenty-five maybe. Sandy hair, cool gray eyes, something of his father's manner already, but with a difference Philip suspected came from his mother. Philip decided to cut off more small talk.

"So Michael, why did you call me?"

The boy gave Philip a slow smile, touched by a winning confusion, yet intimate.

"I liked—like you."

Philip decided, too, to cut this short. "I'm not really available to be liked."

The boy was silent, then, "Oh, I don't have to like you for a long time. An hour will do."

He got up and came toward Philip.

Philip put out a warning hand.

"Wait. Maybe an hour is more time than I have now."

"I hope not, and anyway, I don't think so. Besides, maybe I can give you more than that."

"Go on," Philip said.

"You didn't just stumble out to Faraway by accident."

"So now we both know that," Philip said.

"Are you trying to find out . . ."

Philip cut him short. "I'm just doing a job, like I told your father. He must have told you."

"No, my father doesn't confide in me," Michael said with a wry smile. "Nor I in him."

Philip wondered what this lost boy wanted. Michael was attractive. But he had to be careful. The boy was volatile, probably not to be trusted. And yet, he seemed to want to talk, and more.

"Did you tell him you were coming here?" Philip asked.

"Please. He doesn't want to know about me. I'm not military enough for him. I was there because he has some notion that he owes it to my mother to 'be a father' to me. Most of the time I live away. Anyway, he has his own interests.

"Like what?"

"We have two thousand acres there, and back in the woods he has his own war games to play, without fighting with me."

Philip wondered if General Ferguson's small body of soldier attendants were only the tip of a larger corps. It was not unknown in these days for wealthy men to have small private armies. Otis Ferguson was in the unique position to have that. Or was Michael Ferguson hinting at something else?

"Does your father know about you?"

"Fathers and sons traditionally don't talk much in my family. Oh, sure, he knows that I like boys, but he doesn't believe it. He has his own boys to like."

"I don't follow," Philip said.

"Dad's boys are *real men*, Philip, don't you understand? They're not what he would call fruits and pansies, they're good American boys who, as he would say, have been freed from the weakening influence of women and an effeminate and mongrel American culture, under his command learning how to uphold the true American way of life. If they're close to each other, or to him from time to time, it's not being perverted, it's in the tradition of the noble warriors of ancient Greece: honorable, warlike love."

Michael's voice was tinged with disdain.

"You see, Philip, because I'm his son, he puts up with me. But that's all, Philip, that's all. I'm there because Daddy believes in family, but as far as he's concerned, my blood is tainted. I like boys, I wear immoral clothes, and go dancing and like music; his boys don't do that, Philip. They march, and drill, and salute, and fire rifles, and learn to use weapons he has stockpiled all over those two thousand acres. If once in a while one or two of them find themselves alone in the woods or a barn, and something happens, why, it's just a necessary release from the tensions of their Spartan life—that's how he would put it."

"And that's why you're here? To tell me this?"

"Yeah, that's why, and because—you want me to say more?"

"No," Philip said.

He walked over to Michael, and kissed him lightly. Michael impulsively threw his arms around Philip. Embracing, they sank to the floor, kissing, holding. Philip felt the young man's strength, the lithe body pressed against his. Clothes were discarded, hands caressed, tongues sought one another, flicked nipples, and chests. Fingers touched thighs, armpits. Their bodies welded to each other and rose in unison, in passion and delight.

"Philip, hold me, please, no one ever has. I want it."

Philip's spirit went out to this boy, nearly fifteen years younger than he, yet already weary with the world's knowledge, experienced in its pleasures but not in its passions, adept at lust but an amateur at love. Philip knew that what he was doing was dangerous for both of them. But for the moment—for that burning immediate moment—he wanted Michael as much as Michael clearly wanted him. The curves of their bodies, the flaming touch of their hands, the pressure of Michael's cock, long and demanding against his stomach, the eager entwining of Michael's arms, his fingers silkily running over Philip's body, all of it was right, predestined it seemed, as if each had been half before, separate for an eternity and now were joined after endless searching, divinity restored, become one, and more than one, at last.

Philip was overwhelmed with the certainty that Michael needed someone, needed him. He pulled the boy tenderly to him, they embraced again, turned and took delight from one another, touching, embracing, lips encircling and enticing until with simultaneous and fluid delight, they found themselves one indeed, and lay back, arms entwined, looking wonderingly into each other's eyes.

As Philip walked through the dusky Georgetown night, he thought about the moments he had spent with Michael, moments so short in time but an eternity in meaning. They lay together for a long time on the floor, but finally dressed. Talk was easy, intimate. Michael was quiet, but the edge, the sharpness that had hung about him like a protecting aura had dissipated. Philip had many times been in such situations after sex, when it seemed as if life itself had stopped for a moment in contemplation of the beauty and perfection of the act, but with Michael he felt, and he felt it with dread and alarm as well as joy, that this moment was more true, and therefore perhaps more dangerous than any other he had known. Something deep in each of the two men had been fused this day, for how long, or to what purpose, Philip did not know.

Finally, when their spirits had waned somewhat, and the realities of the day intervened, they had talked, again about Michael, about his life, about his loneliness, about his need, but also about his insistence that his life be his own, lived by him without dependence on anyone, save for the desire to love and be loved.

They talked, too, about other things. Philip learned that the enigmatic Otis Ferguson was not to be thought of as a mad man. He was intelligent, even brilliant, talented, and in command of his life as he was in command of others. What, Philip asked, did Michael know about his politics.

Conservative, of course. No, not a supporter of any politician, not close, as far as he knew, to anyone, but an acquaintance of many. No, Michael had never seen Magnus Hopkenson at Faraway, but he was rarely there himself.

The President? Otis Ferguson did not think much of him. "Betrayed his trust" was how the general put it. And Hopkenson? Michael wasn't sure. Probably too liberal for his father. Philip tried other names: Rideau, Jennings.

"Oh, I think he knows all those people, in one way or another, but I doubt if he would have much to do with Jennings or his kind, though from what I hear, they might very well agree with one another. Dad is constantly ranting about how the nation needs strong leadership and how the forces of corruption and immortality—I think he means me—have taken over the country. But he's not religious. And I think he has some idea that *he* ought to be the leader to restore his "American Way." God help us if he is."

The two sat in silence for a long time. Then Philip asked quickly, "Do you love your father?"

Michael looked at him, suddenly stricken. "Oh, Philip, I always wanted to, but he'd never let me. And now . . ." he stopped.

"And now?" Philip prompted.

"And now I don't think I can. I think he's killed it, any chance."

April 9   7:20 P.M.

Philip weighed the conversation as he walked toward Amos Parr's house. For the moment, the tumult he still felt about

Michael had to be put aside, but not, he insistently knew, forgotten. But he was sure of one thing. The situation that passion had led him into with Michael could be dangerous for this investigation. He deeply felt, and his instincts about people were almost always right, that Michael was honest and good. But it was clear also that the boy was divided, deeply torn about his father. Philip would have to tread carefully if he expected to see Michael much more, or if he hoped to be able to find Michael helpful as a conduit of information about Faraway. He knew, but he wasn't sure why he knew, that part of the puzzle was Otis Ferguson. Though there seemed to be no connection between Ferguson and the other pieces in the puzzle, and Ferguson seemed to be singlemindedly intent on his own perhaps mad, or perhaps grimly sane, quest for order and law in an America he envisioned but which in fact was largely vanished, yet because there was a connection, however tenuous between Bray and Ferguson, Philip knew he could not ignore the man.

He reached Parr's street, and stood in front of the house, preparing himself for the questions he had to ask Amos Parr, who was his ally, and indeed his employer, but who, he realized now, had not been frank with him, had indeed been deceptive. Philip had to know what Parr had not yet revealed.

"Ah, Philip, how nice to see you. I'm glad you could come."

Parr had asked Philip to join him for dinner when they saw each other in New York.

Parr ushered Philip into the study.

"Drink?"

"Scotch, I think," Philip said.

After drinks were made, the two men sat quietly. The summer night wafted through the open doors and the muted sounds of the city served as counterpoint to the calls of birds from the garden.

"Terrible business about Haley," Parr finally said.

"Yes," Philip replied, waiting for Parr to give him the opening he needed.

"Do you have any ideas about . . . ?"

"About who, or why?" Philip finished the sentence.

"Yes, that, and what are we going to do to stop it? I said the other night, and I'll say it again, the whole thing has gotten out of hand. Who knows which of us might be next? Philip, I'm not happy with this."

"Nor am I," Philip agreed. "But you know why we have to go on with it."

Parr nodded. "Yes, I know."

"There's something else you know, too, Amos—I may call you Amos?"

Parr looked comfortable. "Of course, Philip."

"You know a lot about Magnus Hopkenson. About people who are around him, who have been around him."

"I suppose I do, though I haven't been in touch . . ."

"I know that, but I suspect you don't let too much slip by unnoticed, do you?"

"I like to be informed," Parr said with a smile.

"Then," Philip said, "I need some of your information."

"Such as?"

"I'll be blunt. You—I mean you and Beverwyck and Witter—talk about why Hopkenson must be elected . . ."

Parr interrupted, "Because his politics and his liberal . . ."

Philip interrupted him. "I don't want the campaign oratory, Amos, I can read that in the papers. Why do you three in particular want him elected? You are all powerful men. You can, as we have seen, make things happen that you want to happen. What can Magnus Hopkenson do for you that you can't do for yourselves?"

Parr slowly drained his drink, and got up and made another. "Philip, you're right. We can do more privately than any president can. We don't need Hopkenson to—say, enrich ourselves. We're all rich, probably rich enough. Influence in the White House doesn't count for much in our position, since we do, shall we say, control very many aspects of the permanent government. No, we don't need Magnus Hopkenson to fill our coffers, or to see to it that our friends are appointed to high places, or to secure ambassadorial posts; we can do all those things. But you may be surprised to know Philip—indeed from your tone, I suspect that though you work for us you do not think too highly of our motives—you may be surprised to learn that we have higher ideals than you seem to have imagined."

"Tell me then," Philip said.

"I'll tell you a story, several stories in fact. Make yourself another drink. You see, Philip, all three of us—four of us if you count Haley—are men who now, and indeed for a long time, have had, literally, nothing to lose. There is no worry in our lives. Wealth and power can do bad things to men, Philip, and in some cases they can do good things, too. To us, I think it is the latter. We were—are—all agreed, informally, that because of our position in life, and because we all share what we, my dear Philip, share with you, and as you now know, with Magnus Hopkenson, that is our . . ."

Philip interrupted impatiently, "being homosexual."

"No, Philip, no, only that. Certainly we are all, as they say now, gay. Certainly in our time—and with Charles I suspect even now—we have been amused by the sight of a handsome lad, or delighted in the strength and excitement of what they used to call the love that dares not speak its name, but which now, happily, I think, is quite vocal. I am sure—in fact, I know, since we talk, the four of us old men—that we have loved and been loved, loved and won and loved and lost. In short, Philip, we have all had our share of sexual delight. Now that I have begun to see the golden threshold of seventy, I find such things are more delightful in retrospect. Nelson, I

suspect, feels the same, though from time to time he hints—
but no, no indiscretions about my closest friend. Poor dear
Douglas was immersed in his work, and his love—and there
was much of it—went to his son who, I fear, was separated
from him. This was a great and helpless sadness in Douglas'
life. Our friend Charles, who is relatively new to our company
and younger, still is very much . . . but perhaps you already
know all that?"

Philip let the implied question pass.

"Ah yes, you are discreet, too. Good. At any rate, Philip,
it is not only sex, but sexuality that binds us together. And
this is only one of the ties, aside from a web of mutual
business interests that would absolutely dazzle you, my dear,
far beyond what I suspect you could imagine. But now *I* am
being indiscreet. What binds us all closely, aside from our
long and mutual acquaintance, what binds us most is the
freedom which our wealth has given us, and the vision of life
which we all share, a vision certainly formed in part by our
similar background and education, by the fact that all of us
were—shall I be crass—born well, and by the fact that over
the years we have come to understand one another almost
without the need for words. But centrally, Philip—and can
this be understood?—we are bound by a kind of sensibility we
all share, a sensibility that is intimately a part of our sexuality,
intimately a part of our preferences, but which extends so far
beyond the sexual that the implications broaden to touch
every facet of our lives, our tastes, our attitudes, our spirits.

"I sometimes wonder if the last several years, in which
the world has come to accede to the demands of the new
generation to be openly gay, to thrust being gay into the light
as a political *and* emotional force, I wonder if this very
openness has not come about at the expense of a kind of shared
language of the spirit which was, perhaps, more developed
among us when we had to be more secretive, more discreet.
Men such as ourselves—I mean all of us, Philip—you, me,

Magnus, *we* are different, you know. It is not just sex and sexuality that defines us and separates us from *them*. We are a race apart. Plato was right you know, when he suggested that at the creation the Great Forces created gay men, lesbians, *and* heterosexuals, three separate races, three separate identities. We talk in language that those *others* do not understand. We feel feelings that are foreign to them. We communicate in a complexity of nuance and an idiom that finally is not ever theirs to know. All the legends, all the clichés, Philip, are in their way true. We *are* different, we *are* sensitive, we *do* create, we *see* more deeply, more intimately, we have a conduit to the mysteries of sex and to the mysteries of life which always seems to me to be denied to those men and woman of the, as we say, *straight* world with whom I daily and generally associate. Oh, they are bright, often brilliant, competitive, strong, achievers, many of them powerful and rich as I, but what our dear brother Henry James described as "the finer grain" seems to me never quite available to them, even the best of them. Oh, yes, there are among us the dolts and the fools, the pointless twits and the incompetents, but largely I have found that for me there is a hidden language of the heart, an often unspoken dialect of the spirit, connected to deep mysteries and to the very vital instincts of creation itself that is so often shared among men like myself—and like you. Thus, because Nelson and Charles are of my mind, and I of theirs, we have become bound together. And to what purpose, you ask? You must wonder after all this mystic rambling, why I have not in fact answered your question. Well, I will now, and directly.

"Many years ago, we four decided that along with all the complex webs we weave, along with the numerous charities we all quite anonymously support, along with the strings we pull and the destinies we shape, we would do all we could for the purposes—I had almost said, the cause—which was in fact closest to us all. None of us has been left untouched, Philip, by the ancient hatreds which are directed at men like us. None of us have, at one time or another, been strangers to what bigotry and oppression have accomplished against us.

"Thus, we have, for some years now, made considerable though necessarily silent contributions to various organizations that support "gay" rights. We have seen to it that our influence was felt when a certain senator was found to have committed what was to us a quite understandable indiscretion with a handsome young Senate pageboy—I knew them both, but that was some time ago—and certain arms were if not twisted at least pressured, and certain votes were changed, and what was a motion for ouster was reduced to censure. You may remember the situation. We have also seen to it that other public figures whose activities in opposition to certain legislation favorable to gay people were, shall we say, warned that such opposition might be costly to them. I myself have seen to it that the dreaded sickness which descended on so many of our friends in these last years has at last been given adequate funding to research its cure. All of these things have necessarily been secret.

"Now, Magnus Hopkenson, who I loved, who, Philip, I still love in many ways, is about to become our president. There is no doubt in my mind that he will be president, Philip, unless his secret is made known. He will make a great president, his name will rank with Roosevelt, perhaps higher. But if it is discovered that he was—is—gay, then I fear that the aroused bigotry and stupidity of our great nation will send him down to defeat, and pave the way for another man to continue and even enhance what I know for a fact to be his current policy of repression against gay people, and against many classes with whom he is not in sympathy. If we crush"—Parr mouthed the word with a curious force—"if we crush this disclosure, then Hopkenson is safe. And safe for what? Safe to have eight years to begin and perhaps complete projects that will change the face of America, Philip, and to do

something that perhaps no president has dared to imagine—
and there have in our past been at least two who might have
imagined it—that is my dear Philip, to ban with a single stroke
of his pen the bigotry against people who, in Magnus' case, are
his own.

"That is why we want him there, you see. Magnus
knows us, though he does not publicly embrace us. And he
also knows, if I may be direct, that we have done much to
further his career, and will do more. There will be a point, if
he is elected, when it will be clear that he is in our debt, and
deeply. And then, Philip, we will collect on that debt. Not, as
you thought, for gain, or favor, but for what is, after all, only
right."

Philip sat, incredulous at this disclosure, wondering if it
could be true, doubting it, half wanting to believe it, amazed
at the cool revelation of power, wondering that these men,
seemingly so conservative, so exemplary of the highest levels
of the established hierarchy, could have such a radical vision.
Finally, "Can you do this?"

"Oh, yes," Parr said. "We can."

Later that night, after dinner, the two men sat on the
terrace, sipping brandy. During the talk over the excellent
meal, Philip had once again kindled the real fondness he felt
for Amos Parr. Now it was combined with an admiration he
had not felt before, and mingled with a certain sadness that
this fine man was, he could see, a lonely man, with no friend
to comfort his final years.

Out of the silence of the garden, Parr said, "I hope I
wasn't, too . . . ah, eloquent in there earlier. As I've grown
older I've become convinced about certain things and . . ."

"No apologies," Philip said. "You were fine. I was
moved, and, well, Amos, I'm proud to know you."

"If I'm not being too inquisitive, Philip, you don't really
talk much about . . ."

"About my life? No, I guess I don't. My life has been my work. There's not much more there."

"No, ah, friend," Parr said tentatively.

"No, no friend," Philip said, but an image of Michael arose, handsome, in his mind.

"I wasn't even sure you were gay," Parr said, "until, well, until I was sure. You know—magnetism."

Philip smiled. He almost wished he was older, or Parr younger, and then wondered if it mattered. He liked this craggy, principled old man, handsome now in a forbidding way, certainly handsome in his youth, a man now strong and matured into a calm certainty of the purposes of his life. He reached out and took Parr's hand.

He felt the thin strength of the older man, and the shock of surprise thrill through Parr's body, into his.

"Oh Philip, what a kind gesture," Parr said, his voice low, and sincere. "But please, don't. I find you very attractive. But I'm twice your age, and set in my ways, and I have found that my equilibrium is best maintained if my friendships are gentle and unthreatening. But no, don't take away your hand. Let us keep this contact a little longer. But though I would wish to hold you, I think that you might not want, finally, to hold me. I am old, Philip, and have seen much, perhaps enough. I'll be happy with your friendship. Unhappily, at my age, one always suspiciously feels that the attentions of young men are given out of pity or, in my case, greed."

"No, Amos," Philip began . . .

"I know, don't say anything. I know that you mean it, and I knew from the moment we met that there could be between us that curious attraction that older and younger men seem to have for one another in our world, the one offering beauty and vibrancy, the other calm experience and a sense of life, of life felt, and life lived. But now, no more." And Parr released Philip's hand.

The darkness deepened. Philip knew there was more he had to know. He asked Parr about Rideau and Jennings.

"I don't believe for a minute that Louis Rideau has become a Born Again Christian." Parr said smiling. "Louis is an astute but perhaps unscrupulous politician. He too has claims on Magnus, he did after all, help him into politics, and he is, after all, the senior senator. The two of them have drifted apart. Rideau has become more conservative. But for appearances they keep up a front of unity and there is much genuine feeling as well as much real political purpose in their association, however much it may be diminished from its former closeness. I think that Rideau himself would like to see Magnus in the White House, hoping his claims on Magnus would, could, then be realized. I suspect he sees Jennings as, in effect, a large block of votes, now I fear, very large. I expect that promises have been made, by Rideau, and by Jennings. I am sure that Louis despises Jennings personally, even though he may publically embrace him."

"Could Rideau be behind any of the things that have happened?"

"I don't know. He could. He is powerful enough. But the question is, Philip, why would he? Murder is a dangerous game. It can be found out. No, I think Rideau has too much at stake in his own career to chance dirtying his hands with any such thing."

"And Jennings?"

"Ah, Billy Jennings. Scum, Philip, scum. But not to be ignored. He is a dangerous man, because in essence he does not, I think, believe in what he preaches. Or if I'm wrong, and he does believe in it, then he is even more dangerous. Ignorance and faith have always seemed to me more appalling than hypocrisy. But Jennings wants power. He has amassed a lot of it. He is rich from the contributions of Tennessee dirt farmers, from the advertising of Kentucky hardware stores, from the tuition of stupid boys and girls who believe life can be changed if they go to college and learn and preach Billy's gospel of hate. And he has an arm in Congress. Seven

representatives and at least two senators are members of his
church, and, I believe, in one way or another on his payroll.
I'm working on those disclosures now. He has chosen
corruption as his theme, and he has chosen what men like him
always choose, down through history, gay people to be the
scapegoat. What can not be proved, as Gibbon said, is
implied, and the big smear rides in the land again and if he has
his way, there *will* be laws against gay people and our love, as
well as laws against abortion, against any kind of sexuality not
blessed by the words of his own brand of belief. And there
will be worse things. He is trying to sponsor an act in
Congress which will make the old Family Protection Act seem
benign. He wants to get into the schools. He wants to expand
his newspaper network, and control the news. And there are,
God help us, many who believe he is right. I see him as the
real danger, Philip. But as a murderer, no, not that, at least I
can't believe it to be so."

"But why is he willing to support Hopkenson?"

"Two reasons, I think. Our president in effect double-
crossed Jennings. Jennings brought him votes, but the Great
Man didn't deliver. Jennings wanted a bill passed; he wanted
federal money. He didn't get it, because political realities got
in his way. Jennings doesn't forgive and he has vowed revenge
even if it means having Hopkenson in the White House. I
suspect Rideau had told Jennings that he has Hopkenson's ear,
and that if Jennings delivers enough votes—and money—that
Hopkenson will have to listen. That may, by the way, be
true."

"What do you know about Rideau and Jennings personally?" Philip asked.

"If you mean, are either of them suspect, I don't know.
Louis married very young, and remains happily, as I suppose,
married to the same rather dull woman. There has been no
hint of anything improper in his life."

"Could he know about Hopkenson?"

"He could, but as I said, Magnus has been so discreet, that well, it seems unlikely."

"And Jennings."

"Jennings hates anything that is not made in his own image. He despises, despite his public announcements, anyone who is not white. And he loathes gay people with a passion bordering on hysteria. Psychologists would say he is homosexually repressed himself, but I doubt it. Sex itself is appalling to him. He is, I understand, personally chaste, indeed fanatically so. And I am sure he knows nothing about Magnus. They have never met. It is unlikely, unless it is necessary, that they will, unless Magnus is compelled to accept Jennings as a necessary part of the campaign, which may happen, I fear."

"Then," Philip said, "he could be investigating Magnus. He could be Bray's client."

"Yes, that is certainly possible."

"I have to ask you another question, before I go," Philip said. "Can you tell me about Hugh Tilden."

Parr looked at him with a steady gaze.

"Hugh Tilden, as far as I know, is dead. I knew him briefly years ago. He was an aide to Magnus. Then he left Magnus, got some kind of job in the State Department perhaps, and left because of a scandal. There was talk that the scandal was arranged. I don't know. All I know was that Tilden disappeared from Washington. That was years ago, and as far as I know, he is dead."

"I don't think he is dead," Philip said. "There's a connection here between Tilden and St. Pierre, and possibly between Tilden and Magnus. Any idea?"

"No," Parr said quickly. Then, "Yes, there is something, and I've been wrong to keep it quiet. But I'll tell you. After Magnus and I ended our, what will you call it, our involvement, Magnus and Hugh Tilden saw a good deal of each other. I once suspected it was Tilden who, ah, interfered between us, but I was wrong. Tilden was Magnus' aide then, but as soon as Magnus went to the House of Representatives, Tilden left, if voluntarily I don't know. I suspect Magnus got him the other government job. Shortly after that Magnus married and then no questions were ever asked. I knew about Magnus and Tilden. I doubt if anyone else did."

"What was Tilden like?"

"Oh, Hugh was not of Magnus' caliber, but he was loyal, and essentially decent. No, I don't think he broke us up. Magnus was young, we were all young, and experimenting. I suppose to say he interfered is too strong. No, he's not to be blamed. I am sure his departure from Washington was arranged, but by whom, I don't know. Magnus wouldn't do it."

Philip rose and extended his hand to Parr.

"Thank you, Amos," he said warmly. The two men embraced, and looked at one another.

"Philip, dear Philip," Parr said. "It has been good to talk. I hope it won't be our last conversation."

"No, it won't," Philip said. "If you're . . ." Philip paused, not wanting to hurt, ". . . if you're lonely, I'm here."

Philip thought he caught a tear in Parr's eyes. But the older man's quick smile obscured it.

"Thank you, I know."

Parr walked Philip to the end of the garden, to the gate that gave out on the street.

"There's one thing I have to say," Parr said.

"Yes."

"I have a number of sources, ways of getting information, loyal employees, whatever. I often hear things, sometimes I hear things I don't want to know about. I know who you saw today."

Philip stepped back, surprise evident in his face.

"The investigator investigated?"

"No, nothing like that, I assure you. Please believe me. I'm afraid that I, well, I own the hotel in which you stay and the bell captain . . ."

"I see."

"Philip. Otis Ferguson is a mysterious man, as you have discovered. I know little about him. The worlds knows less. But I urge you, if you have much to do with him—or anyone connected with him—be careful."

15.

L ord, let now thy servant depart in peace."
      The priest made the sign of the cross over the coffin,
and the pallbearers lifted it and slowly paced down the aisle
toward the open door.

Tim followed the coffin, the tones of the organ shudder-
ing through him. He scarcely felt his mother's hand clasped
around his arm. In back of him, Ada, who had been with the
family for many years, audibly wept as she followed the coffin
of Douglas Haley, who she had served for so long.

Tim was comforted by the surety that Randy was
walking a few paces behind him. He felt the strength of
Randy's support and love as an almost tangible thing.

The church, filled in pew after pew, smelled of incense
and the ancient rites of that Episcopal heritage which, Tim
knew, had meant much to his father. The choir, walking
behind him, chanted one of those royal and stately Anglican
hymns that Tim had not heard for years. He was strengthened
by its melody. The sun haloed through the arched door of the
church, and for the moment it seemed as if his father's coffin
was going to disappear into a blaze of light, a prefiguration,
perhaps, of his certain entrance into glory. The coffin passed
into the light; Tim followed it out into the Boston sun. The
hearse awaited; behind it was the Haley limousine followed

by a long procession of cars attesting to the long procession of
men and women who claimed friendship or acquaintance with
Judge Douglas Haley.

Tim stood on the steps and pulled his mother close to him
while the pallbearers continued their measured tread to the
hearse. Since the burial was to be private, the congregation, as
it filed out, stopped and gripped Tim's hand, held his mother's
briefly, exchanged glances or nods if they were not well
known, a few words if family friends.

"The president has asked me to convey his sincere
sympathy," a tall, well-dressed man said, taking Tim's hand.
"He hopes that if there is anything you need, you will call."

Tim smiled wryly to himself, knowing the president was
only too happy to offer help to Douglas Haley now that he
was dead, when he had done much to hinder him, usually in
vain, while the judge was alive. Tim could only imagine that
the president was relieved so outspoken a critic of his
administration would now speak no more.

Tim felt Randy come up beside him.

He gave him a smile, and was happy to feel the pressure
of Randy's hand on his shoulder.

He heard his mother saying, "Thank you for coming,
Mr. Mayor. I know Douglas would be pleased that you were
here."

Tim thought, "How do you know what he would be
pleased about, Mother, you haven't laid eyes on him in three
years."

"But then," he thought with pain, "neither have I. We
both abandoned him."

Other voices swam out of the crowd. "A great man, Mrs.
Haley. We'll miss him in Washington." "He did so much for
our hospital." "A force to be remembered in this nation, Mrs.
Haley." "I don't know where the library would be without his
kindness."

"Oh, Marion, this is too much for you," a matronly

woman said. "Come, you don't need to face anymore of this," and started to lead her away.

"Thank you, Mrs. Saltonstall," Tim said. "Take her to the car; I'll be along in a few minutes."

Tim's mother looked at him bewilderedly.

"Go ahead, Mother, we'll be along."

"Just a few more minutes," he said to Randy. "Then we'll go, too."

The congregation continued to file out. Tim shook hands by rote, smiling, responding when necessary.

"Thank you for coming, Governor."

"I appreciate it, Your Eminence."

"I will call, Mr. Ambassador, I promise."

"Thank you Rose, I'm sure we'll always remember. I know he did."

The hum of voices blended into a kind of chant.

Reach out, shake a hand, say a few words. Repeat the gesture. Try to be kind. But while the litany was going on, there were other thoughts pressing in, thoughts he wanted to banish forever, and others that were just beginning to have coherent meaning. Again and again, replacing the faces that smiled sadly into his, he could see the anguished and shocked face of his father, the pallor of death upon it, the surprise of life's extinction reflected in the wide staring eyes, the face he had for so many years avoided, and which he had come home to see and to kiss at last, only to find it thus, deprived of life, and he, Tim, now forever deprived of love.

And other thoughts came, insistent, demanding: *Why did this happen? Who did it? They had to be found, and he, Tim, must make them pay, bring to their eyes the terror he saw in the poor face of his father who he would now never know.*

In the dazed hours after the discovery of the body, throughout the police questioning, after the return to New York, Tim's mind was filled with a chaos of despair and anger. He let Randy support him, fell into that powerful protection which Randy could offer. But as the days passed, the day after the death, a day after that, the morning of the funeral, his anger and purpose crystallized. Why had his father called him? The answer to that was soon clear. His father's secretary reported that the judge had booked a flight to Pennsylvania the day before he died. Where?

He was at the Jennings rally. Why? No answer. The secretary didn't know. But one thing was clear. Haley must have seen Tim there.

"He had to have been there, Randy. He must have seen me."

"But why would your father go to a rally like that? He wasn't a supporter of Jennings, was he?"

"I don't know. I doubt it. He was a pillar of the Episcopal Church, but like he once said, no one could accuse him of being a Christian."

"Then why?" Randy repeated.

Tim shrugged. "Maybe a coincidence, but he was there, and so was I. If he saw me there, then that must have prompted him to call."

"To say what?"

"It was important. Randy, his message. He never said . . ." Tim couldn't finish the sentence, but the memory of that recorded message brought a clutching to his throat: "One thing more. I love you."

"He never said that before," he sobbed, as Randy took him in his arms.

And now, as the last of the mourners filed by, Tim was sure he must find out why his father died, and discover who had done it.

"Mr. Haley?" Tim realized someone had been speaking to him. He pulled himself out of his memories to find three men standing in front of him, one of them holding out his hand. He took it mechanically, starting to say "Thank you for coming." But one of the men said, "Mr. Haley, I'm Nelson Beverwyck. I am—was—a very close friend of your father's." He emphasized "very." Tim looked at the man. Tall, graying hair, dark eyes that looked intimately into his, skin tanned and healthy; a man, Tim thought, who radiated purpose, and to whom he felt drawn, who seemed by his very presence to project comfort. "And this is Charles Witter and Dr. Amos Parr."

Tim held out his hand to the other two men. The first one introduced was trim, younger than the others. Handsome, Tim thought. The second, older, the oldest of the three, was solemn, did not smile, but Tim saw in his eyes curiosity and a look he could only describe as fondness and compassion, as if the man somehow knew him, or knew something intimate about him.

"We were all very close to your father," the man named Parr said. "We regret—deeply regret—his loss. Believe me, Mr. Haley—"

Tim interrupted, feeling somehow impelled to do so. "Please, it's Tim."

"Thank you," Parr said. "Believe me, if there is anything any of us can do, call on us."

Tim liked the courtly manner of the older man.

"We mean it," the younger man, Witter, continued. He looked at Tim, and smiled hesitantly. He too seemed to look at Tim in a way that suggested he knew him. Perhaps his father had spoken of him to them.

"Mr. Haley, Tim," Nelson Beverwyck said, "here is my card. It has a number on it that you must not hesitate to call if you feel the need to . . . to talk. Your father meant the world to me, and to each of us. In some ways he was my closest friend, though perhaps each of us felt that about him. You are his son and well, you're important to us, too."

Tim became aware of Randy at his side. Why he did it,

he wasn't sure, but later he said it was right, that the moment called for honesty. He said, "This is Randy Asher, my lover."

The moment hung in silence. Parr's face stiffened, Beverwyck looked impassive, only Witter betrayed an emotion, which Tim felt somehow was not unsympathetic.

"Who are these men?" flashed through his head, as each in turn shook Randy's hand. Beverwyck seemed about to speak, then instead, put his hand briefly on Tim's shoulder and said, "Good-bye, Tim, you have friends in us."

The three men smiled and walked down the steps of the church. From the limousine Tim saw the pale anxious face of his mother peering through the window. He realized he must join her. He and Randy followed down the steps and got into the car, Tim on one side of his mother, Randy on the other. The car moved slowly away, taking a son to bid his father a last farewell.

April 10   *3 P.M.*

"Who are they, Randy?" Tim asked when they were at last back in the house after the funeral.

"Nelson Beverwyck, Beverwyck International," Randy read from the card. "You know who he is. Money. Power. He owns half of everything."

"That I know," Tim replied. "I mean who are they in connection with my father? Why did they seem so concerned?"

"Yes, that is strange," Randy agreed. "It seemed that they knew something, almost that they wanted to tell you something. Did your father have business dealings with Beverwyck?"

"He could have. I wasn't party to much of his life in these last years. You know that. The name of Parr I may have heard before, I'm not sure. I never paid much attention to his friends. But I think we'd better find out about these men. I have a feeling they could tell me something."

"I have another feeling about them, too," Randy said. "How about you?"

"Yes. I know what you mean. They seemed, well, they seemed gay."

"There have always been rumors about Beverwyck," Randy said. "But there are always rumors about prominent men. He's not seen much in public, but when he does appear, he's always described as the wealthy bachelor head of Beverwyck International, and is shown with some starlet on his arm. I've always thought that was mostly publicity."

"Randy?" Tim asked. "If these men are gay, and they claim to be my father's closest friends, well, what does . . ."

"What does that say about your father?" Randy finished the sentence.

Randy said, "Let's find out about them. We know their names, it won't be hard to check them out. When we get back to New York, I'll call around. If they are gay, then it will be known to someone, no matter how much they're in the closet. We have friends who move in those circles. I'm sure we can find out what we need to know."

April 10   3:00 P.M.

"So Nelson, what's your opinion of young Haley," Parr asked as he settled into his seat for the flight back to New York.

Beverwyck completed his instructions to the captain and turned to Parr and Witter who sat around the table about to begin the light lunch Beverwyck served aboard his plane.

"I think the poor kid is in shock. But he seems to be a bright young man. Remarkably possessed, given the circumstances."

"I think," Witter said, "we ought to keep an eye on him.

He could be volatile. If he's anything like his father, he isn't going to let this thing go without questions."

"He's very much like his father in that way," Parr said quietly.

"And he's also very outspoken," Witter said, reminding them of the introduction of his lover.

"Who is this Randy Asher?" Parr asked.

"He's in the news a lot lately," Witter said. "An activist. He has a very good chance of being elected to Congress from the Greenwich Village Congressional District."

"Yes, of course," Beverwyck said. "We have funneled some money into his organization, I believe."

"I think so," Witter said. "At any rate, both these young men are activists, and I think they bear watching, as I said."

"Perhaps we should put Philip on them," Beverwyck suggested. "Or should we wait for them to call us?"

"No, I don't think we should wait," Parr said. "I think we should get in touch with them. I know that Haley and his son were not on good terms. Young Haley is likely to be suspicious of older friends of his father's. It seems to me they would be hesitant about calling us. It does appear that for some reason Haley and his son were going to meet. It was Tim who found the body. I think we should go to them."

"I agree," Witter said. "Asher has a large organization. They could be very useful. It would be very interesting to find out what they think about, or even know about, Michael Ross. I don't think Ross had made any liaison with Asher, but Asher could not have been unaware of him."

"Do you really think they would be helpful to us?" Beverwyck said doubtfully.

"Yes," Witter said, "I do, for the reason that they—at least Tim and presumably Randy—now have a stake in what we're doing. After all, we all need to know why Douglas Haley is dead. Let's not forget we are all in danger. We might find these young men helpful, and for that reason, I agree that we send Philip Kristopher to them, not wait for them to come to us."

"If we do," Beverwyck said, "we're going to have to tell them about us."

"Yes," Witter said, "but I think the time has come when we will have to take off the masks."

The men sat in silence for a time. Beverwyck said quietly, "But my friends, can we be responsible for taking off the mask that our friend Douglas wore? Do we have a right to do that? Who among us is going to tell Tim Haley what his father never told him?"

"I will," Parr said. "I am sure Douglas would want it that way, and I am sure also, though I do not know the boy, that it will give Tim Haley something now that he never had before. I believe Douglas was going to tell his son about his life. Douglas would want Tim to know, and in knowing, I think Tim will find his father at last."

16.

Parr had returned to Washington after Haley's funeral with the conviction strengthened that the investigation must be continued. He had spent the last few days catching up with business that had been untended; met with the hospital board, gone to a luncheon meeting of the Museum Conservancy and entertained Senator Cooper of Idaho and Frederic Moore of the EPA with whom he was working to see a bill on wetlands through Congress.

But during all of this, even as he discussed a new head of surgery for the hospital, as he pledged to lead a new campaign drive for the museum, as he diplomatically convinced the senator his reelection would be aided by supporting the wetlands bill, his mind was always on the events of the last several days, events which played an obligato to the melodies of his daily life. He could not forget the stricken face of Timothy Haley, and he could not suppress the fact that Douglas Haley was gone, a fact which he was now only beginning to realize fully.

Hovering in his consciousness now, also, was doubt. There were too many questions and too few answers. One by one, people who got close to the question of Magnus Hopkenson were eliminated. People who might potentially be dangerous were, like flies, mercilessly killed. It was possible, sickeningly possible, as Philip had suggested, that the very man they were trying to protect, Magnus Hopkenson, was himself this merciless executioner. Amos did not want to believe this; he could not believe it because it ran counter to everything he knew about Magnus. And yet, now, it was the only answer that made any sense.

Uncomfortably, there was a small part of him, the coldest and most pragmatic part of him, that said: "Yes, and it's right. Whatever has to be done to protect Magnus must be done." But then the specter of Douglas Haley would arise, that cold pragmatic self would be banished, and Parr would know that such thoughts, however unwanted, must be banished as well.

Most unpleasant of all, however, was the sense that he was himself in danger. He, after all, knew the most. He, after all, was the source of everything that had happened, and he had brought others with him: Nelson, Charles, Philip. A complex edifice was in danger. What to do?

Perhaps, he thought, he should appeal to Magnus directly, confront him with what was happening. Vow once again that he would never disclose what he knew.

But what would that accomplish? He had not really spoken to Magnus confidentially for years. They met, of course, in public, encountered one another at dinners, at party gatherings, saw one another at the round of social events where much of the real politics of the Capitol was transacted. But they had always kept a distance. If it were Magnus who was behind it all, what would that accomplish save to tell him that Parr was now a clear danger to him?

If Magnus were not involved, if he was still unaware of the drama playing around him—as could very well be possible—then to alert him to it would be contrary to everything he and his friends agreed upon. "Magnus must not be told." That was the essential article of faith, for such a disclosure would taint their potential relationship with Magnus. The ground was delicate, and he must tread carefully.

Parr sat at his desk, the midmorning sun gleaming across the carpet, etching a path to the fireplace, its rays lighting the memorabilia of a lifetime scattered around the room.

"I have been able to accomplish so much, and I am so powerless now," he thought. "So powerless now."

But, he decided, he must begin his day. Put these things aside for now. A stack of mail lay in front of him. His calendar was on the desk. Leon, both butler and secretary, had filled in the blank spaces for the next few days with notations, indicating calls to be made, lunches, dinners, appointments, the round of events which Parr used to relish, but which now seemed to be an irritation and a futility.

He pulled the desk calendar to him. Better get started. On the page that indicated calls to be made there were three numbers, calls to be returned. One was from Louisa van Velsor, a wealthy old lady who was hovering on the brink of donating her large collection of nineteenth-century American paintings to the museum. Parr was sure that a call, some conversation over tea, perhaps a lunch would be enough to insure the bequest. He had a way with women like that. Another call was from the State Department. Parr recognized the number, even though no name was added. The undersecretary kept him informed about certain events in a certain country where Beverwyck, he, and Charles had some interests. The third one was Philip Kristopher's office in New York. He decided to call Philip first. As he reached for the phone, he glanced at the other page where his appointments for the day, if any, were listed. There was only one: In Leon's precise hand it said: "Otis Ferguson. Lunch at 1 P.M.."

Parr put the phone down. Otis Ferguson? Why? Except to arrange the meeting with Philip, he had not spoken to Ferguson in years. He had once seen to it that a certain senator had arranged that a particular amendment to a minor bill had its wording slightly changed. This small change had been useful to Otis Ferguson. Parr called in that debt when he

asked Ferguson to see Philip. He wondered why Ferguson
wanted to renew what had never been a close relationship. He
pressed the call button on the phone, summoning Leon. In
minutes, Leon appeared, carrying a tray with coffee.

"Sir?"

"No, no more coffee, Leon, thank you," Parr said. "Tell
me, this lunch date with General Ferguson. When did he
call?"

"Yesterday, sir. He said he would send a car at 12:30."

"I see. Did he call himself?"

"No, sir, it was apparently his secretary."

How like Ferguson, Parr thought, to assume that Parr
would be free. He glanced at his watch. It was nearly noon.

"Thank you, Leon, that will be all. Oh, yes, I'll dine out
tonight so don't prepare anything. And I suppose I'll have to
have lunch with Ferguson. Would you call Miss van Velsor
and ask her to tea tomorrow or Thursday? Then you can have
the rest of the day off."

Leon nodded. "Will there be anything else, sir?"

"No, thank you."

Leon left the room. Between Parr and Leon there was
always a strict formality, coupled with a hint of humor. Leon
had been with him for seven years now. He had worked as the
maitre'd at a hotel Parr had a share in, in Baltimore. There, at
dinner, Parr had been impressed with his efficiency and was
aware that he was gay. Soon, Leon left the hotel and came to
work for Parr. Since then, Parr had come to depend on Leon
to make his complicated life run smoothly, and underneath the
veneer of the domestic relationship, Parr felt a fondness for
the young man, and determined to reward him well, for Leon
was devoted and very protective. When Parr was gone, Leon
would not be in need. And why not? Parr had felt when the
decision was made to write Leon into the will, he had no one
else to leave things to, save for various trusts and foundations
which would receive the bulk of his estate, his paintings, the

furniture collection, and the books. Why not reward Leon, who had been, if not a son or lover, at least someone he could trust.

Someone he could trust. He realized he had not called Philip. There was another young man to whom he was drawn, more than he had admitted when Philip was here last week. Drawn not for physical reasons, though Philip was indeed handsome, very handsome: a fine jaw, chiseled and firm, eyes that looked into you and made connection, an amiable smile, a purposive handsomeness, with the strength that was seen often in those portraits of young Americans painted in the early years of the last century. Yes, Parr thought, Philip. He wondered if it were possible to get to know the young man better. If behind the cool impeccability of his manner there was the chance for—for what?—for no more than a simple friendship, Parr knew, but that would be itself a rich gift. He had caught a glimpse of Philip's warmth at dinner. He hoped time would ripen their friendship. Young men always were problematical to him: They at once made him feel younger and older. Their youth was infectious, giving him vital energy, and yet it was sad as well, since he was incapable of avoiding the fact that he was, in Leon's case, in Philip's too, old as their fathers must be, and older.

The insistent summons of the door knocker echoed through the house. It was nearly twelve-thirty. He had not called Philip. He had wanted to call Ferguson to cancel, or put off the lunch. He had nothing to say to that man. But now, it must be the car Ferguson said he would send.

He heard Leon going to the door, down the hall, past the row of family portraits. At the door, someone would be standing, having alerted the house by the thunderous and ponderous door knocker that had alerted the house to callers for two centuries.

Parr wearily rose. Leon entered the room.

"Sir, General Ferguson's driver is here."

"Thank you Leon. Bring me a jacket and a tie, please."
Leon returned quickly with a jacket and a tie.

"Nice choice," Parr said. He always trusted Leon to choose the right combination of things. He knotted the black tie and slipped into the brown tweed jacket that Leon held for him.

The two men stood for a moment, and impulsively Parr reached out and touched Leon's arm. They exchanged smiles and then the masks were resumed and Leon held the door as his master went down the steps to the limousine that waited at the curb.

"I think we should call them," Witter said to Philip.

Chuck Witter and Philip were having lunch in Witter's office. Witter told Philip about Haley's funeral, and about Tim Haley and his friend Randy.

"What do we know about them?" Philip asked.

"Not too much," Witter replied. "Young Haley: almost nothing. I gather that he and his father had a serious disagreement, were estranged. The boy came to New York. His friend Asher has become quite a force in downtown politics. He runs the VID, and heads the coalition. He's heading for a serious political career."

"And you think," Philip said, "we ought to bring them into this?"

"I think we have to. Young Haley is bent on finding out what's going on. I think he suspects that his father's death is more than the robbery attempt the Boston police have called it. Of course he's right. If we don't get some control over the boy, then he may start getting in our way. I suggest you meet them. I'll set it up. They're young and impulsive. They may be trouble, and they could get themselves hurt. I think we owe it to Douglas to see that nothing happens to his son."

April 11   1:00 *P.M.*

The chauffeur held the limousine door for Parr. From inside, a voice said, "Amos, how good to see you."

In the car Parr was surprised to find Otis Ferguson himself.

"Hello, General," Parr said.

"Now Amos, we go far enough back not to be so formal," Ferguson said, extending his hand.

The car pulled away, and threaded through the Georgetown streets.

"I hope you don't mind having lunch with an old friend, Amos," Ferguson was saying. "I know it's short notice, but I thought, I haven't spoken to Amos Parr since he sent that pleasant young man—what was his name—Kristopher, out to see me. I shouldn't let old friendships slide that way. So I called."

Parr thought, We're not friends. We have barely spoken in years. He was surprised by the warmth of Ferguson's tone. It was too warm, too friendly.

The car had turned out of Georgetown and was now heading out of the city, toward the Virginia countryside.

"I thought you wouldn't mind having lunch with me at Faraway," Ferguson said. "Much nicer than restaurants in town these days. Don't you agree? Cheaper, too," he smiled.

Parr knew that Otis Ferguson did not have to worry about the cost of a meal.

"Well, Otis," he lied, "I do have an appointment later today, and I'm dining out tonight . . ."

Ferguson cut him off. "Oh, we'll have you back in town in plenty of time, Amos."

Parr clearly had no choice. The car sped across the

Potomac and into Virginia. Ferguson said, "Lovely here, isn't it, Amos. Much nicer than the city. I fail to understand just why anyone would choose to stay in that town when they could be out here." They were silent for a while. Then, "Oh, yes, one thing Amos. This young man, now just who is he? Of course, I was helpful to him, gave him what he needed, I think. But I must say Amos, if it hadn't been you, I wouldn't have done it."

Parr was distinctly uncomfortable with the direction of the conversation, but he didn't want Ferguson to know it. Assuming the same friendly tone, he said, "Yes, Otis, Philip *is* a pleasant young man, isn't he? He's just doing some work for me. Nothing very important, but confidential, I'm sure you understand that."

"Important enough, I gather," Ferguson replied, "to require a little, shall we say, extralegal snooping."

Parr smiled what he hoped was a knowing smile. "And I'm sure you understand *that* too, Otis."

Ferguson was silent, clearly feeling bested, then, "Anything more I could be of help with, Amos?"

"No, you've already been of immense help," Parr parried. "Anyway, it all came to nothing." He hoped he sounded convincing.

"Well," Ferguson said, appearing to drop the inquiry, "I certainly won't pry. I know some things need to be kept confidential. That's the trouble these days, everyone talks too much, not enough action."

Parr nodded, not sure if he was expected to answer. He decided to be noncommittal.

"Now tell me, Amos," Ferguson went on, "when was the last time we had a good talk, must have been, oh, when you and I were both on the board of Anaconda, wasn't it? Yes," he said, not giving Parr time to answer. "That was it. Good five years ago, I expect. I do want to thank you for those strings you pulled then Amos, great help it was. That's why I let your boy come out to see me. I felt I was in your debt, and I wanted to clear the slate, so to say."

"Well, I appreciate it, Otis," Parr replied, wondering how long this would go on. Otis Ferguson was not, normally, a man for small talk. His way was stern, demanding, and he was used to being listened to, not to listening. His manner, Amos felt, did not ring true, he seemed too obliging. But perhaps he had mellowed in these last few years. After all, it was surprisingly easy to gain entre for Philip. Perhaps age was smoothing out the hard military edge of Ferguson's personality.

Parr realized Ferguson was going on. "Debt of honor, Amos, that's what I considered it. Not too many honorable men around these days, you know, don't you agree? We're a vanishing breed, Amos, and don't you forget it."

"Oh surely now, Otis, it's not as black as you paint it," Parr said, feeling he was required to say something.

"Not as black as I paint it? Why it's worse. Worse," he said, and Parr saw the general's fists tighten, clench, and unclench. "Now that young Philip, he seemed like an honorable man, ah, sorry, you're right, no need to talk about him. But at any rate, Amos, there aren't many others, not many real men around at all so far as I'm concerned. Congress is full of nincompoops, fellow travelers, people in it just for the money. No patriots, Amos, that's clear."

Parr could see the conversation was developing into a tirade.

"How are your horses, Otis?" he asked, hoping to get Ferguson on a subject he knew to be dear to him.

"Horses? Damn sight better than most people I know these days," he went on, not to be deflected. "Why Amos, you wouldn't believe what is going on around us. Mongrelization is what it is. No honor, no one any good at what they do, no standards, Amos. It used to be a decent world, in my Daddy's time, even when I was young, but we let anyone in anyplace. I resigned at the club, you know, when they let that Asiatic join."

Parr remembered that "the Asiatic" was an eminent Japanese businessman who later became ambassador.

"Now surely, Otis," Parr said, drawn in against his will, "surely you can't believe that someone like Ambassador Sumayama is . . ."

"I don't care what he is or isn't," Ferguson said. "What I'm talking about is the fact that you can't rely on anyone these days. Why look at that man in the White House. Now Amos, I supported that man, I voted for him, and I will tell you, between us, that I saw to it that a very large piece of cash went to get him where he is. Now I know you didn't agree with me about him then, but I have seen my error, Amos. I have seen my error. Weak, vacillating, big talk and no action, that's the man I got for my money, Amos. Why he had the chance to bomb . . ."

Abruptly he stopped. "Well, I guess I was getting a little bit riled up. My doctor tells me I have to calm down." He smiled full on Parr, as if to pull himself back to calmness. Parr felt Ferguson take a breath, and then, more calm, he said, "I suppose, Amos, that you see something of Nelson Beverwyck?"

Parr knew it would be pointless to deny that.

"Why yes, Otis, you know Nelson and I have many interests in common."

Ferguson smiled. "Yes, I know, Amos, many."

Parr felt a distinct edge to Ferguson's tone. What was he implying?

As if to answer, Ferguson asked, "Nelson involved with your Mr. Kristopher? Or is it your friend Witter? Works for him as I recall."

Parr wondered if Philip had given Ferguson that information.

Noncommittally he said: "I expect you know about as much as I do, Otis."

"Well, now, I hate to admit it, but I don't, Amos, I don't. I'm sorry to keep coming back to this, and I know you said it was confidential, but surely you can tell an old friend. After all—"

Parr could feel it coming—

"After all, I did bend the law just a bit to help you. Now I'm grateful for what you did for me, and well, it's not as if I'm not, but I think you take my meaning."

Parr decided that he had to answer Ferguson, but without revealing anything.

"All right Otis," he said, deciding to play the game instead of opposing Ferguson.

"Philip *is* doing some investigating for us. Now I can't say why, but let us say there are large sums at stake. You know we don't take risks." Parr hoped that would satisfy Ferguson.

The general digested the information for a moment, then, "One thing bothers me, Amos. Why did you call me?"

Parr was unprepared for the question, expecting more probing into the nature of the investigation.

"You? Why, uh, Otis, you're the obvious man to call."

He felt Ferguson look at him strangely.

"Obvious? Mmm. Well, I'll tell you one thing. I liked that young man. He had something I like."

Parr was surprised at the abrupt change of subject. He risked, "What was that, Otis?"

Ferguson was quiet for a while. Then, "He was in control of himself. Didn't reveal anything. Very businesslike. I like men like that, Amos, men who can hide their feelings, who can play rough if they have to. I wouldn't mind having someone like him working for me. Too many people around me reveal too much. Let the world see too much. Infirmity"— he drew the word out—"infirmity should be hidden, Amos, kept hidden for everyone's good. But some people just flaunt their ways in front of everyone who will watch. It's a weakness, Amos, a damned weakness. Thank God I've been able to master it, to control myself. We all have to, for the good of the country. I like that in a young man."

Parr felt that once again Ferguson had let himself go, lost control.

"We need real men these days," Ferguson went on. "Men of action, who don't have to rely on anyone. That's what I'm proud to be. I always thought *you* were a man like that Amos. You are, I know it. *That's* why I helped you and that young man. Not because of *any* other reason. *Do* you understand me? Not because of *that!*" He stressed *that*, and went on, his words falling in a torrent, "You are honorable men, I hope, Amos. You *do* understand me, don't you." His remark was not a question.

They had come by now to the gates of Faraway. Parr saw the gatehouse was guarded. They drove down the long drive and stopped in front of the mansion. A young man came briskly out of the house and saluted Ferguson as he got out of the car.

"I expect you'd like to freshen up, Amos. Private Somers here will take you to your room. I'll see you later. I have some inspections to make." Ferguson turned on his heel as the young private saluted with a snap.

"This way, sir," he said to Parr, taking his arm.

Parr realized that something was very wrong. He wondered why he felt no longer like a guest, but like a prisoner.

17.

Randy sat at his desk, a pile of unopened mail in front of him. Since he and Tim had returned from Boston, he had been puzzled and obsessed with the murder of Judge Haley. Tim had subsided into a quiet calm which Randy knew hid his anger. Randy was not as sure as Tim that the judge's death was anymore than the result of a robbery attempt. What was so horrible about it was that it seemed Tim and his father might have had a reconciliation if death had not stepped in and ended forever that possibility.

"But what *can* we do?" Randy said once again to Tim, when, the night after getting back from Boston they went over and over the facts.

"We can try to find out why he was killed," Tim said angrily.

"Tim, I know it's hard," Randy said, trying to be gentle, "but sometimes there isn't any reason for this kind of thing. People are killed everyday in senseless muggings, for no more than a few dollars. There's no proof that there is any other cause. After all, it looks like a robbery."

"Looks like it," Tim said, "but I just have a feeling that it isn't."

The two men discussed the situation well into the night,

getting nowhere. Tim refused to relinquish his "feeling" and Randy could not convince him.

The next morning, Randy went into his office, and now sat at his desk, wondering how to shake Tim out of the obsession that seemed to grip him.

The phone buzzed. Randy picked it up.

"Yes," he said.

"Mr. Asher, my name is Philip Kristopher. You don't know me, but Charles Witter asked me to call you."

"I don't believe I know Mr. Witter either," Randy said.

"No, you don't, but you did meet him at Judge Haley's funeral in Boston. He wanted me to call you and ask if there was anything he could do for the judge's son."

"That's very kind of him, Mr. Kristopher, but I don't think so." Randy was wondering just why this call had been made.

There was a moment of silence, then, "Mr. Asher, I called you, rather than Mr. Haley, because we think it is important that you meet with us. We didn't want to upset Mr. Haley, but we do think there is something about the judge's death that ought to be discussed. We would . . ."

Randy interrupted.

"You say 'we,' who do you mean?"

"You met them in Boston," Kristopher said, and went on, not giving Randy a chance to comment. "We feel you might be able to throw some light on the situation. Could we talk to you?"

Randy's mind was racing. Why did these men want to talk to him? Who were they? Who was this Kristopher? He asked the last question.

"I work for Mr. Witter as an investigator," Kristopher replied. "When can we meet?"

"I think it ought to be both of us, Tim and I," Randy said.

"Fine. When?"

"Tonight, at my apartment. It's near . . ."

"I know where it is," Philip said crisply. "I'll be there at seven-thirty."

April 11   *7:30 P.M.*

Philip studied Randy Asher. The eyes of a prophet, he thought. Tim Haley, slight, sandy haired, sat on the floor next to the TV, clutching a beer. Philip refused a drink. He noticed Randy didn't drink either.

"So, Mr. Kristopher, you want to talk to us. What about?" Randy asked.

"Did you know my father?" Tim asked, not giving Philip a chance to respond to Randy.

"No, not well, though I had met him," Philip said. "I'm very sorry for what happened."

"Just what did happen?" Tim asked pointedly.

"We . . . I don't know," Philip said. "I hoped you might know something I don't."

"All I know is that my father was . . ."

"Tim, please," Randy said, coming over next to him and laying a hand on his shoulder. He sat down next to Randy on the floor and took his hand. Philip liked the natural intimacy of the gesture.

He warmed to the two young men, liked what he saw in the relationship.

"Tim, your father's death is a terrible thing. My employers want to find out about it as much as you do. They worked closely with your father, admired him. I think I can even say that they loved him. His death has been a blow to them as well as to you. They've hired me to investigate it."

Randy looked at Philip. "Do you think there is something to investigate? The police say it was robbery."

"I don't know, at the moment."

"Just why do your employers want to go deeper into this?" Tim asked. "And who are they?"

"You met them in Boston. They were business associates of your father's."

"Is it because of business that he's dead?" Tim asked.

"Look," Philip said, "there are some things I can't really discuss. Let's just say they don't feel the police explanation is adequate. What we—what I would like to know from you is if you spoke to your father, knew anything about his movements, who he might have seen, in the week or so before he was . . . before he was killed." Philip saw that Tim still could not hear the words without pain.

Randy had gotten up and was pacing across the room, from the window back to where Tim sat.

"Mr. Kristopher. You want us to give you some information. And we want to help. If there is something more to this than the police say, we want to know it, too. But how can we trust you? You refuse to tell us why you need to know this. You avoid answering any questions about your employers. You want something from us, but we don't get anything back."

Philip weighed what he should and should not tell them. He could see that Tim Haley was determined to pursue the causes of his father's death. It was obvious that the two of them were intelligent, but amateurs, and that they could get hurt if they became involved in a game which was being played for stakes higher than they knew. But it was also clear that it would be better to have them on their side than running amok in the middle of things, and possibly causing even more trouble. Yet he could not reveal the central fact to them. Hopkenson's name must not come into it. And further, he was not at liberty to discuss other things. Could he explain to these young men, who were clearly inflamed by their own idealism, that Beverwyck, Witter, Parr and Haley were bound together by the same tie that bound him and Randy, and that he himself was also gay? His employers from the beginning were adamant that their private lives must not be exposed to public scrutiny of any kind. And there was more. Could he, a stranger, even intimate to Tim Haley what Tim Haley clearly did not know—that his father would have understood his son's way of life, understood, approved, and sympathized. Perhaps Tim would want to know this, Philip thought, but he was not willing to be the messenger. He decided his job now was only to lay some bait. Tim and Randy would take it or not. If they took it, they could be valuable allies, but only on Philip's terms. If they rejected it, he would have to find a way to deal with that, too. He knew the success of his work lay in the still all too volatile hands of Tim Haley. Randy, clearly a peacemaker, would be reasonable.

"I'll tell you what I can. Your father, Nelson Beverwyck, Amos Parr and my immediate boss, Chuck Witter, were—are—involved in a very delicate—ah—project that now seems to be endangered by your father's death. It is vital that this project be brought to a successful conclusion."

"Mr. Kristopher," Tim said with evident irritation, "we're not children. What is this project? What are these men doing?"

Philip looked at them levelly. "If I tell you that I would be involving you with knowledge that might be as dangerous to you as it seems to have been to Judge Haley. Do you want that? There are things you may not want to know. All I need from you is what I've asked. You don't need to know anymore than I've already told you."

"Unless we want to get hurt. Is that what you're saying?" Randy asked.

Tim stood up. "Mr. Kristopher, I want to know why my father is dead. You come in here, lay out a story that more than confirms my suspicions that there *is* something to suspect. Then you back off. Now, I want to know who you are, and who these men are who sent you here. So let's start with one simple fact that seems obvious to me."

"Which is?" Philip said.

"Which is that your employers are all very powerful men and they seem if I'm not mistaken, to be gay men."

"I don't think that's the point," he responded.

"Well, what is the point, then?" Tim said coolly. "What is the point of this visit? The point of your questions? You're sent by your obviously gay employers. We're gay. We don't hide it, and I suspect you are, too. Whatever this is about, we all have something in common here, yet you're treating me like a straight cop interrogating faggots at a raided bar. If you or your boss have something you want to know, then ask it, but don't hide behind your macho secrets."

"I know who you are," Philip said. "And I know that this must be frustrating, even enraging for you, but it's not for me to say anything about my employers. And my life, at least right now, is private, too. If you want to help find out who killed Judge Haley, then you can. If not, then I'll say good-bye now."

"Then I think we'd better say good-bye," Tim said angrily.

18.

April 11　　　*7:15 P.M.*

Parr was awakened by a knock at the door. He pulled himself up, realizing that he must have fallen asleep. For a moment he was confused; did not remember where he was. Then he remembered the afternoon: the ride to Faraway, the rantings of Ferguson, the escort to the room. He looked at his watch, it was eight at night.

"Come in," he called.

Was it his imagination, or before the door swung open was the lock gently, quietly, released? Had he been locked in?

One of the uniformed young men entered. Parr shrunk back against the bed, now no longer sure what would happen. But the young man saluted and said, "The general sends his compliments, sir. Dinner will be in fifteen minutes."

Parr found his way downstairs. Every now and then he caught glimpses of a guard standing at a window or pacing across the lawn. He paused at the bottom of the long staircase. The front door was across the tiled floor, a dozen feet away. To the right, French doors led into the garden. Perhaps he could slip out, make a run for it.

"Sir, the general is at table. This way please." The same young man who had awakened him pointed down the galleried hall toward mahogany doors. Parr saw he had no choice.

"Amos, I hope you rested well," Ferguson said, rising from the table. "I am sorry I had to leave you, but urgent business, you know; things like that come up. Come, sit down." He indicated a chair at the end of the long table.

Parr sat down. The servant who stood behind his chair placed a plate of soup before him, and poured the wine. Ferguson nodded, and the servants quietly left the room.

"Well, Amos, it is nice to have you here. I so seldom see people these days who I feel, how shall I say, equal to. We should really renew our friendship. After all, we have so much in common, so many interests that are the same." He looked at Parr like a hawk watching its potential prey.

Parr decided to confront the general.

"Ferguson, why are you holding me here? Why was I locked in my room?"

"Holding you? Why Amos, how can you imagine that? We're old friends, and I am sure your room wasn't locked. Did you try to get out and couldn't?"

Parr had to admit he had not tried the door. Perhaps the sound of the lock was only his imagination.

Cooly changing the subject, Ferguson said, "My grandfather built this house. His father started the farm. We've all added to it over the years. Father to son, father to son."

Parr decided he would watch and wait to see where the night was tending. It was clear Ferguson was enjoying whatever game he was playing.

"And you," Parr said, deciding he too could fence. "Father to son as well?"

Ferguson looked darkly at him.

"My son, ah yes, my son. Perhaps not cut quite in the same pattern as others of us. Do you know him?"

Parr admitted he did not, and added with deliberate ambiguity, "Though I know of him."

"I see," Ferguson said with a trace of irritation.

"What I don't see," Parr decided to risk, "is just why I am

here tonight. I do have engagements in town. I will be missed." He hoped his threat was clear.

"Oh, Amos, please, don't worry yourself about that," Ferguson said. "I took the liberty of calling your butler to let him know you would be staying here for a few days."

"A few days! What do you mean? Otis, you can't do this."

"Amos, we are on Ferguson land now. You must realize we are far out in the country surrounded by several thousand acres of my very private home. I would think that you would welcome a chance to have a few days away from your busy life, your friends, your investigations into the doings—ah—of others."

"I don't know what you're implying, Otis."

"I'm not implying anything. We are, after all, two civilized men. Surely we can enjoy an evening of gossip and talk of old times."

Parr decided it was useless to protest. Ferguson had quietly made it clear there was no way to escape from Faraway. Parr decided it would be best to let Ferguson have his way, and to see the evening out.

The dinner continued, the servants coming and going, removing courses, bringing others. All the while Ferguson kept up a steady conversation, light, often witty, yet, Parr could not help feeling, laced with a kind of menace, a hint of unspoken subtext.

Parr decided the only way to deal with the situation was to take the offensive again.

"Otis, why am I here?" he asked directly.

"Comradeship, Amos, I've said that."

"Please, Otis, no games. We have never been, as you put it, comrades. We have never been friends. Bluntly, you owed me a favor, I collected on it. That has been the nature of our relationship. Now, you bring me here, and keep me here against my will. To what purpose? When I leave, this will not go unforgotten."

Ferguson looked at him without commenting, and Parr had the chilling feeling that perhaps Ferguson did not intend to let him leave.

Instead, Ferguson smiled and said, "Come, let's have some brandy in the library. Sit by the fire and talk about life. I'm an old man, Amos, I have few friends, few friends of my age who are understanding as I know you can be. Perhaps I have been rather peremptory, but that's the prerogative of command, you know. I forget sometimes that civilians don't always see things the way we do." He got up and led the way into the library.

"Leave us," he said to the servant who brought in the brandy. When they were alone, Ferguson poured each a brandy, and settled into a large wing chair by the fire.

"Now, Amos, I hope you feel a little less threatened. I'm a lonely old man. Retired from the world. I need someone to talk to. I am very disturbed these days, Amos, as I am sure you are, by the course things have taken in our country. Certain values have been lost, principles betrayed. Random violence stalks the streets. Why the horrible death of Douglas Haley is an example of this. A fine man, Haley, yet struck down by some vicious rabble, looking no doubt, for money to buy drugs or support a whore. That is the kind of thing I am talking about, Amos, the end of civilization is what it is."

"Yes, Haley's murder was a terrible thing," Parr said.

"Terrible, exactly the word," Ferguson went on. "Terror walks our streets, and does anyone do anything about it? No, our leaders, our so-called leaders, allow the permissiveness to continue. The moral decay is all around us, Amos. The rabble are given bread and circuses, and decent men are forced to cower in their homes, and even there they are not safe. What can we do? I'll tell you, we must have a strong leadership, a leader willing to take the reins of government out of the hands of the weak sisters and the do-gooders."

"I had thought our president was to be such a leader," Parr said. "I believe that you once thought so."

"I did think so, I am ashamed to say," Ferguson said, "but no, I was wrong. He is trapped by the system itself. It is the system that has to be changed, radical reevaluation, that's the answer. We must return to certain earlier values, to a time when our nation was ruled by an elite."

"And who are these elite?" Parr asked.

"Men like yourself, Amos. Like yourself. And your friends, Witter, Beverwyck, Haley. Strong men who agree with me that power is the answer. I know that you are powerful men, who have many ways of using your power. I suspect you are involved in some power play even now. Am I right? You know, Amos, we could all work together; you, your friends, and I. I have some resources too, it might surprise you to know just how great they are."

"I'm afraid, Otis, that you are romanticizing my relationship with Beverwyck and Witter. We have a number of business interests in common, which is not unusual. Certainly you and I have had some as well. But we are not really the kind of cabal that you seem to think." He wondered, as he was speaking, just what information Ferguson did in fact have.

"Perhaps so, perhaps not," Ferguson said, "but you do support Magnus Hopkenson."

"Yes, I think everyone knows that," Parr said.

"Would it surprise you if I said that I am leaning toward him as well?" Ferguson asked.

"I would have thought that Hopkenson was not exactly the kind of man you would admire, not exactly the leader you have in mind," Parr said.

"Leaders can be made," Ferguson said. "With the right advice, the right men behind them, certain pressures . . ." He paused, and looked keenly at Parr, as if waiting to see if he would respond. Parr kept silent.

"But ah, speculation, of course. I am sure that Magnus Hopkenson is his own man. Quite incorruptible."

"Yes, I am sure of that, too," Parr said.

"Decent man, no danger of . . ." Ferguson went on. He let the phrase hang in air, clearly waiting for Parr to finish it.

"Of what?" Parr said with deliberate innocence.

"Nothing at all," Ferguson said, obviously irritated. He got up. "If we are to get you back to Washington early, we had best retire. Good night." Abruptly he strode out of the room.

Parr was surprised at the sudden termination of the evening, as if Ferguson had either found out what he wanted or had given up the query for the time. What did Ferguson want? Was he seriously proposing an alliance between himself and Parr and his colleagues? To control Hopkenson? What did he know? The phrase "certain pressures" was ominous. And was Ferguson in fact going to let him go?

April 11   Midnight

He was jolted out of a deep sleep by someone roughly shaking him.

"Wake up, Amos," Ferguson's voice demanded. The light came on. Ferguson was in Parr's room, wearing battle dress. With him were two of his uniformed followers.

"Now Amos, we must talk."

"And must I answer?" Parr said coldly.

"Who is this Philip, and why did you send him to me?" Parr realized Ferguson was no longer playing games. The implicit menace of the interview was clear. He decided he would have to say something to satisfy the man, for the time being at least.

"Philip Kristopher is just what I told you, Otis. He is a private investigator working on a project for me and for my colleagues. That's it."

"Why Walter Bray?" Ferguson snapped.

"Because he is a link in the investigation. I don't know any more than that," Parr insisted truthfully.

"Are you sure I am not the subject of your snooping?" Ferguson said with venom. Parr realized paranoia was joined with his obsession.

"No, Otis, you are not. But you knew what Philip needed to know."

"You know, Amos," Ferguson said in a soft cold voice, "I do not believe a word that you have told me. I am sure you are involved in something very unsavory, something perhaps very dangerous. Is that so?"

Parr realized it was useless to answer, and shook his head.

Suddenly Ferguson leapt to the edge of the bed and pushed Parr back against the pillow, his hand at Parr's throat.

"Who wants to know if Magnus Hopkenson is one of us?" he spat. "Who wants to know?"

Parr tried to push Ferguson's hand away; the grip tightened around his throat. He gasped, "I don't know. I don't know." It flashed through his mind that this was, in fact, the truth.

Ferguson took away his hand, and stood up, staring angrily at Parr.

"I don't know what you're talking about," Parr said.

The two men looked at one another, glances cutting like swords.

"You'll talk eventually," he said.

Ferguson nodded to the uniformed men. The light was suddenly shut off. There was a terrible silence. Parr tensed, waiting. Then the door was opened. The two men left, leaving Ferguson silhouetted in the gray light from the hall. Ferguson said, "There's no middle ground, Amos. Either you're loyal to me, or you're a traitor." The door slammed, and without doubt this time, with solid finality, was locked.

19.

There's only one fact we have," Tim said. "That is that my father was at the Jennings rally. He had to have been. That's where he saw me, and that's why he called me."

"I think we have some other facts, too," Randy said. "If you're willing to look at them."

"You mean about Kristopher and his bosses?"

"Yes. That's what I mean."

"I've been thinking about that, too."

"Does it seem strange to you that your father was involved with these men all of whom seem to be gay?"

"Which means that my father, too . . ." Tim let the sentence hang.

"I don't know what it means about your father," Randy said. "But you may have to face that, too."

"Face it. I can face it. If my father was gay, then a lot begins to make sense, about him, about his separation from my mother. So many things would be clear. But, oh, Randy, why didn't he tell me? Why did he keep us apart all these years, why . . . ?"

Randy could see that Tim was getting increasingly upset.

"Tim, please, we don't know any of this for sure. We don't really *know* if Beverwyck and his crew are gay. We don't even know what they want or what they are doing in our lives, except they said they could help us."

"But they wouldn't trust us," Tim interjected.

"But don't you see, they have a lot of answers," Randy said. "One answer surely must be about your father." Randy continued. "Look at who these men are. Beverwyck: rich, a powerful businessman. Witter: head of a major network. Parr: wheeler-dealer in Washington. Your father: politician and power-broker. Power is the common denominator. They are men who can make things happen, who can control things. They are investigating something which apparently led to your father's murder. The murder is made to look like a robbery, but because of what they know, they are sure it is not. Men like that, Tim, have money and power and what they want is more of it. I'm sorry, I don't mean to say anything about your father, but you know he had a lot of influence, pulled a lot of strings. Now the most important strings right now are those connected with the presidency. Was your father close to the president, or to Hopkenson?"

"He knows—knew—them both. I met the president once, before he was president. He came to our summer place in New Hampshire. What are you getting at?"

"Honestly, I don't think I quite know. But something bothers me about all this. Tim, I'll be blunt, if your father was . . ."

"Say it, if my father was gay—it's okay, say it—God knows I wish I had known."

"If your father was gay, then is there any connection between his murder and Michael Ross? Is there anything involving Hopkenson in all of this? Maybe there's no connection, maybe there is."

"You can't think Hopkenson killed Ross?"

"No, I don't think that. I don't know what to think. All I know is Michael Ross's murder was covered up. Who had the clout to do it? Beverwyck, Witter, Parr and your father. If anyone could pull those strings, they could. The question is, why?"

"To protect Hopkenson, of course," Tim said.

"Sure, one reason. Murder isn't good for a campaign. But we know that Ross was gay. That's what is being covered up. They don't want Hopkenson connected with that either."

"For obvious reasons," Tim said.

"But maybe there's a less obvious reason," Randy said. "Don't you see: if they successfully hid the Ross thing, then they could stop. But they didn't stop. And now your father is dead. There's something else, and it has to do with Magnus Hopkenson."

"Do you think they're the ones who roughed me up for trying to find out about Ross? They could have connections like that. But would my own father . . . ?"

"No," Randy said. "It doesn't seem likely. I doubt if they knew about that. If they did, they would have come to us earlier. No, there is something going on here, and it seems there is a lot at stake. I think maybe that whoever attacked you also killed your father. I think that what's at stake is the career of Magnus Hopkenson, and we've become part of this, whether we like it or not."

"There's one thing I have to know," Tim said. "I have to find out just what my father had to do with the Reverend Billy Jennings."

April 12   10:00 A.M.

The next day, Tim called the offices of God's People in New York. He said that he wanted to see Reverend Jennings about a personal matter connected with the late Judge Douglas Haley.

"Could you wait just a minute please," the operator said.

He waited for some time. Then, suddenly, the voice he

had heard denouncing all he stood for was speaking over the phone.

"Mr. Haley, this is Reverend Jennings. I am so sorry about your father. Can I be of any help?"

"Yes, you can," Tim said. "I would like to see you, if I could. I thought perhaps you might be able to give me some advice about a bequest in my father's will."

"I would be more than happy to be of any aid to the son of such a fine man," Jennings said. "You come over here this afternoon."

"Do you think he knows who you are?" Randy said when Tim had hung up.

"How can he?" Tim said. "He may have seen me at the rally, but we've never met. No one knows me. I let him think I have some money for him."

April 12   3:00 P.M.

Tim arrived at Jennings' 84th Street office, a small townhouse tucked away between First and Second avenues. He was shown up to Jennings' office immediately.

"Well, Mr. Haley," Jennings said, "do come in. Let me say again what a loss your father's death is to us all. I know he was a God-fearing man, and it is a shame that such a dreadful thing could happen. But those are the times, are they not?"

Tim could see that Jennings was looking at him as if he knew him.

"I can't help feeling, Mr. Haley, that we have met."

"No, Reverend Jennings . . ."

"Please, call me Billy."

"No, I don't think we have. But I do believe that you had met my father. He was at your rally in Pennsylvania the night before he was killed. I want to know why he was there."

Jennings motioned Tim to a chair.

"Now that certainly is news to me, Tim. I would have been proud to meet your fine father, had I known that he was there. But I'm afraid he didn't make himself known to me."

"Mr. Jennings," Tim said, "my father was not, I have to tell you, a notably religious man. It seems to me unlikely that he would come to your rally to hear you. There had to have been another reason. Did he meet with Senator Rideau, your co-speaker?"

"No, I can assure you he did not. The good senator left by helicopter immediately after he finished his wonderful talk. Such an inspiration that man. I wish you could have heard him. But then, Tim, I'm sure your good father has instilled in you the same virtues we all believe in. I just thank the good Lord that I had a chance to preach to your dear father on his last night on earth. I hope it was a comfort to him, but as to seeing him, no, I didn't have the pleasure."

"This is a great mystery, Mr. Jennings," Tim said, not sure how to deal with Jennings' smooth denial, unsure, if it were not to see Jennings or Rideau, just why his father would have been there.

"Well, mysterious are the ways of the Lord," Jennings said, rising. "Now, Mr. Haley, I do have many appointments today."

"Oh," Tim said, "one thing before I go."

Jennings smiled, looked expectant, thinking perhaps that Tim would mention the bequest he had dangled over the phone.

"Yes, my boy, any help, just ask."

"I was at your rally that night, too."

"Well, then, you must know why your father was there, after all."

"No, I didn't know he was there. He must have seen me, because he called me and left a message. You see, Mr. Jennings, my father and I have been estranged for some years because of my beliefs."

"Ah, I see, I see," Jennings said, leaping to his own conclusion. "You too are born again, and your father can't accept it. So common these days. But a fine young man like you has to hold on to his faith in spite of everything, even when his beloved elders are opposed to him."

"Yes, Mr. Jennings, you're right." Tim said with a cold glint in his eye. "I do hold on to my faith. My lover does too. We held on to it at your rally while you denounced us. Gay and proud, Reverend, remember that? I was there, but I wasn't marching with you. My friends, my lover, all of us were there to uphold our own life against the bigotry that you preached, Reverend. I think now that my father might have marched with me. In fact, if it weren't for men like you, we might have marched arm in arm years before. But now it's too late. Someone killed him. And I'll never know."

Jennings stared at Tim, his eyes widening, his breath coming in short gasps. But when he spoke his voice was cold.

"So, young man, I did recognize you. My message is the same now as it was then. Give up your evil ways or you will be punished. Anyone who walks in the shadow of that evil will be punished. I warn you, Timothy Haley, your day of reckoning will come. Yes, now I know who you are. And I know who your so-called lover is too, that rabble-rouser Asher. Wherever I go, you people follow, interjecting your unwanted presence into my rallies, trying to mock the words of righteousness that the Lord has given me to say. But you won't win, you and your kind. I know that you are conspiring to support Magnus Hopkenson and pervert him with your poison. But you can't win, young man. We have power, and we will destroy you, do you know that? The Lord has commanded that the children of Sodom be cleansed by fire. That is my mission on this earth, and I will see it through."

Quietly Tim said, "Reverend Jennings, I never pray, because your God, according to you, won't hear my prayers.

But tonight I think I'll say a prayer for you, just in case someone is listening."

"I'll tell you who is listening," Jennings shrieked. "All the angels in heaven are listening, and they will call down damnation upon you. If your father was what you say, then he was punished rightly, just as you will be."

Tim went white with anger, and with difficulty suppressed a desire to smash his fist into Jennings' face. Controlling himself he said, "I won't forget that Jennings, and I can assure you that someday, sometime, I'll see to it that you won't forget it either."

When he got back to the apartment, he told Randy about his meeting with Jennings.

"The man is mad," he said, describing Jennings' rage. "And I'm sure he was lying about seeing my father."

"He had to have talked to him," Randy agreed. "There's no other reason why your father would have gone to the rally. You know where the answer to that is, don't you?"

"Yes," Tim said. "I do, and you're right, we have to contact Kristopher and the others. If they know that my father went to the Jennings rally, and why, then the fact that Jennings denies seeing him will be very important."

"Yes," Randy said, "and there's another reason. I think you found it today. Jennings himself. We can't fight him alone. And we know—you heard him say it—he's going to push forward his crusade against us, against gay people, and he's got more resources than Bryant and Falwell ever had. He can do it. And if he is courting Hopkenson, then he may be unstoppable."

"But men like Beverwyck and Witter may be able to stop him. Is that what you mean?"

"Yes," Randy said. "I think your father saw the danger. We have to convince these men that despite their power Jennings could be a danger to them, too. Men like Jennings can command the power of bigotry, which can destroy even the greatest men."

"Yes," Tim said. "We must contact them. Tell them what we know. But they have to trust us, too. It's got to be full disclosure on both sides."

"I think it will be," Randy said. "We know something they don't. I think they'll have to trust us now."

After Haley left, Billy Jennings sat at his desk, clenching and unclenching his hands. How he hated them, all of them, perverts, degenerates, every one of them. But he realized he had to pull himself together. He picked up the phone, dialed, waited.

"It's Jennings," he said. "Listen, young Haley was just here. He asked if I had talked with his father. No, of course I denied seeing him. But I don't think he believed me. I'm afraid I got . . . carried away. No, no, I didn't *tell* him anything. I don't *know* what to do about it. No, now you wait. I don't want to hear about that. I wash my hands of the whole thing. I'm not responsible. Remember, I wasn't anywhere near Boston when he died. All right, I'll calm down. What do you want to know? Who? His name is Asher. Randy Asher. No, I don't know where they live, the boy just threw it in my face that they were—lovers. Yes, right, Randy Asher is his name."

20.

I want everything—anything on every name on this list: news reports, credit checks, gossip, anything you can dig up."

Walter Bray handed copies of the list to the seven members of his full-time research staff. That was three days ago. Now, in front of him on his desk there was a stack of files, some thin, others bulging. Whether out of all this would come answers, he didn't know. But he hoped so, because so far he had found no answers himself.

The continuing investigation of Hopkenson, the original purpose of it all, had turned up nothing concrete. Smith wanted to know if Hopkenson could be connected with any sexual impropriety. The answer so far was no. There were no scandals, as far as could be discovered, in Hopkenson's seemingly impeccable life.

But the life, as it turned out, was not the central issue. The investigation itself had turned ugly. Digging had not turned up a skeleton, but it had found several bodies, and Bray wanted to know why such violence had been engendered by such a seemingly pointless search. Furthermore, it seemed he was not the only one looking. Someone else was on the trail of the Hopkenson secret, if there was one, and whoever it was now seemed determined to prevent Bray from completing his investigation. If there was nothing to hide, why had so much blood been shed, the blood of Monte Dillon, and, as he knew now, of Aleister St. Pierre?

What had started out as a relatively simple job for a client in search of questionable information had become a complicated dance of murder and intrigue: the investigator was investigated, the client became a suspect, the object of the investigation was perhaps in danger himself. For all these reasons Bray had now begun his own search. He wanted to know who Smith's employer was, he wanted to know who was on his own trail, he wanted to find, and stop, the killer.

In the stack of files on his desk, he hoped to find some clues, some hints as to how he might do all these things.

The first file was small. In it was a sheet on Aleister St. Pierre; the few facts on his life, background information, and the photos. They were not pleasant photos, but Bray looked at them coldly. They showed St. Pierre, or what could be identified of him. His body was twisted strangely, there was little left of his face, his hands were crushed. The body had been found five days ago in the weeds by a small stream. It had lain unidentified and unclaimed in the Washington morgue until, as part of the blitz of investigation that Bray had set in motion, George Ferrall had followed through and made a positive identification from the remainder of a fingerprint. So much for Aleister St. Pierre.

He had gone to St. Pierre to find Hugh Tilden, and to find out if St. Pierre could provide anything that might touch on Hopkenson. Apparently St. Pierre had something, and was killed for it. Perhaps it was his knowledge of Tilden himself. Of Tilden, there seemed to be no trace, His file was small, too. After his arrest, he disappeared. But what was interesting was that item by item, his life was being obliterated, too. Bray did not immediately realize the significance of the information in the file until he saw that as the years went on, there was less and less to know about Tilden. His life was sparse enough: college, a teaching job, volunteer with Hopkenson, then a job in the State Department, then his arrest. Then after that he left the city. A trace or two in San Francisco. A small FBI file. Bray had ways of getting that. But the file was closed a few years ago. Nothing in it for the last seven years. Bray had had some strings pulled at IRS. Tax returns were procured. San Francisco address. An address in Denver. Then, nothing, no returns. Driver's license allowed to lapse. Last known bank account in San Francisco. Bank loans: one. Paid up. No recollection of anyone like him. Hugh Tilden had simply disappeared out of the world. Denver police: no record of any missing persons. No death reported. Bray had hospitals checked for the last seven years. San Francisco police, California, Colorado. He called upon the vast network of information and less than legal sources he had put together in his many years at work. If there was a Hugh Tilden, dead or alive, some trace would be found. But no trace was found, dead or alive.

The next file bulked large. It was thick, and cross-referenced. Magnus Hopkenson's file—Hopkenson, the cause, yet seemingly innocent object of this web of violence. Bray had asked his staff to put together a digest of Hopkenson's movements for the last two months, and a compilation of every news and magazine item connected with him. Underline any name that crops up connected with Hopkenson, he had ordered. I want to know where he's been and who he has seen.

Hopkenson had travelled extensively in the last months: a trip to Germany to discuss options with the EEC ministers; campaign trips across the States; two weeks in Washington at hearings for the environmental secretary's appointment; day-trips to Idaho, Wisconsin, and Vermont; meetings with Senate leaders; breakfast at the White House; conferences with key governors. His schedule was hectic and crammed.

The newspapers were full of Hopkenson.

Senator Hopkenson condemns President's position on the Arab Question.

Hopkenson says it is Only a Matter of Time until Farm Prices will be a "Disaster Area."

Hopkenson Denies White House Allegations that he would Raise Taxes.

Bray ran his eye down the list of headlines, a recital of the name calling, innuendo, and political maneuvering that characterized the preparations for the presidential campaign. It was clear that Hopkenson and the president were squaring off to begin the battle in earnest.

Bray ran his eye down the list of stories, the excerpts from articles the staff thought valuable.

"Senator Magnus Hopkenson insisted today that he was the candidate of no one faction. He hoped to be able to lead his party to victory in November, he said, without relying on any special interest group. Was it true that he was seeking the support of Billy Jennings? Hopkenson said he respected Mr. Jennings, but believed that religion and politics were subjects which the Constitution adequately addressed."

"Neat avoidance," Bray thought.

"Magnus Hopkenson, interviewed outside the Senate chamber, insisted that the president would have to 'pull a rabbit out of the hat' in order to save his farm bill."

"It cannot be doubted," The *Times* editorial said, "that Magnus Hopkenson has the integrity and the talent to lead us now. The present failure of government—for that is what it must be called—under the current administration can only be laid at the doorstep of the president himself."

Unless of course, Bray thought, someone finds out that Magnus Hopkenson has a shady past, and uses that information. Even the *Times* couldn't save him then.

His eye was caught by another story.

"When asked if he thought the death would be detrimental to Hopkenson's campaign effort in the state, Larry

Farnsworth, the New York campaign manager, responded, 'We're all pretty broken up about Michael's passing, but we'll go on just the same. No, Michael was a good man and a valuable asset, but we've already gotten someone at work where he left off.'"

Walter Bray looked back at the story. At the head of it, one of his staffers had written in red: "Michael Ross. Sudden death. Hopkenson NYC campaign. Heart attack."

Bray leafed through the Hopkenson file to the other cross-referenced files. Nothing on Michael Ross. He wanted everything. He punched his intercom button.

"Alice, this Hopkenson file. See who was researching it and pull everything on a Michael Ross mentioned in it. As soon as you can."

The most recent story in the file was a filler from the *Washington Post*. The headline read:

"Douglas Haley Buried in Boston." Underlined was the pertinent fact: "Magnus Hopkenson, though unable to be present, sent condolences to the family, saying that Douglas Haley was one of the nation's most learned and respected men of law. 'He will be sorely missed, for men like him are sorely needed,' Hopkenson said."

Haley. Yes, Bray recalled. Judge Douglas Haley. Found dead in his Boston home. Murdered. He had seen the story. Haley was an important behind-the-scenes man. One of the party kingmakers. Quiet, not much known to the public, but very influential. Bray remembered that the Boston police had tagged the murder as a robbery attempt. He had thought nothing of it at the time. But now, he decided it would be worth a little extra effort. He wasn't sure just why. But Haley certainly knew Hopkenson. Haley knew everyone. Was there some reason why Hopkenson wasn't at the funeral? He checked the dates. The funeral was last week, Wednesday. Hopkenson was in—Idaho. Perhaps a legitimate reason. He looked to see if the staff had cross-referenced Haley. Yes, they had. A thin file again. Nothing in it connecting him with Hopkenson for the last two months. A photo showing him with Hopkenson two years ago, shaking hands at some party function. The only recent item was the obituary and news report of the funeral from the *Boston Globe*. He scanned the item.

"The service was conducted by the Rt. Reverend Sandford Winthrop, Episcopal Bishop of Boston. The eulogy was delivered by Ambassador Franklin Adams Morton, a close friend of the Haley family, and the lessons were read by Senator Marion Pierce of Massachusetts and the Mayor of Boston. The large congregation heard the ambassador describe Haley as 'one of the major figures of American jurisprudence, and one of those men whose loss will forever be keenly felt.' Among the mourners were Secretary Everett Keene as representative of the president; Arthur, Cardinal Hayes; the President of Harvard, Dr. Simpson; and many local, national and international figures, among them Baron Wedekind-Brunspach; Nelson Beverwyck, head of Beverwyck International; Elizabeth Simpson Harding; Lady Shawcross; the Chief Justice and Justices Hardy, Marston and FitzGerald; Charles Witter, of Communications ITV; Leonard Rothstein; Weyland Clarke of the Metropolitan Museum; Dr. Amos Parr of Washington, D.C.; Frederick Corcoran of the Corcoran Trust, and Robert Anderson, junior senator from Massachusetts. The mourners were led by Haley's wife, the former Anna Peabody Milligan, and his only son, Timothy Milligan Haley. The burial was private."

Bray had to read the item again before the connection leapt out of the thicket of names: Dr. Amos Parr. But no, that was not unusual. Haley clearly knew everyone in Washington as well as across the nation. Parr was an important man. Parr was one of the people he had interviewed in the course of his investigation. He was a schoolmate of Hopkenson. Bray decided to file the information away for the time being, but to check out Parr more thoroughly. He pressed the intercom again.

"Alice, the obit on Douglas Haley. Check out every name mentioned on it. See who is connected with whom. Find out if there are any other connections between Parr and Haley than just the usual men-in-high-places acquaintance. Anything yet on Ross?"

"No," Alice Copley's voice came back, "nothing yet. Give me another hour."

Bray turned back to the files. On a yellow legal pad he drew several lines into columns. At the top he wrote *St. Pierre*. In that column there was one word: *dead*. In another he wrote *Tilden*. In that one there was a question mark. Another column was headed by the name *Ross*. That was left blank. The fourth had *Parr* written in large letters at the top. In that column he scribbled *Haley*, *Hopkenson*, *Tilden*. The intercom buzzed insistently.

"Yes," he said.

"Mr. Bray," the receptionist's voice responded, "I have a call from Senator Rideau."

"From his office?"

"No, the senator is on the line personally."

"Put him on."

"Hello, Mr. Bray, this is Senator Louis Rideau."

Bray wondered why Rideau would be calling him.

"You recall, Mr. Bray, that we had a chat some time ago, about, oh, various things. I wonder if I might drop by and see you, for another chat."

"Well, of course, Senator." Bray was surprised. Senators didn't usually call; it was the other way around.

"I happen to be in your neighborhood," Rideau said. "I could be there in half an hour."

Very strange, Bray thought, remembering what a difficult time he had seeing Rideau the last time, and how uncommunicative and in fact unhelpful the senator had been. He said, "I'd be glad to see you, Senator."

"Good to see you again," Rideau said, extending his hand. Rideau came expansively into the room. His presence was powerful. Bray pointed to a chair, which the senator took with a proprietary air. Bray somehow felt as if the office had become Rideau's. The senator's gray hair was brushed back, his eyes, gray also, looked sharply at Bray.

"How can I help you, Senator?" Bray said, retreating behind his desk.

"I'll be brief. I learned you are a good, no in fact, an excellent investigator. I must admit, when you interviewed me about the Stark Commission, I didn't realize what you were, but that is only a tribute to your skill, isn't it?"

Yes, Bray thought to himself, he hoped it was. When he had last seen Rideau, he had used the Stark Commission, on which Rideau and Hopkenson had both served, as a pretense for trying to find out something about Hopkenson. Rideau was clever, and noncommittal, and Bray had learned nothing from him he had not already known. He had obliquely raised the subject of homosexuality, but Rideau had parried with bland disclaimers, and Bray had not felt it would be wise to pursue it.

Rideau was continuing. "Yes, but skill is what you must have in a sensitive job like yours; skill, and discretion."

Bray nodded, saying nothing.

"Mr. Bray, I have a task which requires skill and discretion."

He waited for Bray to respond. When Bray did not, he went on. "I wonder if I might be able to employ you—exclusively—to pursue it?"

"I guess," Bray said, "that depends on what the job is."

"Well, Mr. Bray, it's not anything I could really discuss unless I knew that you would be able to handle it. Sensitive issue, national security sort of thing."

"I really don't take on a job, sight unseen, Senator," Bray parried.

"I could probably double your normal fee," Rideau said.

Bray decided to spin the game out.

"Why don't you let me sleep on this Senator and I'll—no, you get back to me tomorrow."

Rideau sat for a moment as if he had more to say. Then, "Thank you for your time, Mr. Bray."

Bray held the door, the senator left. He wasn't exactly happy, Bray thought.

Alice Copley was standing outside the office as the senator left. Rideau brushed by her.

"Here's the Ross information," she said, handing Bray a file. He took the file and went back into his office, bothered by Rideau's visit. Why would Rideau come to him? He can find anything he needs to know. He's got a staff and access to the FBI and CIA if he needs it. There had to be a catch. And then the offer of money. Double the fee. Then Bray had the catch. Rideau wanted to find out if Bray's firm was engaged in anything that might preclude Bray from giving the senator his "exclusive" services. "Exclusively" was the key word. Rideau was angling to find out if Bray could be hired, exclusively. If Bray had said no, then Rideau would know that Bray was working on something else. Was it Hopkenson that Rideau also wanted to investigate? But why would Rideau want to investigate Hopkenson? If anyone knew the intimate details of Hopkenson's past, it was the man who was his political mentor and associate. No, Bray decided. It didn't make sense. Rideau was angling for something, but he wasn't sure what. But one thing, at least, was clear. Rideau couldn't be Smith's employer. There was someone else out there whose identity was still hidden behind the mask of the mysterious Mr. Smith. But now Bray wondered if Rideau might have hired the other investigator, a man behind another mask, whose path kept crossing, and recrossing his.

Bray took up the sheet that Alice Copley had given him on Michael Ross. He read:

"Michael Ross. Born December 17, 1942. Ogdensburg, New York. College at Lawrence University. Yale Law, ending up in NYC with Horner, Barton Fields in PR work. Three years there. Lived in four apartments in New York, all in the Village area. Changed jobs twice. Good credit risk. No police record. Volunteer worker with Village Independent Democrats for Abzug, later for Koch. Worked as a paid staffer for the governor's New York office, later went on to party headquarters in the city and then into media and PR for Hopkenson campaign. Lived alone. Died suddenly, apparent heart attack. Survived by a sister in Ogdensburg. No information on associates, friends. Seemed to be a workaholic who kept pretty much to himself. New York source says he was well liked by colleagues at headquarters. No information about private life, though possibly gay. Sports: tennis and jogging; member of New York Athletic Club."

Bray stared at the report, then picked up the phone. He consulted his Roladex and dialed a number.

"Jim," he said. "This is Walter. Check something out for me, will you. Do you have something on a Michael Ross? Get back to me."

He hung up and impatiently drew diagrams on the legal pad in front of him. Michael Ross, he wrote, over and over again. The intercom buzzed.

"Yes."

"Mr. Bray. About Amos Parr."

"Yes?"

"He and Haley go back a long way. Old cronies. Same political club, lots of social contacts in common."

"How about others on that list?"

"They both seem to know Lady Shawcross, the Cardinal, Nelson Beverwyck, Frederick Corcoran, and Leonard Rothstein."

"Thanks, Alice."

He looked at the list of names. He crossed out Shawcross. Next went the Cardinal. Rothstein followed. Two remained, Nelson Beverwyck and Frederick Corcoran. Beverwyck of Beverwyck International and Corcoran, head of the multinational Corcoran Trust. Both rich and powerful men. Now he had to look into these lives as well.

His phone rang.

"Yes? Ah, Jim. What did you find?"

Jim Cavanaugh, his contact inside the New York Police Department, and an old friend of Bray's, simply said, "Nothing, Walter."

"Nothing? The guy's dead. You know that?"

"Yes. I know that. But I can't get at the records."

"What do you mean, can't?"

"There is a file, but it's been sealed and I can't get it. Someone doesn't want that file to be seen. In fact, it may not even exist. All there is is a reference to it. The file itself is gone, taken to the chief's confidential section. No access."

"Thanks, Jim."

Walter hung up. Michael Ross. A jogger and tennis player. In apparent good health. Dead. No records. No access. Something wasn't right about that.

He buzzed the intercom again.

"Alice, did you dig up anymore about Ross?"

"No, Mr. Bray, there just wasn't much to dig up. Even the news report of his death was just a filler in the *Post*. Only three, four lines. There's just nothing there."

Bray scratched his head. Just nothing there. A sealed file. There was nothing there about Hopkenson either, yet two people were dead. He wondered if maybe the toll had just risen to three. And he wondered if Michael Ross hadn't, in fact, been the first.

21.

The next day at Faraway Parr was pulled out of bed before the morning light by one of Ferguson's men. He was not gentle.

"Good morning, Amos," Ferguson said. "We're going into the field today. I want you to see what discipline can do." Without breakfast, Parr was hurried out of the house. A small convoy of jeeps waited outside, engines running. Ferguson, still in battle fatigues, returned the salute of the driver and the other men in combat uniform standing by the jeeps.

"Help our guest in," he barked. He leapt into another jeep and the convoy sped away down the dirt road. Through fields and into deep woods they drove. As they passed, Parr could see men drilling. They passed what appeared to be a barracks. In one field there were five armored tanks lined up, another parking area held more jeeps and larger convoy trucks.

Jolting in the jeep, his guard pressed in next to him, Parr could hardly believe what he saw. *He has an army here*, he realized. *His own private army*. They drove for another twenty minutes, deeper into the hills in back of the estate. Finally they came to a deep bowl-shaped area, where Parr saw what must be the main detachment of Ferguson's army. There must have been nearly a thousand men, standing in formation.

They snapped to attention as Ferguson's jeep drove onto the field. He jumped out.

"Present arms," a sergeant commanded. With a clash the troup of men gave him a salute. Ferguson walked with the sergeant up and down the ranks of men, a general on parade.

He's mad, Parr thought, *mad and dangerous*.

After the review was over, Ferguson signaled the jeep to drive to a group of buildings lying near the edge of the field. The jeep stopped and Parr was told to get out.

"So, Amos, you see. Power. You thought I was not serious when I said I have resources. This is only a small part of it. Come with me."

He led Parr into the barracks. The room was bare, save for an army cot, a small desk and a chair.

"Now, Amos. You've seen that I am quite serious. Sit on the bed." Ferguson continued to stand, looking down at Parr who had nearly fallen onto the low cot. Ferguson began pacing back and forth, describing the line from window to door.

Parr felt himself seized with despair. The man was clearly insane. How could he get out? Who would help him? But he knew he mustn't give in to those feelings. Instead, he got to his feet.

"Ferguson, you know you can't get away with holding me here. I have friends. I will be missed. My butler knows I am here. If I do not return, he will see to it that I am traced."

"Then, Amos, we will have to discipline him," Ferguson snapped, not breaking his stride. "And we may have to discipline you as well. Sit down." He thundered. "Now Amos, I have been gentle, until now. But the time for that is past. You have a choice, Amos, you are either for what we believe, or against it. You are loyal to me or you are not."

Parr realized that to argue with Ferguson in his present state was impossible.

"I have nothing to say."

"Nothing? Well, then, let me tell you something, dear Amos. I know what you're doing. You think I don't. You think I have been deceived by your young Philip Kristopher, by your secret machinations. Well, I know exactly what is going on. I know about you, about your friends. And I know about Magnus Hopkenson."

Parr started to speak, but restrained himself. Ferguson caught the gesture.

"That surprises you, eh? Don't let it. I have my sources too, you know. After all, I did run intelligence for this nation once."

Parr decided that no matter what the cost, he had to find out what Ferguson knew. Summoning his strength he said with as firm a tone as possible, "Just what do you know Ferguson?"

"What I know is that you and your friends are trying to stir up trouble. You have been nosing into Hopkenson's life, prying into mine, digging up things that ought to remain buried. Well, you see what it has cost."

Parr, enraged now, cried out, "Hopkenson won't put up with a man like you. Once he finds out what you are, he'll repudiate you, he won't be party to this kind of thing. You represent everything he despises, everything he has fought against."

"But, Amos," Ferguson said, his tone cold, "he doesn't know that does he? He doesn't know about all of this. Few do, few will, until the right time. When that time comes we can march to victory over the bodies of the mongrelized rabble. And once we've won, even Hopkenson will come around to our way of thinking. But until then, Magnus Hopkenson will serve a very useful purpose. Don't you see that Amos? If he steps out of line, we will know how to handle him. That's why we need you and your friends, Amos. You can be part of this. Surely you want to see things as they should be, not the way they have become. Oh, I know who you are, and *what* you are. Oh yes, I know that too. But I can ignore it. It can be quelled in a man. It can be repressed and hidden. It takes sacrifice and discipline, but such a thing does not have to be master of real men. I know that. I am proof of that Amos. Join me Amos. Convince the others. You can help bring Hopkenson to victory, and through him, our cause can triumph. Then, once we've won, we won't need Hopkenson anymore."

Parr felt his stomach knot into sick nausea, but he forced himself to say, levelly, as coldly as he could, using anger and fear to give him strength, "I will never willingly march by your side, Ferguson. I despise you and everything you stand for."

Ferguson stared at Parr with a cold, curious stare.

"I see," he quietly said.

He walked to the door."

"Guard," he barked.

The guard entered. "Sir."

"Arrest this man. Imprison him, and tomorrow, when you have my order, execute him for treason."

22.

Bray had been standing in front of Amos Parr's house for over an hour. There was no sign of life. No one had come in, or gone out. That morning, after Rideau had visited him, after he had puzzled over the Ross information, he checked out other friends of Haley. None of them, save one, had any long connection with Haley and Parr. That one was Nelson Beverwyck. Their names appeared on the lists of several charities. They served jointly on the boards of several major corporations. They sponsored the same museums. It was not at all uncommon, Bray knew, for wealthy men to be connected in that way, and yet not be close. But far too often he would come upon the names of Parr, Beverwyck and Haley in association. Also, cropping up was the name of Charles Witter, a New York executive. Then he had it. The sealed file. If Michael Ross died from natural causes, there would be no file at all. The police kept no files, no records unless a crime had been committed. Not only was the Michael Ross death not natural, but someone was trying to hide it. A loner, Bray thought. Possibly gay. Gay and dead. Gay and murdered? Hopkenson and Ross. Could that be what he was looking for? But wait. What was he looking at? He was looking at the possibility that a member of Hopkenson's staff had been murdered. Because he was gay? Or because he knew something about Hopkenson? And someone, someone with a lot of clout, with influence enough to seal a police file and choke off the news had changed the story entirely, changed it so much that apparently Ross's own co-workers did not suspect that anything had happened.

This was another twist, and a nasty one. Only Magnus Hopkenson would be damaged by something like that, Bray realized. And only someone like Magnus Hopkenson had the power to make such things disappear. Maybe there was nothing in Hopkenson's past that could be found. But Bray wondered if there might be something even more damaging in the present.

Was Hopkenson also connected with Haley? Was Haley's death connected with Hopkenson? Questions? But about Haley and the others, he did have some answers.

What had excited Bray most about these men was that save for Haley, they all seemed to have in common the fact that they were, as the columns sometimes put it, eligible bachelors, and Haley had been separated from his wife for ten years. Parr however, was well into his seventies, Beverwyck sixty-three, and Witter forty-five. These men, all of them highly placed, also seemed to be placed in that group of wealthy and influential men whose single lives were in fact a mask for a different kind of preference. Bray wondered if he was right. A group of powerful gay men, closeted, behind the scenes. If it was so, certain things began to fall into place. If Magnus Hopkenson had a gay past, then these men might want to know it. They could be Smith's employers, or they could be behind the other investigator. But what would they do with this information if they had it? Use it against Hopkenson. Blackmail him with it? It didn't seem likely. They all had reputations for high-minded dealings. Though there was nothing to connect them in the public eye, Bray had discovered that they had made contributions to the Hopkenson campaign separately, and as a group.

He wondered if Rideau was part of the group. As he put the pieces together in his office that morning, he referred to his yellow pad. The columns had begun to fill up with notes. There were fewer questions marks. Under Ross he had scribbled: *Murdered? Cover up?* Under Hopkenson there were many question marks. He had written *Gay? Killed Ross to keep him quiet?* Later he put down under Ross: *Murder could be hidden by someone like Hopkenson.* He drew columns for Beverwyck, Witter, Parr and Haley. He made entries under each of them, indicating their place in life, the kinds of power they might wield. Then, like a light going on, it came to him: *Someone* like *Magnus Hopkenson.* No, not Magnus Hopkenson, but someone with his kind of power, in fact with more than his kind of power. He was suddenly sure that the Michael Ross death had been covered up by people who could change the news, people like Douglas Haley, like Charles Witter, like Nelson Beverwyck. The question was, were they covering up their own tracks? Did they hide Ross's death as well as commit his murder?

He had to know for sure if what he theorized was true. There was a chance that the connections he had found among these men were in fact only the chance connections that business might create. Could there be more? Haley was dead. Beverwyck and Witter were in New York. Amos Parr was in Washington. Go see him. But, not him, Bray realized. Go to where he lives. See what can be found out there.

Dusk came slowly, but there were no lights in Parr's house. Bray slipped down the street, and into the garden entrance. At the back of the house he disarmed the alarm and easily opened a side door. He reflected that no house was safe from someone who knew how to get in. He came in through the kitchen. A flight of stairs led upward. He followed it and came out in the central hallway, lined with pictures, heavily carpeted, and quite dark. Off the hall to one side was a dining room. Another door led to great double parlors. Near the end of the hall a third door led into a library. Here was where he might find what he was looking for. The fading light gave him enough to see.

Photographs covered the piano: Parr with numbers of people, some famous, other familiar. The desk stood near the French doors. Bray rifled through the drawers. Various files, notebooks, appointment books. There it was, an address book. In it were the names he was looking for, but with a host of others. Not enough, he decided.

He needed something more telling than that. He looked at the photographs. Too many. His hand reached up to the bookshelf. Many volumes, hundreds. He opened them, one by one. Each one had a bookplate: Amos Parr. Some had been signed by the authors. Bray picked up book after book. No clue here either. He pulled out one more, inside it said: "To Amos, fond memories, Ann." He took out the one next to it: "For Amos, after many years, Leverett Saltonstall." A third: "Lyrics from the heart, Amos dear, Noel." Bray began to pull out the books in the shelf. Each one was inscribed to Parr. From many people, known and unknown. He checked a book from the next section of the bookcase. This was not inscribed. There were five shelves. He chose books from each corner, top and bottom. All inscribed. These were books given to Parr, he realized. One after another, he took the books down, looking at each. At last, one: "To Amos on a happy day, Nelson Beverwyck." Good, Bray said, but not enough. One book, still another. From Roosevelt, from Cardinal Spellman, from Lord Romsey. Halfway down, third shelf, he pulled out a leatherbound book. Its title was *The Intersexes*, written by Xavier Mayne. Inside, written on the flyleaf it said: "To our dear friend Amos. We know how rare this is, but then, so are you. Love, Nelson, Charles and Douglas. Many more happy days and years."

Slowly, Bray put all the books back on the shelf.

Turning, he walked out of the silent house, treasuring what he had found.

Upstairs, Leon, sprawled across his master's bed, vaguely heard the sounds from below. But he could do nothing about them, neither call, nor raise an alarm. He knew he should try to find out who was intruding in his master's house, but everything seemed vague and dark. His face was pressed into the heavy quilt which now was wet with blood. Leon wanted to call out, but his life, weakly pulsing now, was slipping away, disappearing into a void. As the sounds died away, the quilt, made by Amos Parr's grandmother for her son, received the last of Leon's blood, and softly comforted his final passage.

23.

April 12   Midnight

Randy threw an arm over Tim's shoulders, and snuggled closer to him. He had been lying awake, it seemed for hours. His mind was filled with disturbing images, questions half-formed, threatening and anxious feelings that made no rational sense, but kept him from sleep. He turned one way, then another, trying to find a position which would allow him to settle at last into sleep. The dial of the clock next to his bed shone. It was midnight.

Finally, he could not stand it any more and gently shook his lover.

"Tim, wake up."

Tim, always a heavy sleeper, took some time and a few more shakes to drift up out of sleep.

"What is it?" he said, half sitting up. More awake, he said, "Ah, can't sleep. Want to talk?"

"Yeah, please."

Tim inched closer to Randy, putting his leg the length of Randy's, rubbing Randy lightly in the back of the neck.

"What's up?" he said.

"It's that Kristopher. All this bothers me."

"Yes," Tim said. "It bothers me, too. I'm sorry I was so difficult with him, but he made me mad."

"Yes, he was pretty secretive. That's what bothers me. What's the secret? And what does it have to do with us?"

"And with my father," Tim added.

"Look," Randy said, "I think we'd better get in touch with them. We know your father was at the Jennings rally. Maybe they don't know that. That's one thing we've got to tell them."

"And what's the other?"

"That I think I know what they are doing."

"What do you mean, what they are doing?"

"Try this. Your father is a member, apparently, of a group of very powerful men, who are concerned enough about something to hire an investigator to look into the problem. Your father gets killed because of it. Connected with this is Billy Jennings. Jennings is himself powerful, and the biggest and most vocal enemy gay people have these days. These men may be gay. Not only that, but—as you pointed out, and now I believe it—Michael Ross's death may have been murder, and if it was, it was covered up. Who could do such a thing? Men like these could do it. Why would they cover it up? Because Ross was gay. And who did he work for?"

Tim looked at him, fully awake now. "Magnus Hopkenson."

"Exactly. His murder, and his being gay, could be a serious problem for the Hopkenson campaign. Whoever killed Michael Ross was trying to sabotage Hopkenson. Beverwyck and your father heard about the death. They stopped the news. And so whoever killed Ross . . ."

". . . killed my father," Tim said grimly.

"I think that's how it is," Randy said gently, pulling Tim closer to him. "I think that's how it is."

Tim looked at Randy helplessly. "Hold me closer," he said, his voice shaken. Randy took his lover in his arms, and kissed him on the cheek, on the lips. The two melted into each other, drawing strength from their embrace. They touched each other, hands caressing, mouths hungrily meeting, as if, and it was always like this between them, as if it were the first time. They found solace in each other, a physical sign of the inward grace of their love, a passionate manifestation of the spiritual tie that bound them together.

"Come on, let's go into the other room, into the moonlight." The two arose, and walked, hand in hand into the living room. The moonlight dappled their young bodies, lean, hard, defined, hungering for one another. They stood pressed together, their desire growing, the urgency of their need pounding in their thighs. Randy pulled the large cushions off the sofa onto the floor. With the moonlight streaming through the window, washing their bodies in the pale ivory of the night, they found one another, took one another, drew love and hope and passion from one another, and each gave to each in return the strong and thrusting power of their love.

"Oh Tim, give it to me now," Randy panted, "give it to me." They turned, and sought the source of strength, caressing with tongue and lips, hands touching chests and thighs, moving with the fierce rhythm of passion until, with sighs and cries of abandon and pleasure, the floodgates opened together, and they proceeded up a high road of mutual delight.

The moon saw them lying now, hand in hand, looking happily into the pale light, tired, but the fear washed away, replaced by their mutual affirmation, comforted by their love.

Suddenly, there was a clatter on the fire escape and a crash from the other room. A shattering of glass, and then six repeated sounds, dull thuds, and then the clatter again on the fire escape, certainly someone running down. Then there was silence. The two lay there, shocked into full awareness. Tim jumped up and started to turn on the light. "Wait," Randy whispered. "Don't."

They listened. Still no sound.

"Come on."

They went quietly into the bedroom. The window opposite their bed was shattered. Glass lay on the floor. Tim edged to the window, and peered out. "Nothing," he said.

Randy turned on the light. Their bed was indeed covered with glass. The sheets and pillows were torn, penetrated by six rough holes.

"Oh my God," Randy said. "Those are bullet holes."

They stood staring dumbly.

"If we hadn't gotten up," Tim said.

Randy nodded.

"I think this has gotten too big for us," Tim said. "We'd better see Philip Kristopher."

April 13   *10 A.M.*

"It's Hopkenson, isn't it," said Randy.

"We're sure of it," Tim added.

The others in the room made no comment. Witter looked at Beverwyck, silently querying about the appropriate response. Philip stood, his back to the group seated at the conference table in Nelson Beverwyck's office. Instinctively he liked Asher and Haley, knew they could be valuable allies. He waited for Beverwyck or Witter to respond.

Early that morning Philip had gotten a call from Beverwyck.

"They've been in touch with me," Beverwyck said. "Last night someone tried to kill one or both of them. They said they want to talk. I've set up a meeting here, at 10:00 A.M."

"Mr. Asher," Beverwyck started to say, "I'm not really sure what . . ."

Philip decided to short circuit the whole thing. Turning, he walked back to the table, went to the head of it, assumed command.

"I think these men deserve better than they've gotten," he said.

"All right," Beverwyck said, after a pause. "You're right. Douglas Haley deserves better than we've given his son. The fact is, gentlemen, you have hit upon the object of this whole thing. It is Magnus Hopkenson."

Randy said: "It has to do with Michael Ross, doesn't it? He didn't have a heart attack, I'm sure of that."

"You're right about that, too," Witter said, "and I'm afraid, Tim, that what happened to your father is connected with this as well."

"You see, Tim," Beverwyck said gently, "your father, Charles, Amos Parr, and I, have been backing Magnus Hopkenson for election, as, we know, you have. Up until now, our support has been largely in the form of substantial financial contributions which we have ways to see are used for his benefit. Though some of us—your father and Amos Parr—were personally acquainted with Hopkenson, he did not know that we were so materially aiding him, nor in fact does he know, we believe no one knows, that we act as a group. That would have been the extent of it, had it not been for the death of Michael Ross. Philip here learned of the death—you're right—of the murder. We realized that it was imperative that this not become a potential threat to Hopkenson's campaign. We were able, successfully we had thought, to see to it that it did not. That would have been the end of it, had not it suddenly become clear that even with the Ross death hidden, the threat remained. You see, gentlemen, it appears—and I hope you will forgive me if I do not specify here why we know this, for I must out of loyalty protect *this* confidence—it appears that Magnus Hopkenson himself was—perhaps still is—not untouched. He has in the past, as we all have been . . ."

"Magnus Hopkenson is gay?" Randy said suddenly, explosively.

"Simply put, yes." Beverwyck said, slumping in his chair, clearly aware unsure whether he had done the right thing in sharing this information.

"And the threat?" Randy asked.

Beverwyck told them about the investigation into Hopkenson, and their efforts to find out who was behind it, and stop it if possible.

"Then whoever is doing this, if they find out anything, would have the potential to blow Hopkenson sky high," Randy said. "Why don't you think it's the White House?"

"It could be," Philip said. "But it could be anyone else as well. The facts are that Michael Ross's death effectively removed someone who might potentially have embarrassed Hopkenson."

Philip told them about his findings, about St. Pierre, about Walter Bray. "St. Pierre knew something, and he, I believe, is dead. Walter Bray is trying to find out if there is dirt to be found, and he's suffered losses, too. It's as if the killings are meant not so much to hinder Hopkenson as to help him. That's what we're up against. We don't know why, or who."

"And so," Randy said, "you've launched your own investigation into the investigator."

"And, at this point," Philip said, "into just about everyone else involved. That's why we initially got in touch with you."

"And you men," Tim said, almost in a whisper, "you're gay too, aren't you? Then my father . . ."

Beverwyck shifted uneasily. "Tim, I don't know what to say, I didn't mean . . ."

Tim said, "Please, it's all right, don't you see. It's all right that he is, that he was. It's just that I wish I had known, that he had told me, that's all."

"Your father was a fine man, Tim, and a dear friend. In

these last few days, I have bitterly mourned his loss. I know that he thought everything of you."

Tim got up and walked to the window looking out at the city spread below. The others silently watched him, knowing his grief was still with him. Finally, he turned and said, "I think we know something that might be important."

Tim told them about his father's mysterious attendance at the Jennings rally.

"He must have been trying to see Rideau," Philip said. "I wanted him to get in touch with the senator, to see what he could find out. I wonder if he did."

"Jennings claims my father wasn't there," Tim said, and detailed his visit to the evangelist. "He denied meeting with him."

"But why would Billy Jennings be involved?" Witter said. "He's supporting Hopkenson. For all the wrong reasons, I suspect, but supporting him just the same. Why would he kill Ross, or your father . . . ?"

"I think we're being hasty," Philip said. "There is no evidence that Jennings has done anything, and plenty that he hasn't."

"Wait a minute," Tim said. "After my father went to a Jennings rally, he was killed. After I went to see him, someone tried to kill us. That seems pretty heavy evidence to me. And there have been other things." He told them about the attack on him when he was trying to find out more about Michael Ross.

"All right," Philip said. "I agree that it is striking that these things happened after seeing Jennings. It may be coincidental, but for the time being let's presume it's not."

"What will we do?" Randy asked.

"I think we have to go on the offensive," Philip said. "The question in my mind now is what did your father find out from Jennings. Jennings claims he didn't meet your father. Perhaps he didn't. Perhaps your father managed to see Rideau as I had hoped, and without Jennings' knowledge. I think we all have some avenues to explore. I have work in Washington. I need someone to find out just what Jennings does know. It can't be either Tim or Randy, obviously. I think you two could help me in Washington. I'll introduce you to Amos Parr. We can work from that end. Charles and Nelson, you see what can be found out from—and about—Billy Jennings."

Philip moved away from the table, and paced into a patch of sunlight dappling the floor. Reflectively, he said, "I have no evidence that Billy Jennings has a single thing to do with what has been going on. As I've said before, the logical—and most unpleasant—explanation is that Magnus Hopkenson himself has been trying to cover up the past. He's got the most to lose. But that's not an explanation any of us would like to be true. For obvious reasons, we can't go to Hopkenson. The single basic rule of all of this is that Hopkenson cannot be told about the events swirling around him. If he is the cause of them, it's likely to panic him, or push him further. But if he is not, and we hope that he is not, then the effect could be just as disastrous."

"Yes," Beverwyck said. "Hopkenson could very well withdraw from the race if he felt that there was anything known by anyone that might compromise him. We mustn't have any direct dealings with him."

"What should we do then?" Witter asked.

"I want you to see Jennings. Get him here where he's not on his own ground. Then, rattle him. Let him know you think he is connected somehow with Haley's death. If necessary suggest you can do some harm, imply unfavorable media coverage. Nelson, get him where it hurts—money. Suggest you can cause some of his contributors to dry up with some pressure from you. It's a calculated risk but we have to take it," Philip continued. "If Jennings is not involved, then nothing will happen. I can concentrate on Bray. That's what I'll go to Washington to do. I think Tim and Randy can help.

But if, as you suspect, Jennings is connected with this, then we might see some action. We have to wave flag. It's a chance, just like the chance you take when you wave a red flag at a bull. You don't know where he will run, if he will attack or not."

"And if we don't get a response to our flag?" Randy asked.

"Then," Philip said, "we may have to wave it at Magnus Hopkenson."

24.

What a pleasure, Mr. Beverwyck," Billy Jennings said, striding into the room. "When I got your call last night, I said, now there's a man I admire and want to meet."

Nelson Beverwyck shook hands and said, "Reverend Jennings, this is Charles Witter."

"Charles Witter. Why certainly I know you by reputation."

Beverwyck studied Jennings, motioning him to a chair. Stocky, a shock of blond hair going gray, eyes bright with fervor. A quick smile, and yet a smugness about the mouth, an electric pulse that seemed to beat in his every movement. Beverwyck could see why the man was able to sway great audiences. Even in private, his presence was powerful. Even now he seemed to be on stage, a Bible in his hand. He was, Beverwyck could see, a formidable opponent.

"But," Jennings went on, "when you called, I asked myself why such a powerful man, such an important man, should want to meet me, just a country preacher. But I'm honored sir, honored."

Beverwyck crossed the room and stood behind his desk, a position of obvious power which never failed to impress. The tall windows behind him revealed the glittering vista of New York. On either side, the logo of Beverwyck International was emblazoned heraldically on the wall. The desk itself, a single slab of polished travertine marble resting on a chaste stainless-steel base presented an expanse of dark green, glowing between him and Jennings.

"I think we should get directly to the point of this discussion, Reverend Jennings."

"Why yes, Mr. Beverwyck, I know we are all busy men," Jennings said with a smile of complicity. "Now how can I be of service to you both?"

Beverwyck decided to be direct. "Judge Douglas Haley, a personal friend of mine and a business colleague, attended your rally. The next day, he was dead."

"Oh. Mr. Beverwyck. I didn't know you knew the judge. But what a shock that was for all of us. A great man, a truly great man, and I am sure a force for right and for what we all stand for."

Beverwyck was momentarily irritated at the way in which Jennings could turn every utterance into a stage cliche.

"Yes, he was that, Mr. Jennings. We hoped you might have information that could help explain this curious coincidence."

"You must admit," Witter broke in. "it is odd that Haley should. . ."

Jennings interrupted. "Why gentlemen, I hope you know that if I had information which would be of any use I would have already turned it over to the police. I respect the ways of the law, and no one more than I wants to see such a dreadful crime brought to justice. But I can't help you. Why, I had no idea the judge was even there. Though it is good to know that at his last hour, he heard . . ."

Beverwyck walked from behind the desk to where Jennings sat.

"Mr. Jennings, we are adults, and we needn't pretend. We are gravely concerned about the judge's death. We are willing to do *anything*"—he emphasized anything—"to find out why he was murdered. And we are able to do anything. I hope you understand."

"Mr. Beverwyck," Jennings said, rising, "I'm not unaware of the power you can bring to bear, but I must tell you that I know nothing of Judge Haley's death."

"I expect you know," Witter said, "that through my network, I have some connections with the radio and TV stations which broadcast, I believe you would say, your message?"

Jennings looked darkly at Witter. "I am aware Mr. Witter that certain of the good people who carry my word are affiliates of your network. Why do you tell me this?"

"Just to prepare you," Witter said enigmatically.

"The Lord prepares me," Jennings said, his voice rising. "I am not without resources myself."

"Resources *are* important," Beverwyck said quietly. "Did you know that my corporation is connected with the sports arena in Chicago where you plan to hold another rally next month?"

"Connected?" Jennings said.

"We own it."

Jennings paced toward the window, his shoulders hunched with anger. Then, "I see you seem to hold certain cards, Mr. Beverwyck. Since you also seem to insist on playing a game with them, I will tell you that my hand is not entirely empty either."

"Then play it," Witter said.

"Card number one," Jennings replied, walking toward the door. "I do know something about your Judge Haley. I have spoken to his son. And I suspect I know something about you as well, gentlemen."

"Just what do you think you know?" Beverwyck said.

"The Lord God has always given me strength," Jennings said, his voice rising into the inflections of a preacher, "the strength to bear witness to the truth and to search out sin and vice. That is my mission here. Now I know that you and your colleagues are members of that cult who would destroy the way of the Lord, who would bring the sin of Sodom into the homes of America. I know. . . ."

Beverwyck walked quickly over to Jennings. "Mr. Jennings, it is immaterial to us what you know. Didn't we make it clear just now? You only suppose certain things. We have facts. Let me lay it out. We can dry up your publicity, end your media time, cut your money in half, make it impossible for you to deliver this 'message' of yours. Imagine what you want about us, Jennings. It doesn't matter."

"I see we are at an impasse," Jennings said, his preacher's manner gone. "What do you want?"

Beverwyck smiled and walked toward the door. "Nothing now, Reverend Jennings. You've already told us what we need to know."

After Jennings left, Beverwyck and Witter discussed the meeting.

"He's dangerous, isn't he?" Witter said.

"I think so."

"Does he know about Hopkenson?"

"Hard to tell. He's playing those cards very close. But we did what we needed to do. If he's involved, then he's alerted. We've let the enemy know we're here. We've waved that red flag."

"I just hope," Witter said musingly, "that the flag didn't madden the bull beyond control."

April 15   10:00 P.M.

Bray pulled up next to the limousine. The chauffeur glanced at him, and raised his window; at the same moment, the rear seat window rolled down. Smith beckoned to Bray. Surprised, Bray got out of the car.

They were parked on a dirt road about twenty miles from Washington. As Bray walked toward the car, Smith raised a hand, indicating Bray had come close enough. Bray could just see the figure, masked as always, seated in the back of the car.

"What do you have for me?" Smith asked, without preamble or greeting.

Bray outlined what he had done since they last met, explaining that he had found nothing that could incriminate Hopkenson.

"But there are some disturbing facts," he said.

"Explain."

"A campaign aide of Hopkenson's, a Michael Ross, is a problem."

"Why? I understand he died."

"He did. But not naturally."

Smith sat forward in the seat. Bray saw that the news was disturbing. Even the chauffeur turned slightly, as if to hear better.

"How do you know this?"

"My sources," Bray said. He outlined his investigation of Ross's death, and the closed files.

"I think it was murder, and it was covered up."

"Who would do that?" Smith said.

"Someone who did the killing. Or someone who wanted to protect Hopkenson. I think it was the latter. Ross was gay. I'm sure of that. I think someone saw that he got killed to embarrass Hopkenson. Then someone else found out about it, and to protect Hopkenson, got it hushed up."

"Who could do that?"

"For one thing, Hopkenson himself could have arranged a cover-up. But I don't think he did."

"Why not?" Smith's tone was anxious, eager.

"Because I doubt if Hopkenson himself knows about it.

He was duped, just like everyone else. Someone with a lot of muscle in the right places was able to see to it that the murder was erased from the public record."

"Any theories on who this might be?" Smith said warily.

"Just theories," Bray said. "But good ones." He explained his investigation into the death of Haley and his connection of Haley with Nelson Beverwyck, Charles Witter and Amos Parr.

"I know who they are," Smith said.

"And," Bray said, "I think they are all homosexual. What seems to be coming out is that these men have formed a coalition, a cabal if you will. Their hand appears in other places as well. They could cover up the Ross murder. They've got the connections and the resources and the power."

"Could they be trying to find out something about Hopkenson's past?" Smith asked tensely.

"They could be," Bray said, "but I think they already know somethng."

"But if they were responsible for the cover-up," Smith said, "then they must be trying to protect Hopkenson."

"Perhaps not," Bray said. "They might just be trying to protect themselves. After all, if they did conceal the murder, that would be a very useful tool, at a later date, to bring pressure on Hopkenson."

"I see," Smith said thoughtfully. "All right, you'd better continue. Whatever you need to look into these men, I will supply. I suggest, if I may make a suggestion, that you start with Amos Parr."

"I know," Bray said. "He and Hopkenson were in college together. But there's one more thing. Something that might be useful. Another name."

"And that is?" Smith asked settling back into the seat.

"Hugh Tilden. He was connected with Hopkenson. He was, or is, homosexual. Now he's missing. He's been missing for years."

"He's probably dead," Smith said, exhaling sharply.

"No, I don't think so," Bray said. "He just seems to have disappeared. I think he's still alive."

Smith leaned forward again, the moonlight cut across the mask. "What do you know about this Tilden?"

"Practically nothing other than what I've told you. He seems to have been connected to St. Pierre, to have been caught in a vice raid, to have vanished. That's it."

"Then," Smith said, "what's the point of looking for him? He doesn't seem to be dangerous, not the way Beverwyck and the others may very well be. Not nearly so dangerous as whoever is out there doing the killing."

"You're right. But he might be able to incriminate Hopkenson. Then he is potentially dangerous."

Smith was silent for a long time. Then, "You don't think this Tilden is the murderer, do you?"

"No," Bray said, "I don't, but . . ."

"Then let's divide our labors," Smith said, sinking back again into the darkness, "you had best concentrate on the killer. Let me handle Hugh Tilden. Good night, Mr. Bray."

Smith signaled the chauffeur, and the limousine pulled away, leaving Bray standing in the darkness.

"Bastard," Bray said out loud.

25.

April 15   *1:00 P.M.*

The lunch crowd at the Blue Fox seemed to be the same crowd who drank there later, Philip noticed. He sat in the booth well back from the bar, waiting for Alice Copley. When he got to his hotel that morning, after flying to Washington from New York with Tim and Randy on the early plane, he found a message from Copley saying she wanted to see him at the "same place."

He arranged a room for Tim and Randy and the three men went up to unpack, agreeing to meet shortly for coffee to discuss what they had to do. From his room, Philip called Amos Parr. Cradling the phone on his shoulder, he jotted down notes and questions he wanted to answer; the ringing phone sounded an obligato to his thoughts. No answer. Strange, he thought, the butler should be there at least. He made a note to try Parr later that morning, before going to meet Copley. It was important to get in touch with Parr. There were several things Parr could do in Washington, some doors that could be opened by him, including, Philip knew, the door to Louis Rideau. The enigmatic senator clearly had a connection with Jennings and Philip wanted to find out what it was. He wondered if Witter and Beverwyck in New York had seen Jennings and made any progress. He had no luck reaching Parr. Randy and Tim had come to the room and

Philip gave them Parr's number, telling them to keep trying to call him.

The crowd at the bar of the Blue Fox was clearly getting into its third or fourth round of lunchtime drinks. Philip hoped Alice Copley would have something to tell him that would open a crack in the investigation. It was all so tissue thin, so illusory, Philip thought. Men died, and their killers became phantoms, their deaths were obliterated. Raw facts, the hard and cold fact of death itself, was hidden behind the trappings of power.

Philip traced the names of the players in the glistening water in the table top: Parr, Rideau, Haley, Beverwyck, Jennings, Witter, Hopkenson. Even about his employers he knew little, sensed only the resources that lay concealed behind the rich exteriors, the plush offices, the elegant house, the quiet and efficient secretaries, the manner they all seemed to share in common, a polite but distant geniality that never allowed him to get too close. How then breach the walls that protected Rideau or Jennings? How then break through into the layers of armor that surrounded the life of Magnus Hopkenson himself, a life that was seemingly free from blame, a life that had been orchestrated, planned, designed so no flaw would be seen, or could be found. Slowly, the names on the table began to dissolve. The moisture dried a little here, shifted there, became indistinct and blurred. That was the symbol of it all Philip thought; no definition, no sharpness, only a blurring and constant dissolution, as one thing dissolved into the other, and never an answer. That was the problem. Like names written in water, these men, the ones who employed him and the ones he was trying to define, were legends rather than real. They had public personalities, public definitions, images that had been created, yet they had private lives and private worlds which were impossible to define. Whenever he touched them, the public image would flow in, and the private life would dissolve. It was not just Magnus

Hopkenson he was trying to touch, Philip knew, it was a world of secret power, power which seemed so concrete in its effect, but which, when you tried to locate it on a map, disappeared like a cloud, like the slowly disappearing circles when a stone is thrown into a still pond. He glanced at the table top, the names he had traced were gone.

"Hi, got some time for me?"

Philip glanced up. Alice Copley stood by the table.

"Anytime," he said, smiling.

"Let's start with a Scotch," she said.

Philip went to the bar and ordered a Scotch. He realized that Alice Copley was going to expect more than Scotch from the meeting. He remembered the sadness in her eyes when they last met. He remembered the small apartment, and her husband, silently waiting for her every day, every day of her life. He remembered the intimacy and the question in her glance, the almost desperate touch when she held his hand for a moment at parting. He took the Scotch back to the table, wondering how he was going to avoid hurting this sad, nice woman, who was betraying her boss because she loved her husband, but who was willing to betray him to a man she did not know.

He sat down. She smiled at him, and tipped back the Scotch, sipping it, saying, "Happy days."

"Happy days," he said.

"So, what have we got to talk about?" Alice said.

"I was hoping you were going to do the talking," Philip answered.

"Okay, I will. Right off, I know what's happening. I know who you are and what you're looking for. Okay?"

"Okay," Philip said.

"And I can't do any more for you after today. I can't risk it."

"Okay," Philip repeated.

Philip decided to probe. "Just what *do* you know?"

"I know you are looking for something about Magnus Hopkenson. I know my boss is as well. And I also know it's something unpleasant. That's why I don't want to do anymore. Frankly, I'm afraid. That's what I know."

"Afraid of Bray?"

"That, I guess, though he's a wonderful man. I wouldn't be doing this if I didn't owe something."

"Do you think Bray would retaliate if he knew you had seen me?"

"He should," she said. "But no, he's not that kind. But there are others involved, I don't know them. I don't know much more really, but it seems dangerous."

"Do you know who he's working for?" Philip asked, hoping that the needed clue would fall, casually, easily.

"No, I don't, and he doesn't either. All he does is report to a Mr. Smith. That's all anyone knows. You know that too, yes?"

Philip nodded, he hoped noncommittally.

"Can I ask another question before we sign off?" Philip said.

"Sure, you can ask, two, three. I said you've got me for today. It's tomorrow that's out."

"Has Bray been doing any checking on anyone else?"

"Give me names."

"Beverwyck, Haley, Jennings, Rideau, Parr, Asher, any of those."

"Sure, all of them. I researched some myself. But I don't know what he did with the stuff I got. In fact he's been contacted by one of them."

Philip looked sharply at her. "Who?"

"Rideau."

"What was it about?"

"I think Rideau wanted to employ Walter. I wasn't in on the conversation, but when he left, that was the impression I got."

Philip traced the name Rideau in the moisture on the table. If Rideau had contacted Bray, then he was not behind Bray, and Philip was suddenly almost sure he knew who was.

"Have they been in contact before?"

"So far as I know, this is the first time. Walter interviewed Rideau once, but didn't get anywhere. He was surprised that Rideau had come to him."

Philip reached over and took Alice Copley's hand.

"You know, I think you've earned another Scotch and gotten yourself off the hook. I won't need to know any more."

"Maybe off that hook," she said. "There are others."

Philip looked away. Here it comes, he thought, pay up time.

He got up. "Let me get that Scotch."

"Mr. Kristopher, please sit down," Alice said quietly.

Philip sat down, feeling trapped.

"I'll be blunt," she said. "When I met you, I wanted to go to bed with you. I still do. You're handsome, and young, younger than I am. I don't get much chance for anything you know. I really thought I would like to be held, just for a little while. By someone. It's been a long time."

"I understand," Philip said. "I really . . ."

"Please, hear me out," she said. "I want to sleep with you, make love, or at least, have sex. And I could make it happen. I could tell Walter Bray about you."

She reached over and squeezed Philip's hand.

"But I won't. And I won't go to bed with you either. I thought about it a lot, but I couldn't do it, not to my husband, not to Walter, not to you. Anyway, Mr. Kristopher, Philip, I've been around. I'm no dummy. I can add things up. I suspect that you might not want to anyway. I mean for other reasons than business."

"Alice, you're quite a person," Philip said. "I'll tell you something. I'm sorry. I really am. But you're wrong about one thing. I would like to hold you, and maybe we might make love, who knows."

"But you're . . ."

"But I'm gay," he said. "Is that why I wouldn't want to hold you? Is that what you think?"

Alice looked down at the table, tracing her own line in the water.

"Alice, you're right, I am gay, I like men, but it doesn't make me dead to affection, immune to feeling. You're someone worth loving. Someday I'd like to. But you're right, it can't be now. Not because of me, but because there are other things that need to be done, and I *have* to ask you to do one more thing. I hope you will. It's simple, but it's a risk, because you're going to have to reveal what you've done. I need to see Walter Bray."

Alice smiled. "Is this what I have to do for love?"

"I'll make it all right with Bray, don't worry. I think he and I are suddenly on the same side. Can you do it?"

"Sure, tomorrow?"

Philip nodded. They got up. As they left the table, Philip looked down. Rideau's name had already begun to dissolve, but it seemed to Philip that another name had begun to form, appearing like invisible ink when heated by a flame. Philip was almost sure he knew now who was pulling the strings which made all the puppets move.

Before he left, Philip had told Tim and Randy to keep trying to reach Amos Parr.

"What I need is for Parr to talk to Louis Rideau. If Rideau is both backing Hopkenson and courting Jennings, then I want to know why. I want to wave the same red flag at Rideau that we are at Jennings. Parr can do that. But I'm also worried. We need to know where Parr is. We've got to keep tabs on each other, to be safe."

"And you?" asked Tim.

"I'm going to meet a contact. I'll tell you more when I get back. Let's meet here this afternoon, say about two, and if you've gotten Parr by then, we'll meet him tonight."

"Should I try to see Rideau?" Tim asked. "I could get in to him, using my name."

"No," Philip said. "That wouldn't be wise. We don't know if Rideau is at all involved in this. If he is, then Amos will be the best contact. He has reason to be in touch. You don't."

For most of the morning, Tim and Randy waited in the room, from time to time calling Parr's house. There was never an answer. The time was heavy and they wanted to find out more.

"I think we should go there," Tim said. "Maybe he'll be there by then."

"Do you think we should try to get in?" Randy said, when there was no answer to their insistent knocking.

"Break in?" Tim said.

"Maybe try a door around the side at least. Something might have happened."

Tim was hesitant. He remembered entering his father's house, walking up the back steps, into the entry, through the pantry and into the kitchen, and seeing there . . .

Randy picked up on what he was thinking.

"You stay outside. I'll go in."

"No, I'll go with you. If something has happened I want to be with you."

The two went around the side of the house, along the wall that protected the garden from the street. The garden gate was open. No one saw them slip through it into the garden that Amos Parr tended, turning into a mass of summer flowers, rising in tiers, falling in cascades, bordering paths with swatches of color, edging beds with riots of hue, a garden long and lovingly inhabited.

A cellar door, shoved hard, gave them entry and stairs led them up into the house. It was silent.

"Dr. Parr," Tim called softly. No sound.

They climbed another flight, into the hallway. On one side of the hall, the parlors were gloomy in the filtered light, on the other the dining room, rich with mahogany and silver quietly glittered. In the library they opened drawers at random, sifted through letters on the desk.

"Try this," Randy said. He held up a calendar. "It's his appointment book."

They turned to the page for the day.

"Nothing," Tim said. "Try yesterday."

"Also nothing."

"The day before?"

"Yes, here's something."

1 P.M. Lunch with Otis Ferguson.

4 P.M. Tea, Louisa Van Velsor.

"So what does all this mean?" Tim said.

"It means that Parr had no appointments today or yesterday, yet we haven't been able to get him. Philip says there's a butler, yet there's no one in the house. Two days ago he had tea with this woman and lunch with someone named Otis Ferguson. We should try them."

"Shouldn't we call Philip first?"

"Yes, do that. I'll see what else I can find," Randy said.

Randy left Tim alone and went to the hall. Tim could hear him prowling back toward the stair landing. He picked up the phone and dialed the hotel, asking for Philip's room. No answer. As the phone rang, he caught sight of a Roladex on the desk. He flipped through it. Van Velsor, Louisa, with a number. Turning back he found another name: Otis Ferguson, Faraway, with a Virginia address. There was no answer in Philip's room. He must not be back yet. He turned in the swivel chair. In the door way stood Randy, his face white. Tim had a sudden flash of memory.

"What is it?" he said, putting the phone down.

"I think we'd better call Philip. There's someone, something, upstairs. He's dead."

"Oh no," Tim said. "not Parr too."

"No, it's not Parr," Randy said. "He's too young. I think it's the butler."

"Philip's not there." Tim said. "We've got to do something. Parr may be in danger too. Should we call the police?"

"No, we mustn't yet." Randy said. "Let's call Beverwyck and tell him."

"No," Beverwyck said decisively when he heard. "Don't call the police. I'll have someone in Washington take care of it for now. We can't risk any more until we find out what is happening. If we call the police, it will touch Amos. We may have to fix this one, too. Get to Philip as fast as possible. I'll make some calls. Just get out of the house."

"But what about Parr?" Randy said. "We've got to find him."

"I know," Beverwyck replied. "Is there anything?"

"Only an entry in his appointment book, about tea with a Louisa van Velsor and lunch with Otis Ferguson."

"I know Ferguson," Beverwyck said. "He's strange, lives on a farm in Virginia. About forty miles outside of Washington. I know that Philip contacted him as part of the investigation. A friend of Parr's, I think."

"Should we call him to try to find out if he knows where Parr is?" Randy asked.

"I don't know," Beverwyck said. "I'm in the dark, too. I only know he is mentioned in one of Philip's reports. He may have nothing to do with the investigation. You'd better check with Philip first. In the meantime, I'll try to get Philip, too. You get in touch with the van Velsor woman. At least you can establish Parr's whereabouts for that time. She's a cranky old woman, but she'll talk to you. Mention me. I've known her for years."

"What are you going to do about . . . about what we found?"

There was silence for a moment. Then, "I'm going to arrange for it to disappear. Right now we can't afford any kind of publicity connected with any one of us. Just get out of the house, I'll take care of the rest."

Randy and Tim let themselves back into their room. The desk said that Philip had not returned.

"We can't just sit around waiting. He's late now. We've got to do something," Tim said.

"All right, call van Velsor."

"Nelson Beverwyck, this is a treat," the voice said into Tim's ear.

"No, Miss van Velsor, this isn't Nelson Beverwyck. I'm a friend of his."

"Oh, I see, well, yes, what can I do for you?"

"I'm trying to find out if Amos Parr . . ."

"Amos Parr," the crackling voice interrupted. "I'm curious about him, too. I was supposed to have tea with him yesterday and he wasn't there. Now I know he wants me to give my paintings away, but I can tell you that is certainly no way to treat me."

"Excuse me, ma'am, but you didn't have tea?" Tim asked.

"I certainly did not. I went to his house. Now I would normally have asked him to to come to me, but I had an appointment earlier and so I said to his man, Leon, think his name is, I said Leon now you make some nice tea for me and Dr. Parr and I shall come to you. Well, I did. But there was no one there. I waited in the car for twenty minutes and I had Simpson, he's my driver, go around the house knocking on all the windows. But there was no one there. Now isn't that a fine thing?"

"Thank you, Miss van Velsor," Tim said. "I appreciate your information."

"And what is your name? You're not Nelson. Then who are you?"

"Tim Haley, Ma'am."

"Not Judge Haley's son. Oh you know, I knew your dear father many years ago. I was just a little bit sweet on him, but he married your mother. But you know that don't you?"

"I've really got to go now," Tim said. "Thanks for letting me talk."

"Oh, you young people never have time for anything. Well, then, go. But you tell Nelson Beverwyck to call. Another one who never has time for an old woman."

"Goodbye Miss van Velsor," Tim said, hanging up.

He went back into the bedroom where Randy was pouring over a map of Virginia."

"Louisa van Velsor said she went for tea and Parr wasn't there."

"Then Ferguson might know something about him."

"Right," Tim said.

"Or," Randy went on, "Ferguson might know more than just something. Beverwyck said that Philip interviewed him as part of the investigation. Look, it's nearly three. Philip was supposed to be back an hour ago. We don't know where he went. The only thing we know is that Parr may have had lunch with Ferguson two days ago."

"Where is Ferguson?"

"His farm is here," Randy said pointing to the map. While you were calling, I asked the desk and they helped me find it."

"Did you call to see if Ferguson was there?"

"Yes, but whoever answered said he was not available to come to the phone."

"Then," Tim said, "I think we had better go to him."

26.

April 15   *3:30 P.M.*

"Phillip," the note read, "call Beverwyck. He'll fill you in." Philip looked around the empty room. Randy and Tim's note lay on the table. He had said good-bye to Alice Copley, who promised to arrange a meeting with Bray at Philip's hotel, and hurried back to the hotel to meet Tim and Randy, realizing he was an hour late.

"Nelson, it's Philip. What's going on?"

Beverwyck told Philip about the death of Leon, Parr's butler."

"I've taken care of it," Beverwyck said.

"Like Ross?" Philip shot.

"Like Ross."

"But Parr," Philip asked, "where's he?"

"Don't know. Are Randy and Tim with you?"

"No," Philip said, "they left a note to call you."

Philip felt that things were getting out of hand. He regretted bringing Randy and Tim with him. They were without experience. They would get hurt.

Beverwyck told Philip about Ferguson's name in Parr's datebook, and that of Louisa van Velsor.

"I'll be in touch as soon as I hear anything," Philip said, hanging up.

"Damn them," he said aloud. He knew he should have

come alone. They were nice people, but they didn't know anything about what he was doing, didn't know how to take care of themselves. What could they have done? They obviously went to Parr's house. And now they were out in the city someplace. What they had was the name of Otis Ferguson. What Philip had was an appointment with Walter Bray. Bray was in Washington and Ferguson was, presumably, in Virginia at his farm. Would Tim and Randy be fool enough to go there?

He picked up the phone.

"Desk? This is Philip Kristopher. Did Mr. Asher and Mr. Haley say where they were going when they left? They rented a car? To go where? They took a map of Virginia."

He hung up and then, checking his phone book, dialed another number.

"Hello. It's Philip. I have to see you. Can I come over now? Fine. Half an hour."

"I'm really glad you called," Michael Ferguson said as he let Philip in.

As Phillip came into the apartment, he sensed the tension in Michael's manner, wanted to break it immediately and get to the point. But he knew he couldn't. He realized he was tense as well. He hadn't wanted to see Michael. But he felt the case demanded it. But now that he was here, there were other things pulling at him too.

Michael talked on while he was making Philip a drink. Philip wanted to ask him not to talk, just to sit quietly for a moment. Suddenly he realized that Michael was talking, but seriously.

"I've been thinking a lot about you. That's why I was glad when you called. I know that you say that you don't want to be involved right now, but I can't help what I feel. It was nice, the last time. And I think it could be nice again."

Michael sat next to Philip.

"Damn it," Philip said, "why are you doing this? I can't, don't you see. I can't get involved, not with you, not with anyone. This doesn't mean I don't like you. That's probably the trouble. I've been thinking about you, too. But I . . ." He was not able to finish. He wanted to say he had never been involved with anyone. He wanted to tell Michael that all his life he had avoided just that because he wasn't sure he would know how to do it, how to carry it through, how to make it real and right. But he couldn't say that. He wanted to talk to Michael. He wanted, damn it all, to hold him, kiss him, love him. But his mind was filled with other things. With Amos Parr, Tim, Randy, Otis Ferguson, Magnus Hopkenson. Big things, important people, events that would and could change the shape of the nation, not just touch two lives of two men who happened to be drawn to one another. Two lives. A small thing next to the lives that had been lost, next to the dangers that were clearly present, next to the disappearance of Tim, of Randy, of Amos Parr, next to the possible destruction of Magnus Hopkenson. Yet right at the moment, with Michael sitting next to him, his face eager, eyes blue and clear looking into his, his hand resting lightly on Philip's, none of that mattered, none of that seemed worth the time. But he said, "Michael. Yes, I know what you mean. I know. But you've got to help me now. I need you to do something for me and after that, after everything else is done, then maybe we can talk. Will you trust me now? I promise that later . . . well, I promise."

Michael got up and walked across the room. He stood with his back to Philip.

"What is it?" he said, turning.

Philip got up and went over to him, and took him in his arms. He kissed him, and held him close. Philip felt impelled to speak.

"I don't know anything about loving. You said I made you feel good, that I was the first who had done that. Well, you're the first for me, too. I've always been afraid of something like that. Sex was easy, but what you want isn't easy. I'm afraid I won't know how."

Michael looked at him, a slight smile on his lips. "Don't you think I know that?"

Later Philip told Michael what he needed.

"It means spying on your father."

"I can do that, for you," Michael said. "I don't owe him anything."

"Call me later tonight, the minute you get to Faraway. Tell me who is there, if you can find out. But don't arouse your father's suspicions."

He kissed Michael good-bye. "Listen," he said. "Be careful. I think we may have a little more business to finish before this is over."

"I think maybe you're right," Michael said, closing the door.

April 15   5:00 P.M.

"I'm sorry, but no one is allowed in here."

The young guard stood stiff and wary in front of the gatehouse, his hand at the pistol on his hip.

"Is Mr. Ferguson at home?" Randy asked.

"I'm sorry, I'm not allowed to disclose classified information."

"Classified!" Tim said. "All we want to do is find out if anyone is there."

"You'll have to leave by the way you came," the guard said. "No one is allowed in. General Ferguson's orders." He moved toward the car, face impassive, but he seemed eager to unsheath the pistol.

"Let's go," Randy said to Tim. "We're not getting through to this one."

Tim backed away from the gatehouse and made a turn in the drive. The guard watched them; as they drove away they saw he picked up binoculars to watch them still.

"What do you make of that?" Randy said. "A guard. Who the hell is this guy?"

"I don't know," Tim said, "but I think we better find out. If no one is supposed to go in there, then there must be a reason, and I think the reason is Amos Parr."

"So do I," Randy agreed. "Let's park the car back along the road and see if we can hike in."

Tim drove for another mile along the empty country road. They came to a smaller road branching off to the left, turned in and pulled the car over to the brush.

"The house is probably about two miles that way," Tim said, indicating a western route. "I couldn't see anything from the gate, so the house is probably quite a way in. But if we go cross country, we ought to see something."

"I wonder if there are more guards," Randy said.

"We should presume there are, but how many can there be? He doesn't have an army here."

"I don't know," Randy said. "That guard looked pretty military. And all that about 'classified information.' Strange."

The two men slipped into the brush and started in the direction of the gate, trying to bear slightly north where they thought the house would be.

"It's beginning to get dark. That should be a help."

"Only if we find it before the sun goes down," Randy said. "I have a feeling this is a big place. I don't want to be wandering around here in the dark."

"We'd better not talk and just get going," Tim said, plunging ahead into the brush.

As they struggled through the tangled thickets, the trees began to get larger. Soon they were walking through a large forest. They walked for half an hour, pushing through the smaller trees that grew among the larger ones. Tim indicated they should slow.

"It looks like a clearing, or a hill up ahead."

They cautiously advanced to the forest's edge. A low hill sloped upward. They climbed the hill. Near the top, they dropped down and crawled the rest of the way. At the crest they looked down into a shallow valley.

"No army?" Randy whispered. "Look at that."

Below them, barracks covered one side of the valley. Trucks were drawn up in formation, a row of jeeps next to it, and behind it, four light tanks. Men in uniform walked across the field or hurried importantly from building to building.

The two men hoped the tall grass was sufficient to shield them from sight.

"How the hell are we going to get to Ferguson with all this in the way?" Randy said. "If all this is here, then there are probably guards posted every ten feet between here and the house, and we don't even know where that is."

"You're right," Tim whispered. "But now we're here, we want to see Ferguson. Right?"

"Right," Randy said.

"So let's let him know he has visitors."

With that, Tim stood up and began waving to the soldiers below.

"Hey," Randy exclaimed, "what . . . ?"

"You want to get in. This is how," Tim said. "Stand up."

Tim began walking down the hill toward the camp. A group of men caught sight of them. Pretty soon others were running toward them.

"Jesus, they've got guns," Randy said.

Ten guards, with rifles ready, surrounded them.

"What the hell are you doing here?" a sergeant barked.

"I guess we're lost," Tim said with a friendly smile. "We were hiking, and here we are. That's quite a camp you've got there. I didn't know the army had a base out here."

"You'd better come with us."

The guards fell in around them and the party marched down the valley. They were taken into one of the barracks buildings and left in a room with two of the guards. The sergeant went into another room, and they could hear him talking to someone, apparently on the phone. He shortly came back in. To the guards he said, "The general wants to see them. Put them in a jeep and take them to HQ. Send four men."

The sergeant saluted sharply as he led Tim and Randy into the library of the big house. They had ridden through the fields for half an hour, and finally come to the mansion. They were led from the jeep into the hall where another guard, this one in dress uniform with sergeant's strips, led them down a long hall. The hall, marble floored and carpeted, was hung with family portraits, pictures of Virginia planters, of nineteenth-century Civil War generals, of early twentieth-century men in the uniform of the American Expeditionary Force. They turned off the hall and entered a large room. A fire crackled in the fireplace, the walls were lined with books. Heavy Oriental carpets covered the floors and a large desk dominated the center of the room. Behind the desk stood a man in the uniform of a general.

"Sir," the sergeant said. "These men were found trespassing near the barracks."

"Dismissed," the general said.

The guards marched out and the doors were pulled shut.

"Good evening, gentlemen. I'm Otis Ferguson. I don't usually treat my guests in quite such a peremptory manner, but then my guests don't usually wander onto my estate uninvited. Who are you, and what do you want?"

"I know who they are, Otis," a voice said, coming from a chair on the other side of the room. The speaker got up out of the chair and came toward them.

"Jennings," Haley exclaimed.

"Mr. Haley," Jennings said. "And you I presume are Mr. Asher."

"Yes, he knows us," Tim said. "And we know him. You are involved in all this after all."

"Now, now," Jennings said, "let's not jump to any hasty conclusions. I don't know what you mean by 'involved.' I'm simply here visiting my good friend General Ferguson. And I don't think that you, Mr. Haley, are in any position to make accusations. After all, you still haven't explained to the general why you were skulking around his house at night."

"Yes," Ferguson said. "Just what are you doing here? I could have you shot for trespassing on a classified preserve. You know that, don't you?"

"Otis," Jennings said, "let's not deal too harshly with these boys. After all, it may be quite innocent."

"I'm sure *your* being here isn't quite so innocent," Tim said to Jennings. He turned to Ferguson.

"Where is Amos Parr?"

"How should I know where Parr is?" he said smoothly, yet as he walked from behind the desk his manner was menacing. "I hardly know the man."

"You had lunch with him a few days ago," Randy said. "And he hasn't been seen since."

Ferguson hesitated a split second, then seemed to decide denial would not be useful.

"We had lunch, but I let him off at his house. I'm sure his butler will confirm that," he said blandly.

"His butler is dead," Tim said levelly.

"Dead," Jennings said, clearly alarmed. "Why, how did . . ."

Ferguson looked sharply at Jennings, silencing him.

"That's a tragedy," he said without emotion. "But it's not important now. The question is, what am I going to do with them."

"Otis," Jennings said, his voice no longer confident,

"perhaps you should send them on their way. I'm sure they intended no harm."

Ferguson turned on Jennings.

"You handle your prayer meetings; I'll handle my command. I can't send them away, you fool, they're spying. That's plain enough. You know the penalty for espionage, don't you?" He said to Tim, "Now tell me, what do you want here?"

Tim, his face tense with cold fury, said, "What I want is to find Amos Parr. What I want to know is who killed my father. I think you have answers to both questions."

"Oh, my God," Jennings said, turning away.

"You want a lot, don't you boy," Ferguson said.

"You're the one, aren't you? I can see it in your face." Tim said, his voice rising. "You're the one who did it. You killed him, you're the murderer."

Ferguson suddenly leaped at Tim. "Shut up, shut up you filthy queer." He slapped Tim hard across the face. Tim staggered back. Randy leaped forward and threw himself at Ferguson, landing a left to his jaw, knocking him to the ground.

"How dare you!" Ferguson shouted. "I'll kill you for that!"

"Stop it, stop it!" Jennings screamed. "He's safe! Parr's safe!"

The door burst open. The guards rushed in, weapons drawn, and surrounded Tim and Randy, pinioning their arms behind their back. Ferguson slowly got to his feet, his face red with anger. He walked slowly, stiffly to his desk, opened a drawer and pulled out a gun, faced Tim and Randy and leveled the weapon at them.

"Otis, no, don't," Jennings whispered hoarsely.

"Jennings," Ferguson growled, "that will be all." He looked at Tim. "Now young man, you want to know some things? I think perhaps you know too much already. But I know something, too. I know who you are, and what you are. I also know what to do with you." He raised the gun threateningly.

"For God's sake, Otis," Jennings said, his voice breaking.

"Mr. Jennings," Ferguson shouted, "do I have to confine you to your quarters for insubordination? But you're right. I may need to know more. Guard! Imprison these men with the other one. I'll question them myself later."

Tim and Randy were roughly pushed out of the room. In the hall their hands were tied behind them and they were led into the waiting jeep.

The jeep pulled away. As it roared down the drive, a small sports car came toward it up the drive. The driver, a young man, slowed and looked at Tim and Randy. His face registered surprise, but he drove on toward the house.

"You must learn, my dear Reverend Jennings, to control yourself," Ferguson said after the men were led away.

"Otis, you've got to stop this," Jennings said. "What if someone comes here?"

"No one comes here unless I say so. Now I suggest you go to your room. You've become hysterical."

"I'm not hysterical. But I didn't get involved in this to . . ."

"You're involved in this to do what I say, Jennings. Remember, no man is indispensible."

"What are you going to do with those boys?" Jennings said.

Ferguson looked at him coldly. "I may have to kill them." He smiled a chill half smile and marched out of the room. Jennings stood, stunned, face wet with perspiration. He hadn't expected this. He hadn't wanted this. Things were out of control. He walked to the door of the library to see if Ferguson was gone. At the end of the hall, he could see the general. With him was a young man, standing half in darkness, carrying a small overnight bag. The two were engaged in conversation. The general seemed to be trying to control himself. Jennings could hear no words, but the tones registered anger.

Quickly Jennings pulled the library door closed and went to the phone. He dialed, waiting tensely for the seemingly endless ringing to be interrupted by an answer. At last, the phone clicked.

"This is Jennings," he said. "I'm at Faraway. Otis is losing control. You better come out here."

April 15   5:00 P.M.

Philip waited for the knock on the door. He was about to meet Walter Bray, the man he had been shadowing for so long. He had come to admire Bray, though he did not know him. The fact was, they both wanted the same thing. There was no point now in working around or against each other. Everything was suddenly beginning to fall into place, and Philip was sure the only course was for he and Bray to meet, and together steer the investigation to an end.

"Come in," Philip said, responding to the sharp knock.

He rose, hand ready near his gun, a precaution that was second nature. The door opened, and Bray came in, as wary as Philip.

"Don't worry," Bray said, glancing at Philip's posture, "I'm safe."

Philip relaxed, and smiled.

"Drink?" he asked.

"Not on the job," Bray said, relaxing also.

"So," Philip said, "here we are."

"Yes," Bray smiled. "Maybe we have some information to exchange?"

Philip liked Bray. The man was forthright, to the point.

"We do," Philip said. "I think we're after the same thing. Right? I'm looking for whoever has stirred things up around Magnus Hopkenson, and you are, too."

Bray nodded.

"Who are you working for?" Bray asked.

"I think you know," Philip said. He outlined his involvement in the case, and the names of his employers.

"Yes," Bray said. "I did know."

"Do you know who hired you?" Philip asked.

"I was hoping," Bray said ruefully, "that you'd be able to tell me." Philip smiled. The last piece fell into place.

"In that case, I know who it is."

"Can you tell me?"

"Not yet," Philip said. "I'd like to, but you've got to trust me when I say I'm still not at liberty to do that."

The phone rang, startling both men.

Philip picked it up.

"Yes. Hello. Who's there, I can hardly hear you."

A whispered voice said, "It's Michael. I'm at Faraway. My father's in a rage. I don't know what's going on, but he's pulled out all the guards, and declared an alert. As I drove up, I passed a jeep with two men in it. They were being driven off toward the barracks and they didn't look happy."

"Tim and Randy," Philip said. "They did go to Faraway. Then Parr is there, too."

"What shall I do?" Michael said.

"Just stay out of the way. I'll see you soon."

Bray was listening, his face registering the possession of suddenly discovered information.

"Bray, we're going to Faraway, that's where the answer is. You're going to find out who your boss is sooner than I thought."

"I think maybe I already know," Bray said.

Philip picked up the phone and dialed. Then, "This is Philip. I need help, and now. Pull all the strings you've got to get some police muscle out to Otis Ferguson's farm in Virginia. I mean a lot of muscle, state police, anything you can get. Nelson, hurry. I know where Parr is."

"I think maybe you have a call to make, too," he said to Bray, handing him the phone.

"Smith," Bray said. "It's Walter Bray. I'm with Philip Kristopher. Yes. That's right. There have been developments."

Philip signaled for Bray to give him the phone.

"Mr. Smith," Philip said. "I don't know who you are, but I know who you work for. Everything's in danger now. There's more at risk than just a memory from the past. I think we'd better meet. At Faraway."

April 15   *6:30 P.M.*

Tim and Randy were pushed from the jeep and led into one of the barracks which was used as a prison, its windows boarded up. They were prodded by the guard along the hall, made to stop before a door, and when the door was unlocked, shoved into the room.

There was little light, save from a naked bulb. In one corner, on a cot, a man stirred, and sat up, clearly afraid.

"What is it?" he said, alarmed.

The door slammed shut.

"Dr. Parr, don't be afraid, it's me, Tim Haley."

"You here?" Parr said. "Why?"

"Yes," Tim said. "we're all here. This is my friend Randy. How did you get here?"

Parr explained the circumstances of his capture. And Tim and Randy in turn explained to him about their own journey to the cramped little room.

"You went to my house," Parr said. "But was no one there? Surely my butler must have been there."

He caught the glance the two exchanged.

"Leon," he said thickly. "Has somethng happened?"

"I'm afraid something has," Tim said. "I'm sorry."

Parr slumped in the corner, turning his back to the two. He sat for a while, silent, then they saw that his shoulders shook with sobs. Randy and Tim went to him, sat next to him, and Tim held him in his arms while the old man wept, wept for someone who was barely ever his.

Time passed, and finally Parr said, "I guess we've both lost someone to this terrible thing, haven't we?"

Tim nodded, without speaking. Finally, he said, "Could you tell me about my father?"

Parr sat up on the bed and pulled himself into the corner. "Come sit next to me, my boy," he said softly, "and let me tell you about Douglas Haley. He was the finest man I ever knew, and the best friend I ever had. Tim, whatever there was between you, I know he didn't want. I know he wanted to love you, to hold you like you held me a moment ago, to call you son, like I will now, for I feel if you will pardon me, that we need one another. I can hardly replace him, Tim, but I can offer to, I can try to be in some small way a friend. I know he would have wanted that."

"Why didn't he ever tell me about himself?" Tim said, near to tears.

"Oh, Tim, you are so young, so innocent. You and your friend live in a different world than we did. it's easy now, it seems, to be what you are, to declare yourself, to live with pride. But it wasn't like that when we were young, Tim. It was something to be hidden, if we knew it, as I always did. But many did not know, did not let themselves know. I think—I know—your father was like that. He fought against his knowledge, Tim, denied it, suppressed it, and though it lay beneath the surface, he could not face it. And when you came to him and bravely told him about yourself, giving him, as I told him, the greatest gift you could offer a father—your trust—he could do nothing but reject it. But you must forgive him, Tim. He suffered from that rejection terribly. But toward the end, before he died, I know he decided to face himself as well as you. I feel in some small way I helped him make that decision, helped him look inside himself and make the choice that was so right and even easy for you, but which was so agonizing for him. Tim, my boy, may I say, my son, you have no idea how many men of my age have lived hidden lives, secret from the world, secret even from themselves. We wouldn't be here now if such a thing could have been spoken in the open, accepted by the world. It is because of *this* secret, kept by your father, by me for years, and by Magnus Hopkenson whose cause we are all serving, that we have been thrown into this little cramped room and live at the whim of a man who is, I fear, quite mad. Tim, forgive your father. Love him. He loved you so much."

Tim trembled, a sob hung brokenly in the room. He looked helplessly at Randy, who reached out and took his hand. Together, the three men sat on the bed, the dim light casting their shadows large against the wall, hands in each others' hands, a circle of love and comfort, and at last, of power.

The time passed in silence, each one meditating on his own thoughts. Outside there were no sounds save the muffled tread of the guard outside the door. Parr dozed off on his cot, and Tim and Randy, in one another's arms, made do by leaning up against the wall. There was a noise in the hall, the sound of marching feet. The door was opened, and a man was shoved into the room, falling on the floor.

"Here's another roommate for you," the guard said.

The door slammed and the lock was turned. The man on the floor looked around.

"I didn't know this room was occupied," he said with a bitter smile. "I'm Michael Ferguson. Who are you?"

April 15   8:15 *P.M.*

"That must be their car," Philip said as he and Walter Bray pulled to a stop on a lonely back road in the Virginia countryside. The two men got out and immediately pushed forward into the underbrush.

"The house is this way," Philip said. "If we go in this direction, we'll come to it."

They worked their way into the woods, pushing through stands of low growth, into deeper forest. As they moved on, they could see little in the darkness, save the dim outlines of the trees.

"What's that ahead?" Bray said.

Through the trees they could see, filtering through the branches, a glow of light. They advanced until they came to a clearing. Beyond the top of the hill, there was a definite bright glow.

They moved up the hill, crouching down, as close to the ground as they could. At the crest they stopped.

"Jesus Christ," Bray said.

Below them, the valley was bathed in the bright glare of floodlights.

"So that's it," Philip said.

The lights etched bright patterns on the valley floor, and blocking out against them were the low forms of buildings, each of them ablaze with light as well. In the center of the field, standing stiff and at attention, a body of men stood in ranks. On a platform in front of them they could see Otis Ferguson. He was addressing his men, his arms punctuating the air as if making a point. They could hear the tones but not the words of his speech. Suddenly he turned and apparently gave an order to a soldier standing at the head of the column. The soldier saluted and ran on the double across the field.

"Let's see if we can get closer," Philip said.

On their bellies the men crawled along the crest of the hill toward where it declined toward the field.

"If we can get into the cover of that building," Bray said, "we can get closer. It doesn't look like anyone is there."

They crawled and scrambled down the hill, staying in the shadows of the line of trees until they managed to slip down to the level ground behind the furthest building.

"No one in sight," Philip whispered.

Crouching low, they ran from building to building until they were behind the center of the compound. A narrow alley gave them a clear sight line to where Ferguson stood. They could hear him clearly now.

"You men have signed on with me because you believe in the values and principles of this nation," he was shouting. "You want to fight against the creeping decay which has overwhelmed our great land, to destroy the mongrelization and the corruption which threatens to destroy us if we let it. Well, the time is coming when we can march together to fulfill our great purpose. But all around us, the enemy is mobilizing. The evil empire which threatens to engulf us with its moral rottenness has powerful forces as well, and we must be constantly vigilant, constantly on our guard against their inroads."

Ferguson stood, spotlighted. His men were drawn up in front of him. Philip could see that the "army," was not as impressive as it appeared from a distance. Not all of them wore uniforms. Some were dressed in khaki fatigues, others in air force jumpsuits, others in nondescript civilian clothes. Only some had guns, others only knives strapped to their belts. As Ferguson harangued them, what seemed like discipline from the crest of the hill was seen to be restlessness. As Ferguson shouted, Philip could see some of the men look at one another and shake their heads, as if they doubted the sanity of their leader. Others shifted impatiently from foot to foot, barely concealing boredom or impatience. Only the front lines, some thirty men, were fully dressed in battle gear, and stood at rigid attention, seeming to be the elite guard of Ferguson's army.

"I have called this alert," Ferguson continued, "to show you that it is no idle fantasy that we are in danger, but to show you also that we will triumph. This very night our defenses were breached by two spies. I want you to see them, to know just what you are facing." As he spoke, a detachment of guards marched out, surrounding four people. They brought them to the foot of the platform.

"Bring them up here," Ferguson commanded.

The guards parted and the four men stood on the platform.

"My God," Philip said in a hoarse whisper. "It's them!"

Blinking in the glare, the four stood on the platform, hands tied behind their backs. Ferguson stood facing them, two guards, rifles at ready, stood on either side.

"These are the spies of the rabble who presently control our nation. These are the degenerates who claim to lead us. Look at them," Ferguson taunted, "look at them. Do you know who they are? Do you know what they are."

Ferguson went over to the small group, roughly he pushed one of them forward.

"Look men. Look at this young man, no older than many of you, yet corrupted. Do you know him? His name is Haley, Timothy Haley, and he is the son of an ancient family, a family that made our nation great before it was sucked into the maelstrom of decay which corrupted it like it has corrupted our land. He is a spy, men, a damned spy who has forced his way in here to find out our secrets and betray us. Well, he has failed. And with him is another one, another spy. The two of them came here to do their destructive work. And do you know what else there is to say, men? Do you know what other secrets these two carry? Let me tell you." Ferguson's voice lowered. "These two young men"—his voice dripped with mockery—"they claim, are you ready, men, to hear this— they claim to be lovers, to love one another. They live together like man and wife, doing what things I will not mention. You know what they are don't you? I don't have to spell it out to you what kind of enfeebled and moral degenerates these two are. In our new nation, the nation we will build on the bodies of such filth as this, there will be no place for this kind of weakness, no place for such immorality."

"But there is worse, men, even more shocking than this is this old man here, this seemingly feeble old man. Here is a monster of depravity. Amos Parr. You must have heard of him. If you have not, you have been touched by him, for his power touched many of us. Oh, but no longer. He is one of them as well, one of these degenerates. But unlike these two young men, he is more dangerous. They simple skulk in the night. He has fingers on the pulse of the land. He can control destinies and therefore, men, he is a thousandfold more dangerous. But they are all in league, men, in league with one another against right thinking decent men like you and me. You see here in Amos Parr the worst of the species. He is a traitor, a traitor to the very ideals that his own forefathers built upon. But we can deal with traitors."

Ferguson's voice had risen to a shout, and he paced in front of the group of prisoners. Philip could see that the men in the field were getting more restless, more disturbed by the ranting of Ferguson. Glances were exchanged, there was doubt in many a face. Ferguson came to the edge of the platform.

"Over the years I have fortified Faraway. I have carefully built up a force here which will have the power to lead those who think like I do into battle. I have collected weapons, material, trucks, tanks, planes, and they are now at the ready.

The time is drawing near. And we are not alone. There are others like us across this great nation, waiting to rise against those who would destroy us. But before we do this, we must cleanse what we can, destroy what we can so that our purposes will be pure. And now I will show you the most terrible thing of all."

Roughly he pulled the fourth prisoner into the glare. Philip started forward. "My God, it's Michael, his son."

Michael stood in the swath of light, looking frail against the darkness. His father stood next to him, visibly shaking with a barely contained inner rage.

"Men," he thundered, "there is only one thing worse than spying, than disloyalty, and that is treason against blood. Do you know who this man is? Yes, many of you do. Many of you have seen him here for years, growing up, changing, leaving Faraway, denying all that he was taught. And now, tonight, he came back here, and why? To spy against me, his father. To bring his own corruption into the very place he was born, to spread his own degenerate evil into this house which I have purified, made safe from the viciousness which he represents. My son," Ferguson raged, "my son is a traitor, a traitor to me, to his manhood, a traitor to you. He is like these scum here. He knows their ways, practices their vice and their corruption. In ancient days, men, it was not unknown for fathers to sacrifice their sons for the good of the land, to cut off, as it were, their own limbs so that the tree might grow. I am made in that mold, reared in that righteousness. I will see to it that we march forward into battle pure and untouched by vice and corruption. We will win our fight against the evils which surround us. Tomorrow morning at 0700 hours I will raise the sword of vengeance and I shall strike. Tomorrow morning these men will be executed for treason. Company dismissed."

Ferguson abruptly marched off the platform. The troops stood in shock, not moving, not carrying out the order for dismissal. Ferguson got in a waiting jeep and sped off into the night.

Philip and Bray, too, were shocked by Ferguson's brutal speech. The soldiers on the field did not seem to know what to do. The guards on the platform hesitated not sure if they should return the prisoners to the barracks. Philip realized the time to act had come.

"Do you have your gun?" he whispered to Bray.

In answer Bray pulled out his automatic.

"Then use it," Philip said. With that he pulled his own gun and fired at one of the guards, catching him in the leg, Bray picked off the other one, and the two men ran quickly behind the next building. The troops on the field exploded into chaos.

"Quick, get to them," Philip shouted.

Bray and Philip snaked their way across the field toward the four men on the platform.

"Get down," Philip shouted. "Get down. It's Philip."

Tim seeing what was happening, jumped off the platform. Michael and Randy followed. Only Parr, confused, remained standing there. Bray ran across the field to the platform, firing as he went. Philip fired into the group of soldiers, and raced to the other side of the field, ducking behind a building. The line of elite troops was looking wildly around, trying to find the source of the shots. Philip, from in back of the barracks, began a fusillade of fire, drawing the attention of the troops to him. Bray leaped to the platform and pushed Parr to the ground.

He quickly untied Tim.

"Get the others loose and get to cover." Tim untied Randy, who released Michael, while Bray loosened Parr's ropes.

Philip was firing at random into the crowd of soldiers. Some were hit. Other soldiers began firing in the general direction of Philip's position. The cross fire was chaotic, confusing the soldiers still more. Men dove to the ground, others took cover behind the barracks, firing wildly into the night, at whatever enemy they imagined might be there. Several men were hit. The lieutenant of the elite patrol was wounded, but lay on the ground shouting orders that no one heard.

Bray and the others ran across the field to Philip and the shelter of the barracks.

When they were at last together, they scrambled into the darkness and up the hill, reaching the top, where they dropped to the ground. Below them, the scene was confusion. Men were running aimlessly, firing into the night. Officers shouted commands, but were ignored. Still other men commandeered jeeps, loading them with boxes, ammunition, rifles and driving off into the darkness.

"It looks like mutiny," Philip said.

At Faraway itself, Ferguson pulled his jeep to the front door and strode into the house. In the hall, Jennings was hurrying toward the door, suitcase in hand.

"Just where do you think you're going, Jennings?" Ferguson said. He pulled his pistol and herded Jennings back into the library.

"You can't do this," Jennings cried. "You can't keep me here like this."

"Shut up!" Ferguson said. "Do I have to execute you as well?"

"What do you mean?" Jennings, panicking, cried.

"I mean that I am in command here, and the decisions are mine. Now get in there."

"Why are you doing this?" Jennings said, cowed and sinking into a chair.

"Because you, all of you, are too weak to handle this situation the way it should be handled. It calls for command not weakness. I ought to shoot you now for desertion."

"I think there has been enough shooting, Otis," a cold voice said from the door. Standing in the library door, was Louis Rideau.

"Louis, thank God you've come." Jennings quavered. "He's insane."

Rideau walked into the room.

"Otis, what is happening?"

"How did you get in here?" Ferguson demanded. "I gave orders that no one was to be admitted to the grounds without my permission."

"There are no guards at the gates," Rideau said.

"No guards," Ferguson shouted, his voice shaking with rage. "Jennings, get to your room. Rideau, if you hadn't been so lily-livered, so indecisive, none of this would have happened."

"If you hadn't gone kill crazy, Otis . . ."

"I'll show you who's crazy," Ferguson said. He rushed from the room, shouting for a guard.

"What are we going to do?" Jennings said to Rideau.

"I don't know," Rideau said. In the distance, they could hear the sound of firing.

"My God, what's that?" Jennings said rushing to the window.

Through the window he could see lights breaking the darkness.

"There are trucks or jeeps coming."

"We've got to get out of here," Rideau said.

"I don't think so, senator."

"What is this?" Rideau said. At the door stood Philip, gun in hand. Behind him were the others, armed as well.

Jennings jumped up, terror in his face. He ran toward the French window, threw it open and leaped into the darkness.

"Let him go," Philip commanded.

Outside, the shots were coming closer. There was shouting, the breaking of glass.

"Michael, you and Bray had better cover the door. Tim, you and Randy search for weapons. There are sure to be some," Philip said.

Michael and Bray left the room, followed by Randy and Tim. Parr looked at Rideau.

"Louis," Parr said sorrowfully. "Why? How did this happen? Why did you start this insane slaughter?"

"I didn't want to," Rideau said, sinking exhausted into a chair. "I didn't do any of it. I didn't plan it. I didn't want it. It was all Ferguson. But he went too far, killed too many."

"But why?" Parr asked again.

"I had to protect Magnus."

"Of course," Philip said, "of course, that's the answer."

Rideau looked curiously at Philip.

"Go on," Philip said.

"I had to protect him. Someone was looking too deeply into his past. Sooner or later they would find out that . . ."

"That he was homosexual," Philip said.

"Yes," Rideau said. "It would ruin his chances for election. I had to find out who it was. I had to stop it."

"Instead you only killed innocent men." Philip said. "In the name of what, for God's sake?"

Rideau looked stricken.

"In the name of justice," he said quietly. "I wanted him elected because I believe in him, in what he wants, in what he can do."

"But," Parr said, "why did you ally yourself with Ferguson, with Jennings?"

"Jennings is simple. He can command votes," Rideau said. "Ferguson was necessary. He had ways of making things happen. He could clean up unpleasant details." He covered his face with his hands. "But I didn't think he would kill. He said he could take care of things, take care of . . . embarrassments."

"Like Michael Ross and Aleister St. Pierre?" Philip said.

"I didn't think he would kill Ross," Rideau said, his hands whitely clenching the chair arms. "I told him to frighten him to get him to leave the campaign. I would have paid him off, or gotten him another job, or arranged to have him just go someplace else. . . ."

"Like you 'arranged' for Hugh Tilden?" Parr said.

"But Ferguson did kill Ross," Philip pursued, "and he killed St. Pierre as well. You know that, don't you? Or did you manage to ignore that like so much else that was going on, ignore it for the sake of your principles."

"And did you ignore Douglas Haley, too?" Parr said.

"That was a mistake," Rideau cried. "Jennings panicked. He should have called me, but he called Ferguson. By then it was too late to stop Ferguson. He was out of control. I thought I could control him."

"Like you thought you would be able to control Magnus," Parr said, "using his past against him?"

"No, that wasn't it," Rideau shouted. "That wasn't it. Ferguson threatened me, too. He actually threatened me. Ferguson said that once Magnus was in power, then we could make him do whatever was necessary. But that wasn't what I wanted. That was Ferguson's idea. Ferguson threatened to expose Magnus. I came here tonight to stop that. I was going to do . . . to do anything."

"Even kill him?" Philip said.

Rideau stared at the open window. "Even kill him," he said quietly.

Suddenly the window was shattered by shots. Glass exploded into the room. Shouts and firing were heard outside.

"You two," Philip commanded, "stay here. Don't go out." He dashed from the room.

"It's all over, Louis," Parr said. "You know that, don't you?"

Rideau nodded. "I know. What should I do?"

"You'll have to decide that," Parr said. "You did all this, set all these dreadful things in train to keep a secret, to protect a man. . . ."

"A man I loved, Amos. Do you know that?" Rideau said in a strangled voice. "I had to protect him from whoever was trying to find out about his past. It was you, and Nelson, I suppose, wasn't it?"

"No, Louis, it was not. I *know* about his past. You see, I loved him, too, Louis, but in a different way than you did. You loved him because you helped him to rise, to become the man he is today. I loved him before that. I loved him because he loved me, once. You saw in him the patriot, the statesman. I saw in him the man who, when we were young, held me close—oh, no, don't be shocked Louis—don't withdraw from this—you know about Magnus. You may not understand that love, but you were willing to kill to keep it a secret. You would have killed me if you had known what I'm telling you now."

"No, Amos, you must understand," Rideau said desperately—"I didn't sanction the killings, I didn't want them . . ."

"But you let them happen, Louis, you let them go on, because you weighed one thing against another and felt that the end finally justified the means. And so you allied yourself with Jennings, a man who Magnus would despise, for the sake of votes, for the sake of money, no doubt. And you allied yourself with Ferguson, a dangerous madman whose insane schemes and distorted and vicious delusions have perhaps damaged irreparably exactly what you wanted to protect.

"And there's more Louis, more than that. You have deprived men of life, been party to the destruction of one young man, taken a father from another. And all in the service of your blind delusion that Magnus's secret must be kept. You say you love him, but you know nothing of love. You declare principles, yet you do nothing but violate them. Do you see your own mask, Louis? Do you see that you're as evil as

Ferguson, as bigoted as Jennings? Have you looked into your heart, Louis, to see what lies buried there? Are you sure that once Magnus is elected you wouldn't betray his secret so as to control him? Are you sure that in your heart you don't despise him for what he is, despise him because long ago he held me in his arms, and we loved? Oh, Louis, you have much to answer for and I am not sure that you ever can."

Outside the house, everything was in chaos. Philip, Michael and Bray crouched inside the front door. Outside the darkness was punctuated by the lightening of rifle fire. Ferguson's troops, realizing the situation had collapsed, were swarming toward the house, out of control. The men who Ferguson had recruited, not from the decent and principled as he claimed, but from the butt ends of the criminal and the disaffected, ran toward the house, loot and larceny clearly their intent.

"I hope Beverwyck has gotten some reinforcements," Philip said, pumping another round into the darkness.

Suddenly, in the midst of the running men, Ferguson appeared, on horseback, waving a pistol, shouting for order. He galloped among the men, firing wildly into the night. He took aim and gunned down a man who was breaking a window, trying to enter.

"Rabble," he shouted, "filthy rabble." He fired again, hitting still another man. Ferguson spurred his horse toward a group of soldiers who were carrying boxes of silver and pictures from the west wing, and fired into them, hitting two in quick succession.

"Otis, help me, help." From the darkness, Jennings ran. He rushed toward Ferguson, crying for him to save him. Ferguson reigned in his horse and turned in the saddle, looking for the person who was calling him.

"Otis, please!" Jennings screamed.

Coldly, almost abstractly, without evident passion, Ferguson raised his pistol and fired point blank at Jennings. Once, twice, catching the man as he stumbled toward him. The force of the shots pushed Jennings back. He looked up at Ferguson, surprise and horror in his face. Ferguson fired again, a shot into Jennings' temple. Jennings fell. Ferguson spurred his horse over the man's body.

"Traitor," he screamed. Riding toward the door of the house, Ferguson fired again and again. Then other shots punctuated the night and suddenly Ferguson seemed to leap upright in the saddle. A look of outrage crossed his face, and his body slumped forward, slipped from the saddle, and toppled to the ground.

"Father," Michael called, and started to run out of the house.

"Wait," Philip shouted and threw himself against Michael, knocking him back into the hall. As he fell against Michael, Philip saw Louis Rideau standing in the open window, staring out into the courtyard at Ferguson's body.

Why was he standing there like that, Philip thought, he should get down; he'll get hit.

But the firing was suddenly silent. Ferguson's men, shocked into action by the fall of their leader, stood staring at his body sprawled and twisted on the flagstones of the yard. And then Philip saw why Rideau was staring out the window; why he was standing numb and still. In his hand he held a gun. Philip knew without looking that it was the gun Rideau had just used to shoot down Otis Ferguson.

Rideau looked up dully at Philip, and without speaking turned and walked back toward the library.

Panicking, Ferguson's men started to run into the night.

The darkness was suddenly illuminated by light. Sirens were heard. The roar of motorcycles filled the night and searchlights swept the area, picking out the fleeing men, pinning them in circles of light against the trees.

Out of the tunnel of blackness a squad of motorcycles

roared, escorting a black limousine which pulled up to the front of the house, followed by cars full of armed state police. The police quickly ringed the house. Philip, Michael and Bray stood up from the positions they had taken. The limousine stopped and sat silently for a moment. Inside was a man, a hat pulled down low over his face.

"It's Smith," Bray said to Philip.

But Smith did not get out. Instead the driver's door opened, and the chauffeur got out and strode into the house. He passed Philip and Bray, not acknowledging them, and headed down the hall, toward the lights coming from the library door.

"I think we'd better follow him," Philip said.

"I have to go to my father," Michael said to Philip.

"I know," Philip replied.

Michael went out and knelt beside his father's fallen body. Philip and Bray followed the chauffeur into the library. Inside were Parr and Rideau. The chauffeur entered the room. From the hall, Philip could see Rideau, who staggered back, as if struck.

"Magnus," he said. "What are you doing here?"

Rideau collapsed into a chair. The chauffeur removed his cap and dark glasses.

"I don't understand," Rideau said wearily. "How did you get here?"

Not answering, Magnus Hopkenson crossed the room looking warily at Rideau.

Philip went to Rideau. "You were in this together?" he asked.

"No," Rideau said. "He was never part of it. He knew nothing. I did it all. I did everything. It was all done for him."

Philip looked at Hopkenson for confirmation. Hopkenson nodded.

Rideau continued, quietly, to himself.

"If only I could have found out who started the

investigation, I could have stopped it then. Everything would be different."

"But don't you see," Philip said patiently, as if talking to a sick child, "you couldn't have stopped it. It was Hopkenson himself. *He* started it; and now *he*'s stopped it."

Rideau turned to Hopkenson. "Magnus, it was you?"

Philip continued, "He knew if he became a candidate his life would be gone over with a microscope. He wanted to find out if there was any danger of exposure. I believe I am right in saying there wasn't, until you, Rideau, began your own investigation and turned Jennings and Ferguson loose with the information you gave them. You see, the only person, aside from Parr, who knew the secret, was Hugh Tilden, who now works for Hopkenson. He's the Mr. Smith who hired Walter Bray. But now Rideau, thanks to you, and thanks to the things you've caused to happen, Hopkenson has a choice which he didn't have to make before."

Rideau pulled himself from his chair and walked over to Hopkenson.

"But Magnus, I did it for you, can't you accept that?"

The two men stared at one another, Rideau helplessly straining forward, as if pleading with Hopkenson to open his arms in forgiveness. Instead, Hopkenson turned away and walked toward the window.

"How *can* he accept it?" Philip broke the silence. "If he accepts that, he accepts your crimes on his own shoulders. He can no longer pursue his own destiny, not with blood on his hands. How *can* he accept you?"

"Or," Parr said, "keep his secret. But now, he may not want to."

"*That* will have to be his choice now," Philip said. "*That*'s the choice he didn't have to make before, but which, I think, he must make now."

Rideau looked imploringly once more at the solitary figure of Magnus Hopkenson, who stared out into the now silent night. With a great sigh, almost a sob, seemingly torn from him, Rideau turned and left the room, brushing past Randy, Tim and Michael who were standing in the doorway entranced, as if watching the final scene of some great drama.

The men in the room waited for Hopkenson to speak. Slowly he turned. His face was lined with weariness and sorrow. He crossed the room, nodded to Philip and Bray, and extended his hand to Amos Parr. Parr took it, and the two men stood looking long and deeply into one another's eyes, while all the past flowed between them, while all the hurt of distant days was healed, loss and betrayal forgiven, and there were secrets no more. Silently, Magnus Hopkenson turned, and left the room.

EPILOGUE

The New York Times   *Editorial*   *Sept. 1*

The nomination last month of the vice president for his party
and of Senator Magnus Hopkenson of the opposition shows
that our system is still vital. There is no doubt which way this
newspaper will lean when an endorsement is officially made.
While the vice president has tremendous support, the president's administration has significantly alienated large blocks of
the electorate. We believe the serious questioning of the
administration policy is all to the good. We further believe
that Magnus Hopkenson is the man to ask those questions.

November 7

"Ladies and gentlemen, tonight we are broadcasting from the
hotel suite in Washington where Senator Magnus Hopkenson
is waiting for the election returns to come in. The network has
already projected a close race. The senator has consented to be
interviewed. We switch now to the suite of Senator Magnus
Hopkenson. Jack Newfield is there."

"Senator, are you confident of victory tonight?"

"Only a fool is confident of such things, Jack. But I'm
hopeful."

"Do you have any comments you might like to make
about the direction your administration might take, if you are
elected?"

"I think my record will be able to answer any such question, Jack, if I am elected. But it's going to be a close race, or so your computers tell me. I don't think I have anything to say about that now."

"There are rumors, Senator, that you will make some radical changes and proposals if elected. Such as . . ."

"Let me interrupt you, Jack. There are always rumors about a candidate. I prefer to wait and let the facts speak for themselves."

"I know it's a hard thing to discuss on a night like this Senator, but will you miss the help of Senator Rideau?"

"The nation will be at a loss without Louis Rideau. He was a great man."

"Do you feel his suicide tarnished your campaign?"

"It was a terrible thing of course. But we went on, as he would have wanted us to do. Now Jack, I think I'll go back in and watch the returns, just to see if you're right."

Beverwyck motioned to the servant for another drink. The yacht rode at anchor in the Potomac, the dark water swirling around it, the lights of Washington pinpointing the night from the shore. Beverwyck, Parr and Michael Ferguson were in the forward salon, watching Hopkenson on television.

"That was neat," Michael said.

"Yes," Parr said. "He is nothing if not a master of language."

"Do you think he will be elected?" Beverwyck said.

"I would hope so, Nelson," Parr said. "We have a considerable investment in this." The men looked at one another solemnly, knowing that their investment was not only in money, but in emotion and lost friends.

"Of course he'll win," Michael said. "And so will Randy."

"I expect Tim will see some politicking, too," Parr said.

"Isn't that nepotism," Beverwyck said with a smile. "Can lovers both be employed by the government?"

"Only if they make full disclosure," Michael said wryly.

"And what about your full disclosure," Parr asked Michael. "Are you and Phillip . . . ?"

Michael reached out and took Parr's hand.

"I know how you feel about Philip. And I know why; I do, too," he said. "Yes, Philip and I have some plans; take it easy at first. But don't worry, we're both going to be there for you, too . . . if you want us to be."

"You know that," Parr said.

"Do you plan to move to Washington if you win, Mr. Asher?"

"I'll probably have to keep a place there, but my lover and I will work out of New York primarily," Randy replied.

Randy Asher sat behind the desk at the coalition. Around him his campaign workers moved excitedly. The TV camera panned across the scene, pausing on Tim, who sat next to Randy, then moving to frame Randy's face, ready for the next question.

"There's a rumor, Mr. Asher, that if Senator Hopkenson is elected, he will make a major statement on gay rights. Is that true?"

"I can't speak for the senator, but that is certainly what I'm going to work for. We all have our choices to make, and I've made mine."

Chuck Witter flicked off the monitor and turned to Philip who sat with him in the dark media room.

"Well, Philip, there's our bright boy," Witter said.

"Yes," Philip replied, "he is that, isn't he."

"So now it's over, what are you going to do?" Witter asked.

"Oh, I think Michael and I are going to take a little trip,

maybe some skiing, maybe some sun, who knows. And then maybe Walter Bray and I have some plans."

"Oh?"

"Nothing I can talk about here, but Hopkenson has asked Bray to consider the possibility of heading an agency, and well, who knows . . ."

"If he's elected," Witter said smiling.

"Oh, of course, if he's elected."

Witter flicked on another monitor. Magnus Hopkenson's face loomed on the screen.

"We went on, as he would have wanted us to do. Now, Jack, I think I'll go back in and watch the returns, just to see if you're right."

"Fortunately," Witter said, "we were able to keep Magnus out of it."

"The fact was," Philip replied, "he wasn't involved. He was innocent of any wrong doing. He was as much a victim as the others."

"Do you think it was worth it?"

"Let's see what *he* says."

"Intense and loving comradeship, the personal attachment of man to man . . . underlies the lessons and ideals of the profound saviours of every land and age . . . and seems to promise . . . the most substantial hope and safety of the future of these States . . . It is to comradeship that I look for the counterbalance and offset of our materialistic and vulgar American democracy, and for the spiritualization thereof . . . I confidently expect a time when there will be seen, running like a half-hid warp through all the myriad . . . interests of America, threads of manly friendships, fond and loving, pure and sweet, strong and life-long, carried to degrees hitherto unknown—not only giving tone to individual character, . . . but having the deepest relations to general politics."

Walt Whitman
"Democratic Vistas" 1871